Chekhov's Gun

Steve Schach & Sharon Stein

Wandering in the Words Press

To request permission, visit www.wanderinginthewordspress.com.

PUBLISHED BY WANDERING IN THE WORDS PRESS

WANDERING
IN THE WORDS
PRESS

Print ISBN: 978-1-7332126-9-4
Digital ISBN: 978-1-7360927-0-5
First Edition

To Jackson and Mikaela

Also by Steve Schach

Old Bach Is Come
Highly Satisfactory
A Matter of Trust

Also by Steve Schach and Sharon Stein

Coopers Island
Bakerloo Line
Double Two
The Book Buyer
Crossword Traitor
A Case of Wine

PREFACE

by Rabbi Dr Benjamin J. Elton
Chief Minister of The Great Synagogue, Sydney

The great Rabbi, Simeon ben Azzai, taught (Ethics of the Fathers 4:3) that every person has their day. In other words, everyone has some special aptitude and they should be recognised and respected for that.

When it comes to the authors of this volume, we find an extraordinary range of outstanding abilities, in scholarship, medical expertise, community organisation, culinary arts, Jewish learning, and, of course, literary skill.

It is my privilege to have Sharon Stein and Steve Schach as members of my community at The Great Synagogue in Sydney, and the entire congregation benefits from their presence in a vast range of ways; were they not here the Synagogue would be a much poorer place.

I am particularly flattered that they appear to listen to my sermons, because an idea I quoted from Anton

Chekhov helped inspire this new novel. I am sure its appearance will be greeted warmly by the readers who have enjoyed their earlier creations. I won't give away the story but only wish all readers much pleasure as they enter the world and explore the mystery laid out before them.

Remove everything that has no relevance to the story. If you say in the first chapter that a rifle is hanging on the wall, in the second or third chapter it absolutely must go off. If it's not going to be fired, it shouldn't be hanging there.

—Anton Chekhov (1860–1904)

CHAPTER ONE

"**A**re you expecting anything interesting in the mail?" I asked.

Marina and I were seated, as usual, at the second marble-topped table from the left on the pavement in front of our favorite café on Boulevard Nicolas Bourbaki, sipping coffee and watching the world go by. The early summer sun shone softly on the sandstone-faced buildings on the other side of the road. A heap of unopened envelopes lay on the table in front of my wife; she empties our mailbox in the foyer of our apartment building every morning on the way to the café and opens the letters after finishing her second cup of coffee.

Claude, the plump waiter, bounded up before she could answer my question.

"More coffee, *madame?*" he asked Marina in his heavily accented English.

After a few weeks of married life in the Paris apartment she'd inherited, I'd given up attempting to teach Marina to speak French; it was a hopeless task.

1

And Claude loves to show off his mastery of the English he's picked up from tourists.

Marina shook her head, her shoulder-length chestnut hair swinging from side to side. Then she smiled at Claude, who smiled back broadly, his gleaming white teeth perfectly arrayed below his pencil moustache. Claude looked—and spoke English—exactly like every French waiter in the Hollywood movies of the thirties and forties. This firmly endeared him to older American tourists and guaranteed an endless supply of huge tips.

I'd once asked him why he didn't retire to the South of France and live like a millionaire on his vast accumulated wealth.

"*Monsieur*," he replied in his rapid-fire French, "I am a patriotic Frenchman, and my country makes its money from the tourists. Without people like me to serve them in the cafés of Paris, the Americans wouldn't come here."

I gave a Gallic shrug. After more than twenty years living in Paris as an expatriate English writer of historical romance fiction—unkind people refer to the genre as "bodice rippers"—I'd finally managed to learn to simultaneously raise my shoulders, stick out my lower lip, raise my eyebrows, and hold out my hands with the palms upwards, precisely in the same way every French child instinctively shrugs from the age of three months. Or younger.

Her second cup of coffee now only a delicious memory, Marina took out her pewter letter opener, methodically picked up each envelope in turn, opened it, glanced at the contents, and placed the item neatly on the top of one of four piles. Soon after we were married, I'd asked her to explain her system. Bad mistake. You see, ours is a marriage of opposites. Diametric opposites. In particular, Marina is a highly organized twenty-six-year old who invariably replies to every email immediately on receipt. I, on the other hand, still have difficulty reading email or even using a mobile phone. Also, I have a foolproof way of dealing with correspondence: I simply let the letters pile up unopened, and when the heap gets really high, I throw everything out.

We've been married for about three months now. Marina is far too intelligent to try to change me in any way. Instead, she's taken over the many day-to-day duties I've neglected for all forty years of my life.

Marina picked up and opened the next envelope, extracted a neatly folded page, and unfolded it. I noticed that flattening the paper took some effort; the letter appeared to have been printed on heavy linen bond. Eventually, she was ready. "Here's something interesting. It's from the lawyers."

"Which lawyers?" I asked.

Marina loves me dearly, so she just smiled and said sweetly, "Quentin, darling, soon after we were married, your bodice ripper *She Loved the French*

Captain became a world bestseller. And since then, we've been inundated with offers from virtually every movie studio in the cosmos for the film rights to the book."

"Yes, I remember that. But didn't we sign a contract months ago with Megalodeon Studios?"

"Not quite, sweetheart. The studio lawyers got extremely nervous when they discovered that a company called Contrapuntal Howitzer Limited paid you a fee to ghostwrite the book but that my name appears on the cover as author. They can't decide who owns the copyright: you because you were the person who in reality wrote every word; me because that's what the copyright notice in the book says; or Contrapuntal Howitzer Limited, who paid you for writing the book."

"Why does it matter?" I asked. "After all, we're married, we love one another, and we share everything."

"My darling," she replied without even a hint of impatience in her voice that might reveal we've had this conversation at least four hundred and nineteen times before, "when a studio buys the film rights to a book, they have to know who's selling the copyright to them."

"Remind me why we decided to go with Megalodeon. I seem to recall vaguely that we received a better offer."

"Financially, yes, but the Megalodeon people have signed up Adrien Legendre to play the lead role of Captain Philippe le Sabre of the French Imperial Guard, the hero of *She Loved the French Captain*. And you know how I feel about Adrien," Marina added with a dreamy look of adoration on her face.

To the best of my knowledge, this was the first time I'd heard her mention Adrien Legendre, but I'd no doubt Marina had spoken about her apparent heartthrob many times before, so I simply nodded. It's not that I don't really listen when Marina speaks to me . . . well, perhaps I don't. When she talks, I gaze into her beautiful blue eyes and I look at her chestnut shoulder-length hair—did I ever tell you about her gorgeous hair?—and somehow my love for my beautiful wife fills my mind and I can't concentrate on what she's saying. Or perhaps, like so many other husbands, I suffer from selective deafness.

I didn't want to talk about the French film star, so I changed the subject. "Have the lawyers from Megalodeon Studios sorted out the contract?"

"Yes and no."

I raised one eyebrow. "Meaning what exactly?"

"They're getting a judge to rule on the copyright issue. In two months' time, a hearing will be held in U.S. District Court for the Southern District of New York and—"

"New York?" I said. "Why New York? We're British citizens. We live in Paris. Contrapuntal

Howitzer Limited is incorporated in the Cayman Islands. And Megalodeon makes movies in Hollywood. New York makes no sense. No sense whatsoever."

"In point of fact, it does. It says in the letter that all the top copyright lawyers in the United States are in New York City, and all the major copyright cases are heard in that jurisdiction."

"And why are they telling us this?" I asked. "Can't the lawyers function without us?"

"We don't have to be in court, but we need to appoint lawyers to represent us—at Megalodeon's expense."

"And once this case is settled, can we sign the contract and get a check for lots and lots of money?"

"That's what it says here, darling."

"In those very words?" I enquired.

She smiled. "Well, not exactly, but that's what this long paragraph of legalese means. I think."

"You think? Do you know of a way we could find out for sure?"

"I suppose I could send an email to Megalodeon to get a translation into English."

"Pray do that very thing," I requested.

And then I started to worry about the other man in her life. Instead of keeping my concerns to myself, I unwisely asked Marina, "And what about your friend Adrien Legendre? How does he feature in this?"

"I assume the people at Megalodeon Studios are keeping him happy while the lawyers sort out the mess."

"I think the best way to keep him happy is for you and me to take him out to dinner. If, as I assume from his name, he's a leading French film actor, he must live here in Paris. I can explain to him precisely how to portray Captain Philippe le Sabre of the French Imperial Guard on the silver screen and—"

"I don't think that's a very good idea," Marina said quietly.

"Why not? Do you think he'll be so smitten by your beauty that he won't be able to concentrate on my words of wisdom?"

"No. That's not the issue."

"Then why not?" I asked.

Marina looked at me quizzically. "Tell me, darling, when was the last time you saw a movie that was anywhere near as good as the book on which it was based?"

I pondered for a while. "D'you know, I can't think of one."

"Precisely. And why's that?"

"I've no idea," I replied.

"Because the movie director's vision of the book is always vastly different to the author's, and the director is invariably wrong."

"All the more reason why I need to educate your heartthrob Adrien."

"He's not my heartthrob. And if you instruct him how to play the role, he'll fight with the director all the time and the film will turn out to be even worse than it's actually going to be."

"Marina, my love, if the movie is inevitably going to turn out to be such a disaster, why are we selling the rights?"

"For the money, darling. It's as simple as that."

"But don't you have artistic integrity?"

"Of course I do, my angel, I have limitless artistic integrity—except when lots and lots of money is involved." She grabbed her stack of unread mail. "Let's stop talking about the film for a minute," she added. "I need to open the rest of this."

Marina firmly ripped the next envelope open and extracted the contents. She unfolded the sheet of paper and stared at it for a moment with widening eyes. "This *must* be a joke. In the worst possible taste."

I felt a shiver down my back. "What is it?"

"I'm not quite sure," she replied hesitantly. "The letter is in French. But it's signed '*Capitaine* Philippe le Sabre.'"

"You're quite right," I replied. "Someone's trying to be funny. Captain Philippe le Sabre, as we both know only too well, is a fictional character. And he's been dead for about two hundred years, to boot. Which makes it extremely unlikely that he's sending out correspondence. Can I see the letter, please?"

Marina handed it over. I began to read, and the hair on the back of my head started to rise. I could feel my eyes widening in turn.

"Darling, what's wrong? What's in the letter?"

"He says . . . he says he's the tenth-generation Philippe le Sabre, all of them officers in the French Army, and that you've despoiled and desecrated the family name by writing a scurrilous novel about his gallant and fearless ancestor who was a captain in the French Imperial Guard during the heroic French invasion of Russia in 1812."

"You're joking."

"No, I'm not," I replied. "That's what it says here. And . . . and . . ."

"And what?"

I struggled to speak. At last I managed to blurt out, "He says that to revenge the insult to his family he's going to kill you."

CHAPTER TWO

Marina took it all extremely calmly. At the age of seven, she'd been sent away for twelve years to an elite English boarding school, where they taught her to control her emotions and keep a stiff upper lip under all circumstances.

"It's only a joke, darling," she assured me. "Someone's trying to be funny."

"How . . . how can you say that?" I stuttered.

"It's obvious. The book was published more than six months ago, and we had heaps of publicity all over the internet when it became a world bestseller. Why did the prankster take so long? And why write in French? He—or she—must've read the book in English."

I lowered my voice. "Marina, have you forgotten that the French translation of *She Loved the French Captain* was published three weeks ago? And look at the envelope. It's addressed to our French publisher, and they forwarded it to you."

Twelve years of exorbitant fees at an exclusive private school went up in smoke as Marina joined me in panic mode. "What's going on? Who's trying to kill me? What do we do? What do we do?"

"Stay calm, my love," I said in a voice that betrayed that I was anything but calm myself. "I'm sure nothing will happen to you."

Then, much to my delight, Marina's greatest fear—being observed in public with a flaccid upper lip—overcame her comparatively minor fear of being murdered by an infuriated French Army captain whose family honor she had inadvertently besmirched. Her *labium superius oris* stiffened; once again, Marina was in full control of herself and the situation.

"Don't handle the letter or the envelope any further," she ordered me. "The sender may have left fingerprints."

She looked around for Claude. She caught his eye, and he came on the trot.

"Yes, *madame?*"

"Claude, where's the nearest police station?"

Marina spoke so calmly that Claude didn't give the obvious reply: *Is something wrong?* Instead he pointed.

"*Madame*, go two blocks to the left, turn right on Rue André Weil, walk about a hundred meters, and you'll see it on the right."

Marina gathered the mail without touching the letter or its envelope and shoveled everything into her capacious handbag. I rose to my feet, left the usual amount on the table for our four cups of coffee, added an additional hefty tip for providing the directions to the nearest *commissariat de police*, and off we raced.

On the way, I gave Marina a lecture on the correct way to address a French policeman. After all, the French are punctilious about such things, and I didn't want her to get off on the wrong foot with the person whose cooperation we needed to save her life.

"Darling, a *gendarme* is actually a police officer with the military branch of the French police. Instead, we're going to the *Police Nationale*—formerly the *Sûreté*—so you must address him as *Monsieur l'agent*. Literally, that's 'Mr. the agent.'"

"And if she's a policewoman? Do I say 'Mrs. the female agent'?"

"No. She's also an agent of the National Police, and the French word for agent is *agent* and it's masculine. So, it's *Madame l'agent*. Or 'Mrs. the male agent.'"

She rolled her eyes. "Even if I could, I'm not going to speak a word of French in there. You handle it. In French."

I sighed as we entered the *commissariat de police*.

The two policemen behind the counter slouched on wooden chairs. The older man looked interested as we walked in. The younger one looked bored. So I made straight for the older one. Hardly had I started talking when the younger man interrupted from twenty feet away.

"Show me the letter," he ordered.

I switched to English. "Marina, he'd like to see the letter."

My wife produced the envelope without touching it with her hands, using another envelope to push it across the counter. The older man took one look at the name on the envelope and exploded.

"You're Marina Haversmith?" He pronounced the name the French way, *Aver-smeet.*

That much French even Marina could manage, so my wife nodded. The older policeman started shouting. "Captain, Lieutenant, come quickly. Marina Haversmith is here!"

The two officers rushed into the charge-office.

"Marina Haversmith?" the captain asked. In French, naturally.

Again, this was within her linguistic capabilities, but only barely. She nodded once more. At this point, all four police officers started shouting simultaneously. It seemed their wives—and, in the case of the lieutenant, one of his two mistresses as well—had bought the book, read it, and couldn't talk about anything else. The policemen wanted Marina to autograph all five copies of *She Loved the French Captain*, but the books obviously weren't in the police station. So they decided to desert their posts and rush home to fetch the books so Marina could sign her name on each flyleaf, together with a warm message to the relevant woman in each of their lives. The police captain, as senior officer, was halfway to the door when I shouted, "Halt!"

They all looked at me in amazement.

"Captain Philippe le Sabre has threatened to kill my wife. Please read the letter, without touching it—the sender may have left fingerprints."

It is simply not done to yell at a French police officer, but for the sake of their wives and one mistress, they were willing to overlook the gross behavior of *Monsieur* Aver-smeet. I decided not to tell them my name is Quentin Pakenham. I also refrained from mentioning that my wife, the former Marina Haversmith, is now Marina Pakenham, because that would confuse the issue, which was already becoming overly confused, even by French standards. Instead, I told Marina to put the document on the counter and asked the captain to read it. He laboriously extracted a pair of wire-rimmed spectacles from an inside pocket, carefully smeared both lenses using a handkerchief that had seen better days, jammed his reading glasses onto his face, and perused the letter.

The captain was a vocalizer—he mouthed each word as he read it—which slowed the process down considerably. When at long last he arrived at the end of the missive, he yelled, "*Sacrilège!*"

That remark tells you a lot about the admirable French attitude to literature. Deliberately taking the life of a man or a woman isn't particularly terrible—that's merely murder. But killing an author is sacrilege.

14

"Excuse me," the captain said to me. "I need to consult my computer."

He retreated to the back room. I heard a low whistle. Then, *"Mon Dieu!"* And finally, *"Merde!"*

The police captain returned. "No such person exists."

"You mean in the French Army?" I asked.

"No, that's not what I mean. No such person exists in the whole world."

Whenever I make up a character for one of my books, to avoid being sued I thoroughly search the internet for the name to be quite sure no one else has it. But I didn't mention that fact, because then he'd realize that I, not Marina, was responsible for writing *She Loved the French Captain.* And sorting out the resulting confusion would be beyond even my fluent French. In reality, even the combined political skills of the members of the worldwide diplomatic corps would be probably insufficient to clear up the chaos.

You're probably wondering why I didn't put Marina's anxiety to rest once and for all by telling her at the café that, a year before, I'd assiduously searched the World Wide Web for the name "Philippe le Sabre." As I'm sure you know, plenty of people don't feature anywhere on the internet, so the fact that I'd checked the name at the time I'd written the book didn't convincingly prove anything. But I had another reason, a much more worrying reason. It's bad enough to receive a letter with a death threat from a real person. It's infinitely worse when you know—or, at least, strongly suspect—the writer is using a pseudonym. If that's the case, the police first have to find out who actually wrote the letter before they can take action against him. Or her. Or them.

Instead of needlessly confusing the lieutenant, I said to him, "In Britain they have the Army List, a book containing the name of every officer in the British Army. Does France have something similar, and if so, would you please check it?"

"I've no idea," he replied. "But I have a cousin who works in *la Direction des Ressources Humaines de l'Armée de Terre.*" The Army Human Resources Directorate certainly sounded like the right place, so I asked the police lieutenant to please phone his cousin and obtain a definitive answer to the question: Was there or wasn't there a Captain Philippe le Sabre in the French Army?

The lieutenant was at least six and a half feet tall, and built like a tank. He must've weighed at least three hundred pounds of solid muscle, probably more. Much more. I was therefore exceedingly surprised to hear him say to his cousin, "Gaspard, this is Doudou." After all, *doudou* is the French word for an infant's comfort object, such as a snuggly teddy bear or a tattered old security blanket. But I kept a straight face.

The lieutenant—no, I will *not* refer to him by his stupid nickname—pushed the speakerphone button on the desk set and told his cousin about the letter Marina had received. Before he could complete his first sentence, Gaspard excitedly shouted, "Did you say Marina Haversmith?"

"Yes, she's here."

"I must tell her how much my wife loves her book. Put her on the phone. At once."

"Gaspard, she doesn't speak French."

"No problem—I speak perfect English," Gaspard insisted, in perfect French.

Yes, dear reader, you've guessed it. His linguistic claim was as much an inspired work of fiction as *She Loved the French Captain.* Fortunately, I was able to translate. Once Cousin Gaspard had eventually calmed down slightly, I returned the phone to the lieutenant.

"Gaspard, the letter is from someone who signs himself *Capitaine* Philippe le Sabre. What can you tell us about him?"

"I'll check."

We waited no more than ten seconds.

"I can't find anything. Could you spell the name?"

The lieutenant obliged.

"That's exactly what I tried. I'll do it again; I may have mistyped a letter. No, nothing. Nothing at all. No one with that name can be found anywhere in the army."

"What about earlier records? He claims he's the tenth-generation Philippe le Sabre, each of them an army officer."

"That's easy. I'll pop down to the library. We have all the volumes of the French Army List going back to at least 1808, maybe earlier. To save time, I'll check every twelfth year or so. That should be more than adequate if they're career officers. I'll get back to you right away."

All six of us stood in awkward silence. Marina and I had no intention of leaving the police station, not even for a quick cup of coffee, until Gaspard had phoned back. However, instead of the welcome ring of the desk telephone, all we heard was the incessant loud ticking of the clock on the far wall of the charge-office.

After about fifteen excruciatingly long minutes, Gaspard called back. The lieutenant considerately pressed the speakerphone button again. "Doudou, it's most strange. I'll need to go back and check more carefully, but I'm pretty sure I've found seven different French Army officers named Philippe le Sabre. The first appeared in the 1808 Army List I told you about. According to that volume, he was born in 1780. And, yes, he fought as an officer in the French Imperial Guard under Napoleon in Russia and survived the 1812 retreat, precisely as in *She Loved the French Captain*.

"Philippe the Seventh," Gaspard added, "fought during the Second World War and died in 1944."

"And after that?"

"Nothing. Nothing at all."

The police lieutenant scribbled some numbers on a notepad. "Gaspard, the dates make some sense. If the first Philippe le Sabre was born in 1780, then successive oldest sons might well have been born at roughly twenty-year intervals, let's suppose around 1800, 1820, 1840, 1860, 1880, and 1900. The last one, Philippe the Seventh, would definitely have been the right age to have fought as an officer during World War II. That part of the story all hangs together."

"I agree," Gaspard replied. "But the issue is the next three men. If you're correct about the twenty-year intervals, then the last three would've been born somewhere around 1920, 1940, and 1960. No, I think somewhat later. After all, men tended to marry in their early twenties in the twentieth century."

The lieutenant changed some of the numbers he'd written. "So Philippe the Tenth may be only forty, or even younger."

"Absolutely," we heard Gaspard say. "Nothing in the letter is obviously wrong . . ."

"Other than the fact that the last three men bearing the name Philippe le Sabre, if they really exist, don't appear on any French Army list."

Until that point in the proceedings, the captain had stood on the far side of the room without saying a word. Without moving, he suddenly joined the conversation. "Gaspard, this is Captain Léopold Montmorency-Fosseux. Can you hear me?"

"Yes, Captain, I can hear you. But only just. Could you please speak a little louder?"

Montmorency-Fosseux moved up to the speakerphone. "Maybe this Philippe le Sabre is trying to be clever and trick us by playing with words. He claims he and his nine forebears were 'officers in the French Army.' I don't have to tell you the French Armed Forces encompass five branches: the Army, which is where you serve; the Navy; the Air Force; the National Guard, which had to be reconstituted in 2017 after a hundred and forty-five years because of the recent wave of terror attacks; and the National *Gendarmerie*. And as you well know, Gaspard, all five branches have the rank of captain."

"Captain, that's an extremely interesting idea. I like it."

"Gaspard, can you contact your opposite numbers in the other four branches and see if they have anyone with the family name le Sabre?"

"I'll do that right now. Fortunately, generals are almost always willing to take calls from fellow generals, so it shouldn't take me too long."

Captain Montmorency-Fosseux looked at Doudou—so I lied when I told you I wouldn't use that ridiculous nickname—as if he wanted to strangle him. Or, more precisely, the look really meant:

Doudou, I'd strangle you here and now with my bare hands if only you were a ninety-five-pound weakling. In practice, the most I dare do is glare at you. Balefully.

"Why didn't you tell me your cousin is a general?" he demanded.

Doudou gave a Gallic shrug. Despite his huge size, he did it elegantly. I marveled once again at the ability of every French man, woman, and child to execute that shrug so gracefully and effortlessly. And so meaningfully.

Once more we all stood silently and waited for Gaspard to call back. Marina couldn't take part in a French conversation and none of the four members of the *Police Nationale* in the room seemed comfortable with English. I'll admit that, even though nearly an hour had passed since I'd read that letter, I was still scared or, more accurately, frightened out of my wits, so I was stupefied into speechlessness. And the police had the good grace to say nothing, because they empathized with our fears and, most importantly, with the greatest dread of all: the terror engendered by ignorance of the facts.

Fortuitously, Gaspard called back even more quickly than I'd hoped. "I assigned each of the four other branches of the Armed Forces to one of my aides, they contacted their opposite numbers, and *voilà!*"

"What did they find?" Doudou asked.

"Nothing. They couldn't locate anyone with that name anywhere in the French Armed Forces, neither an enlisted man nor an officer."

"Thank you, Gaspard. *Madame* Haversmith will be most relieved."

In Greek mythology, Atlas was a Titan condemned for eternity to hold up the sky on his shoulders. But the Atlantean burden of the celestial sphere was a mere trifle compared to the load the general had lifted from Marina and me. The letter was a hoax.

I walked up to the speakerphone. *"Mon Général,* my wife would be delighted to send your wife a personalized copy of *She Loved the French Captain* as a small token of our thanks to you; I'm sure Doudou can give us her name and the mailing address."

I handed the phone back to Doudou and spoke to the four policemen. "And we'll supply five personalized copies of the book for the women in your lives to thank you for all your help."

So now we knew for sure: either the letter writer was a practical joker with the worst possible taste, or else he or she was someone whose name wasn't Philippe le Sabre and therefore couldn't possibly have been insulted and who therefore wasn't going to kill Marina for having written a book she didn't write.

For some reason, it never occurred to me there was a third possibility: someone wanted to kill Marina for a different reason.

CHAPTER THREE

"What now?" I asked Captain Montmorency-Fosseux.

"We call in the police lab technicians and give them the letter and the envelope. They'll search for fingerprints and look for other ways of identifying the culprit, such as DNA. I understand both of you handled the sheet of paper, so before you go would you please be kind enough to allow us to take your fingerprints and a DNA swab.

"After that, you can leave it all in our hands, *monsieur*. I'll make a copy of the letter for you for your records. We'll soon find the perpetrator, and the courts will deal with him. We have your address and phone numbers, and we'll be in touch with you. Soon, I hope."

After Doudou had fingerprinted us and surprisingly gently swabbed the insides of our cheeks, Marina and I left the police station and walked home. Neither of us uttered a word until we arrived at her flat on Rue George Quatre.

"What next?" Marina asked. "The police didn't exactly inspire me with confidence."

"You're not thinking of Inspector Clouseau, are you? It was probably as a direct consequence of those hilarious *Pink Panther* movies that they changed the names of the various ranks in the French police force. Yesterday's inspector is today's lieutenant. And Chief Inspector Dreyfus would now hold the rank of captain. You need have no concerns regarding the competence of the *Police Nationale*."

Marina smiled for the first time since opening the threatening letter. "What do we do next?" she asked.

"Nothing. We wait. The police will contact us as soon as they know something."

"Should we organize some sort of protection? What about armed bodyguards twenty-four hours a day every day?"

"That's going to cost the earth," I replied. "But clearly this is some sort of hoax, so it'll be a total waste of money."

"Maybe we should hide somewhere."

"Under the bed, do you mean?"

"No, silly. We need to flee."

"Darling," I said, "why don't we just wait until we hear from the police?"

"I can think of one good reason."

"And what's that?"

"I might be dead before they get back to you."

"Marina, my darling, please be reasonable. The last Philippe le Sabre who served in the French Armed Forces was killed in 1944. For more than seventy years, no officer with that name has been a member of the French military, which means the bit regarding ten generations of officers in the French Army is nonsense. And that takes away his motive for threatening to kill you."

"But what if he's in some sort of secret unit that isn't listed in the French Army List?"

"Yes, that's possible," I answered. "But the people who serve in secret units are listed as serving in other unsecret units to provide them with cover."

"You won't find the word *unsecret* in any dictionary," Marina insisted.

"And you won't find the tenth-generation Philippe le Sabre either."

"Maybe he exists but he's not in the army."

"It's possible. But then why would he want to kill you?"

"Maybe he exists, he's in the army, but he's changed his name. How about that?"

"Yes, that's also a possibility," I conceded. "But if he's changed his name, why would he bother about the name Philippe le Sabre?"

"I give up. You win."

"Good! Now stop worrying."

"Fine, I'll stop worrying about being killed. Now I'm going to worry about who wrote the hateful letter."

"That's easy," I said. "All we need do is invoke Chekhov's Gun."

"Meaning what, exactly?"

"It's a literary principle: Chekhov insisted that every element in a work of fiction had to be necessary. As the great Russian playwright and short-story writer himself put it, 'Remove everything that has no relevance to the story. If you say in the first chapter that a rifle is hanging on the wall, in the second or third chapter it absolutely must go off. If it's not going to be fired, it shouldn't be hanging there.'"

"Quentin, are you totally out of your miniscule mind? As a writer of bodice rippers, you've no business using the phrase 'literary principle'—something along the lines of 'scribbler's scheme' would be more appropriate.

"More to the point, everything that's happened to us so far in this novel has been a consequence of my receiving that threatening letter. Without question, the le Sabre letter has been the inciting incident. This book has nothing to do with guns of any kind, whether belonging to Chekhov or to anyone else. And there's no rifle hanging on the wall in the first chapter."

"As a matter of fact, there is one, metaphorically speaking."

"And what is this metaphorical rifle?"

"Adrien Legendre, of course. We discussed the man at some length, but he hasn't played any other role in this story so far, and we're already well into the third chapter. If you think back, you'll recall that you didn't even want me to invite him to dinner. I know of only two alternatives. Either I have to delete him from Chapter One, which you wouldn't like, because you have a schoolgirl crush on him—"

"I do not!"

"Yes, you do. You definitely and doubtlessly do. Or, if you won't agree to my removing him, Adrien Legendre has to be the writer of the letter."

"But why on earth would he do such a thing?"

"That's irrelevant. Chekhov was a far greater author than I'll ever be, so make up your mind: either that lounge lizard Legendre leaves—"

"He's not a lounge lizard. He's a charming, suave, handsome Frenchman who—"

"Either that lounge lizard Legendre leaves Chapter One or he has to be the mysterious letter writer. It's one or the other; you choose."

"Don't be ridiculous," Marina snapped. "I see no reason for you to delete Adrien from the first chapter. He's delightful and he adds his screen presence to this book, which quite frankly leaves a lot to be desired— so far, it's nowhere near as good as *She Loved the French Captain*. But it's quite impossible for him to have sent that document. Just give me one reason why he wrote it."

"For the money. What else?"

"Money? You're joking! He must earn at least twenty million dollars for starring in a picture."

"Most of which goes to his agent, his ex-wives, and his legion of hangers-on, and—"

"*Be quiet!*" Marina suddenly commanded in an icy voice underlaid with cobalt steel. Softening her tone, but only slightly, she went on, "Quentin, I know you're trying to be amusing to try to cheer me up and make me feel less scared, but it's not working. I'm sorry to say that it's making an exceedingly bad situation considerably worse. From now on, I absolutely insist you treat this whole affair with the total seriousness it deserves."

I'd never heard Marina talk this way before. I decided the best response was a slow nod to indicate I'd heard what she'd demanded and would comply.

"Now," she went on, "let's discuss this sensibly and methodically. What are the facts?"

Before I could reply, she answered her own question. "We know of seven generations of men named Philippe le Sabre, and all of them have been officers in the armed forces of France. Also, no one by that name has served as an officer since the end of the Second World War. What we don't know is if anyone currently alive is named Philippe le Sabre. The police need to investigate this point; after all, Google doesn't claim to know everything about everyone in the whole world."

I slowly nodded again. It seemed to be an appropriate response. The only appropriate response.

"On the other hand, my life has been threatened. Someone wrote a letter in French and sent it to me shortly after the French translation of our book was published. It therefore seems likely the author is a Frenchman."

She paused, so I quietly added, "Or someone who wants us to think he's a Frenchman. By the way, the author may be a woman. Or the letter may have more than one writer, like a husband and wife; married couples have been known to co-author all sorts of things."

Marina looked at me with new respect.

"Good points. What else do we know?"

She paused again. I took my courage in both hands and said softly, "Marina, you have to believe me when I tell you I was serious when I suggested Adrien Legendre may be involved in all this. Deadly serious."

I heard the sharp hiss of a rapid intake of breath, but no steely order to keep quiet followed. I decided to proceed, but as cautiously as I could manage.

"Marina, I know almost nothing about Adrien Legendre other than he's a French film actor and a heartthrob to millions of women all over the world. I read somewhere that in his Hollywood movies he speaks English with a French accent so thick you can cut it with a knife. It's even thicker than Maurice Chevalier's accent, which is saying something, but then we know Chevalier put on that accent for the English-speaking fans of his many American films. When he wasn't performing, he spoke English fluently, with just a hint of an American accent. I strongly suspect Legendre can speak almost perfect English when he wants to."

Much to my delight, Marina seemed fascinated by what I was saying. I felt I should continue, all the while treading as softly as I could to make sure I didn't hurt my wonderful wife in any way. "I know nothing about Legendre's personal finances. But I read somewhere that he's had at least three wives and that he spends much of his time in Hollywood. California is a community-property state with a high tax rate. Even if he ends up with many millions of dollars for starring in a picture, about half of his earnings go in Federal and State taxes. Then he has to pay alimony to his three or more ex-wives. And I'm sure his current wife will spend whatever is left. I was quite serious when I suggested he might need money—lots of money."

Marina carefully considered what I'd said. Then she replied, "It's quite possible you're right and that Adrien does need a considerable amount of money. But would that constitute proof he wrote the letter?"

"It obviously isn't proof, but how else is he going to lay his hands on multiple millions?"

"By starring in movies, obviously. He's a film star, remember?"

"That's not where you find the big money," I answered, "and furthermore, as I told you only a moment ago, taxes, agents, alimony, and other expenses quickly eat up a large portion of his acting fees. No, what he's after is a share of the earnings. For example, the first *Star Wars* movie had a budget of eleven million dollars. But the world-wide box-office gross earnings amount to more than seven hundred and fifty million dollars so far. If someone was entitled to a 5 percent share of the box-office gross, which is less than what I would expect a star of his stature to receive, that would still be more than thirty-five million dollars. And that's probably how much money Adrien needs at this moment."

"Who gets the profit from a hit movie?" Marina asked.

"That's the sixty-four-thousand-dollar question. In theory, the producers put up the money to make the movie, and afterwards they share proportionately in the profit. But you have to take into account the box-office gross earnings and the net profit; in terms of the contract, various individuals are entitled to a certain percentage of the gross earnings or of the net profit. If someone is entitled to a share of the gross, that'll reduce the net, complicating matters still further. I understand that movie contracts are highly confidential and consequently no one really knows who gets how much. But this I can tell you: if Adrien Legendre's contract for *She Loved the French Captain* includes even a small share of the box-office gross earnings, and if the pundits are right and the movie turns out to be bigger than *Ben Hur*, then his financial worries will be over. And he may also be entitled to a share of the TV income."

"All that makes sense, but what does that have to do with the threatening letter?"

"Neither Legendre nor anyone else is going to make a penny until Megalodeon signs the contract. But the studio won't sign without their lawyers' approval, and the legal eagles aren't going to give the green light until the copyright issue has been decided by the courts. I strongly suspect—but I don't have the slightest proof of any kind—that Legendre is trying to frighten you into settling the lawsuit as quickly as possible, no matter at what financial cost to you, so he can start to collect his share of the box-office gross earnings."

"But we're as keen as he is to settle the lawsuit— aren't we?" Marina asked.

"Yes and no. It's clear the copyright holder can only be you or me or Contrapuntal Howitzer Limited; those are the only possibilities. But the tax consequences for each of us will be very different for each of the three possible outcomes. You'd probably be able to remember what they informed us would be in our best interests—the international tax issues are far too complex for me to even begin to understand. Fortunately, we have lawyers acting on our behalf and giving us loads of advice, all of it incomprehensible.

"Anyhow," I added, "let's hope I'm right and that Adrien Legendre is indeed the letter writer."

"Why?"

"Because if anything were to happen to you, the legal situation would instantly become immensely complicated, which is the very last thing Legendre wants."

Marina smiled.

CHAPTER FOUR

For obvious reasons, neither of us slept particularly well that night. I finally fell into an exhausted slumber around five o'clock in the morning, punctuated by a recurring nightmare in which the hero of *She Loved the French Captain*, in the full-dress uniform of an officer of the French Imperial Guard, was shot by Anton Chekhov who had grabbed a rifle that was hanging on the wall. It was a relief when the sharp ring of the telephone next to the bed woke me around noon.

"This is Captain Léopold Montmorency-Fosseux."

"Good day, Captain. What news?"

"What I have to tell you is truly bizarre, so weird that I originally had considerable difficulty believing it myself. But after what we found, the *juge d'instruction*, the investigating magistrate for this case, issued an order stating that two different police researchers had to independently check every single fact. We've done that, and you can therefore rely on what I'm about to tell you."

"Go on."

"You'll remember that Philippe the Seventh was killed during World War Two."

I racked my brain. "In 1944, if I recall correctly."

"Quite right. We now know that Philippe the Seventh was married and had a son, Philippe the Eighth, who was born in 1925. At the age of twenty, soon after the end of the war, Philippe the Eighth married in turn. He also had a son, Philippe the Ninth, who was born in 1947. Then Philippe the Eighth disappeared."

"What do you mean, 'disappeared'?"

"The documents we found yesterday afternoon and this morning regarding Philippe the Eighth are dated from 1925 to 1947, that is, from his birth until his son was born. What we've located so far is still incomplete, and we may not find anything more, because lots of documents were destroyed during the war. That said, the evidence we have is conclusive. We've found proof that Philippe the Eighth was born in 1925, as I just told you. We know when and where he was baptized. Two school reports have turned up, and we've located a handful of documents regarding his medical history. We've found his marriage certificates, both the civil marriage at the local mayor's office and the church wedding that followed. His wife's name was Odile. And we have the hospital file for the birth of his son, Philippe the Ninth, two years later. But we can't locate any records after that time.

Philippe the Eighth paid no taxes after that date; no one seems to have employed him since 1947; he didn't perform his compulsory military service, which is unusual; no post-1947 medical records have been located yet; and they haven't found a death certificate either. It's as if he suddenly ceased to exist after his son was born.

"Did his wife report him missing?" I asked.

"I can't answer that yet. Odile can't tell us, because she died years ago. Finding police records from 1947 can be done, but it takes time. And we've been working on the case for less than twenty-four hours."

"What about Odile le Sabre? Do you have any information about her, other than her death certificate?"

"Yes, we do. We did a routine search and we found the usual sort of information we have regarding every law-abiding citizen: employment records, bank data, passport applications, pension information, and the like. In short, nothing we've learned so far about Odile is in the least bit suspicious, whereas her husband, Philippe the Eighth, appears to have vanished mysteriously without a trace."

"Could he have gone abroad?"

"Yes, that's certainly possible, but they haven't found a passport record yet. We've asked Interpol if they know anything, and we hope to hear from them in a day or so. But the long and the short of it is that, to the best of our knowledge at this time, Philippe the

Eighth disappeared into thin air shortly after the birth of his son, Philippe the Ninth, in 1947."

"Have you located Philippe the Ninth? He'd be about seventy today, so it's more likely than not that he's still alive and can tell us about his father."

"Are you sitting down, *Monsieur* Haversmith?"

"I'm embarrassed to have to admit to you that I'm still in bed. Why do you ask?"

"Because Philippe the Ninth has also disappeared. An almost identical story: marriage at the age of twenty, birth of a son two years later in 1969, the usual sorts of records between 1947 and 1969. And nothing at all after that date."

"And his wife?"

"Yes, we've located her. Her first name is Nicole. She's living in an apartment in Lyon. She informed the local police that a few days after she returned from the maternity hospital with their child her husband didn't come home one evening. Nicole told us she reported the disappearance to the police but claims we came up empty handed. She brought up Philippe the Tenth on her own."

"Don't tell me, Captain Montmorency-Fosseux. Let me guess. Philippe the Tenth married around the age of twenty or twenty-one, had a child, and disappeared a few days later."

"Not in every detail, *Monsieur* Haversmith, but you're quite close. We've no record here in France of Philippe the Tenth ever marrying, though a wedding could've taken place elsewhere in Europe. However, in 1969 a boy was born out of wedlock in Lyon. In the hospital file, the father's name appears as Philippe le Sabre the Tenth. The mother's name is given as Marie-André de Villiers. Now for the interesting bit. On the birth certificate, the boy's name was registered as André-Marie de Villiers. As I'm sure you're aware, having lived in France for twenty years or so, Marie-André is a reasonably popular first name for a woman, and I've encountered quite a few men named André-Marie. In fact, the unit of electric current, the *ampere*— or *amp* for short—is named after the French mathematician and physicist, André-Marie Ampère. What happened in 1969 was that the child was given the mother's first name in a male format, together with the mother's family name; the father's names don't appear anywhere."

"Captain, that must mean the mother broke off with the father before the child was born and she wanted to have nothing further to do with him."

"On the contrary, Mr. Haversmith, the records in the maternity hospital show that the father was present in the delivery room during the birth, which apparently lasted the whole night and most of the next day."

"I'm amazed."

"Yes, it certainly is unusual. Also, no other documents have come to light that reflect Philippe the Tenth as the father.

"Returning to what we've found so far about him," Captain Montmorency-Fosseux continued, "Philippe the Tenth has never applied for a passport. However, we now have the Schengen Agreement, and as a result, the borders of Europe are open, so we've asked Europol if they have any information about him. But you're right in one respect: Philippe the Tenth disappeared from France around 1990, when he was twenty-one."

"I'm sorry if I'm asking an obvious question, but have you contacted Marie-André, the mother of his child?"

"She and the boy were killed by a hit-and-run driver. They were crossing the road outside his preschool at a pedestrian crossing. The child was only five years old. We never found the driver."

"In other words, Captain, my understanding is that you've uncovered three generations of le Sabres who vanished completely from the French radar from about the age of twenty or twenty-one. Philippe the Eighth seems to have gone missing in 1947, his son Philippe the Ninth in 1969, and his grandson Philippe the Tenth in 1990, and no one has yet found a record of any Philippe the Eleventh."

"That seems to be the crux of the matter, *Monsieur* Haversmith, and I believe that any additional documentary evidence we may find will only reinforce what you've just said. Philippe the Eighth was born in 1925, so he's probably no longer alive. But I doubt if after all this time we'll ever locate Philippe the Ninth or Philippe the Tenth. I'll get back to you if we find anything to the contrary."

"Thank you, Captain. As a matter of fact, something has just come to mind. Suppose a husband disappears. After some years his wife may want to remarry or, at the very least, try to acquire her missing husband's assets. Did you find any legal documents relating to a divorce, a request to have a husband declared dead, a life insurance claim, or even a deceased estate?"

"French legal records are computerized, with a user-friendly retrieval system. For that reason, we looked for those sorts of documents right from the start. Up to now, we've found nothing at all of that kind. Again, something may still turn up, but it seems unlikely.

"I understand. Now, what have you discovered about the identity of the letter writer?" I asked.

"The letter was posted in Paris, in the Eighteenth Arrondissement. That's in the north of Paris, the district that includes Montmartre, as I'm sure you know. It's unlikely Philippe the Tenth put the envelope in the post box himself, for obvious reasons, but he may have given it to someone else to send to you.

"The experts have analyzed the paper, the ink, and the font," he continued. "They reported that the letter was produced on cheap paper available all over

France, using a popular make of printer that you'll find in homes everywhere. They can't determine what computer was used, but they surmise that both the computer and the printer are mired in the mud at the bottom of the Seine or some other French river.

"The laboratory technicians have been able to account for every fingerprint on the letter, including yours and your wife's. The envelope has all sorts of smudges and prints, probably from the postal authorities and from the person at the publisher who forwarded the item to *Madame* Haversmith, so we're focusing on the letter itself for now.

"The results of the DNA testing haven't come back yet. However, in the absence of fingerprints, DNA traces of the perpetrator seem unlikely. But as I promised yesterday, I'll keep you in the picture every step of the way."

I replaced the phone in its cradle and went to find Marina. She was sitting on the living room sofa, staring into space. I repeated to her what Captain Léopold Montmorency-Fosseux had told me.

Marina nodded. "I certainly understand why the examining magistrate insisted that two researchers had to independently check every piece of information. The problem, however, is that it's hard to prove a negative."

"What do you mean?"

"Suppose a witness is giving evidence in court. The prosecutor asks, 'Can you spell hippopotamus?'

The witness replies, 'Yes, I can.' The prosecutor asks, 'Can you prove it?' And the witness says, 'H-I-P-P-O-P-O-T-A-M-U-S.' That's all fine. But what if it goes the other way?" Marina continued. "The prosecutor asks the witness, 'Can you spell hippopotamus?' The witness replies, 'No, I can't.' The prosecutor asks, 'Can you prove it?' And there's the rub: How can the witness prove he *cannot* spell the word?"

For a fleeting moment, I had a vision of a large gray hippopotamus, his head turned to one side, standing in our living room, looking knowingly at me, and winking broadly. Then I caught on to what Marina was trying to say. "Yes, I see what you're getting at. What the French investigators are attempting to demonstrate is that no records exist for Philippe the Eighth, Ninth, and Tenth after the age of twenty or so. How can they prove an absence of records?"

"Precisely, Quentin. Apparently, the police haven't been able to get their hands on any information. However, that doesn't prove the data will never be found. All we can say is that the police haven't discovered anything—yet."

"Tell me, Marina, did you ever see the musical revue *Jacques Brel Is Alive and Well and Living in Paris*? I read in the online *Telegraph* that they revived it in London in 2014, at the Charing Cross Theatre I think."

"No, I missed it. But I think I have a CD of the show somewhere. I love Brel's songs—in translation, naturally. But why do you ask?"

"Darling, you seem to be claiming that Philippe the Tenth and Philippe the Ninth and possibly even Philippe the Eighth, who must be nearly a hundred years old by now, are all alive and well and living in some obscure corner of France. Or even in Paris."

"No, that's *not* what I said," Marina insisted. "I'm not claiming anything at all. On the contrary. All I'm saying is that you cannot prove a negative, so we can't draw any conclusions regarding the history of the males of the le Sabre family since 1945. Which means we're back where we were before Captain Léopold Montmorency-Fosseux roused you as you 'rested peacefully, deep in the arms of Morpheus,' to quote from a recent book by a certain pretentious writer of bodice rippers whom I know."

CHAPTER FIVE

After lunch, Marina sat back in her chair, looked me straight in the eye, and asked, "How about we invite Adrien Legendre to dinner?"

"You're joking, of course," I replied.

"Were you serious when you emphatically declared that he's the mysterious letter writer?"

"Certainly I was, and you know it."

"Then I'm as serious as you," Marina declared.

"Good. I'm sure that, during the course of the evening, he'll let slip something that proves he's the culprit, especially if we were to ply him with alcohol. By the way, precisely how do you propose to contact him? I doubt if his number is listed."

"I've been thinking about that. The traditional way of setting up arrangements with film stars is for our people to get in touch with his people."

"What a superlative idea!" I enthused. "It so happens that we don't have any people and we've no idea of how to get hold of his people, but otherwise that's definitely the way to go."

"Your sarcasm is as biting as ever," Marina replied. "But the fact is that we do have an agent, and Adrien has an agent. And our agent has been in contact with Adrien's agent regarding the contract. And about the lawsuit. That means he must have Adrien's agent's number on speed dial."

"So you want to phone our agent—"

"He has a name, darling. Osbert Oglesby."

"Yes, I know, but—"

"But what, Quentin?"

"It can't possibly be his real name."

"We've been through this before. Several times. Osbert Oglesby is the name on his birth certificate. Just deal with it!"

"If you insist, dearest."

"I do insist. As I was saying, I'm about to phone Osbert and tell him we want to invite Adrien to dinner. I've no doubt at all that he'll be sitting right there at the dining table before you know it."

Much to my surprise, about twenty minutes later I found myself walking to the wine shop two blocks from our apartment. It seems that Marina phoned Osbert Oglesby, or whatever his real name is, and Osbert immediately phoned Adrien's agent, who informed him that Adrien was in Paris and gave Osbert the number. Adrien himself answered the phone when my wife called him, and he was delighted to accept her invitation to dinner that night. She tactfully asked him if he'd like to bring someone along. He thanked her for her thoughtfulness but declared that he'd prefer to come on his own.

Marina then dispatched me to the wine shop to purchase two bottles of what she described as "the sort of thing film stars drink," before dashing off to the local food shops to buy what she needed for the meal.

Uncharacteristically, she omitted to tell me whether she was going to serve meat or fish, so I came back to the flat bearing two bottles of red and two bottles of white that our local wine dealer assured me were fit for the purpose. Characteristically, he omitted to tell me whether the purpose in question was to impress a film star or pay off the entire mortgage on the wine merchant's luxurious holiday home on the coast of Brittany in one fell swoop.

At eight o'clock the buzzer sounded, and I pushed the intercom button to let Adrien into the building. Soon we heard a knock. Marina rushed forward, opened the front door, and there stood her heartthrob, bearing at least six dozen long-stemmed red roses. As you know, I'd worked out that he needed a spare thirty or forty million dollars or so, and looking at the vast bouquet of flowers he'd brought, I wondered if he was going to have enough money in the bank at the end of the month to pay his florist's bill.

Marina rushed off to find a vase, and I greeted the man I strongly suspected of sending the letter containing the threat to kill my wife. He stood in the doorway, immaculately groomed, trim, fit, and tanned. His handshake was firm; too firm, I thought. His smile was a panoply of gleaming white teeth, clearly the product of extensive cosmetic dentistry. And he spoke English with a French accent that, like his teeth, couldn't possibly have been genuine.

Like me, he was about forty, and he was roughly my height. But that's where the similarities ended. You've obviously seen him in many of his movies, so I don't have to describe his features to you. You know his chiseled jaw, and you recognize his thick, wavy black hair, perfectly coiffed even after winning a lengthy fist fight or coupling with the gorgeous leading lady.

I offered him a glass of wine and was stunned to hear him say he never drank anything other than mineral water. I idly wondered whether our villainous vintner would take back the four bottles—rare vintages fit for a reigning monarch—I'd just purchased. What I needed, very badly indeed, was a stiff drink—or more correctly, several stiff drinks—but I was concerned I might insult our teetotal guest by downing even a small fraction of the alcohol that I simply had to have right then.

At that moment, Marina came back into the living room bearing what looked like a huge red mushroom but turned out to be all the roses crammed into the largest vase she could find, one that wasn't terribly big. She placed the vase in the center of the dinner table, thereby precluding all conversation between people seated on opposite sides of the container.

I tried to verbally convey to my wife that our guest didn't drink alcohol. "Marina, would you *also* like a glass of mineral water?"

I don't think she heard the word "also," despite my heavy emphasis. "Of course not, darling. You'll find two bottles of white wine in the fridge; it's the wine we enjoyed so much last week. I'll have a glass of that."

Having failed at my initial attempt, I thought of pulling a face to signal to her that our guest didn't imbibe, and also to point out that once I'd opened a bottle of exorbitantly priced vino, no way could we recoup what probably amounted to half the royalties we'd earned from *She Loved the French Captain* by returning it to the wine merchant. Luckily, I remembered that the last time I'd tried to communicate nonverbally, Marina had enquired if I was suffering from a toothache. Realizing that the situation was hopeless and financial loss inevitable, I went into the kitchen, fetched a bottle of white wine and two glasses, tore off the capsule, pulled out the cork, and poured for each of us. Out of respect for our guest, I followed the French custom of not filling the glasses more than half way.

As I raised my glass in a toast, Marina observed that our guest was about to drink *aqua pura*. She quickly said, "Darling, I've changed my mind. I'll have what Adrien's having."

I took the two glasses of wine to the kitchen, drank them both, returned to the living room with two empty water glasses, took the wine bottle back into the kitchen, quickly poured two more glasses, drank them both, returned to the living room with the mineral water bottle, poured a glass for each of us, hurriedly muttered, "Oops, forgot the ice," went back into the kitchen, poured two more glasses of wine, drank them quickly, grappled the ice out of those fiendish metal trays we have in the freezer compartment of the refrigerator, divided the last of the wine between the two glasses, drank them, and returned to the living room with the ice.

A glorious start to a sparkling evening of wit and repartee.

CHAPTER SIX

Notwithstanding the hours Marina had spent in the kitchen wrestling with the numerous ingredients she'd bought, I don't remember much about the food—because the conversation was considerably more memorable.

About half way through the main course, our guest smiled warmly at Marina. "For many, many reasons, I'm so delighted that you asked me here this evening. But the main reason is that you've given me the opportunity to pay my respects to one of the leading authors of our time. My dilemma is that I don't know who that is. My agent has retained this lawyer who keeps telling me that the copyright holder is one of three parties, but then it turns out that the third party isn't a human being at all—it's apparently a company. I informed him that I couldn't understand how a company can write a book, and the answer I received from him made the whole situation even less clear, if that were possible. I probably need a second lawyer to explain to me what my first lawyer is saying to me. Perhaps you can shed some light on the situation."

He smiled broadly at each of us in turn. Drinking the whole bottle of wine in under three minutes on an empty stomach had sharpened my mind immeasurably. But for some inexplicable reason, I found myself unable to articulate the plethora of brilliant thoughts that were coursing endlessly through my brain, so I looked expectantly at Marina.

"Adrien, it's surprisingly simple. I paid Quentin to write a book under my name and—"

"But isn't that illegal?" Adrien asked with a broad wink.

I couldn't work out if he was trying to be amusing or if he genuinely believed that Marina and I had broken the law. I decided to take a light-hearted approach. "My dear Adrien, if what we did isn't allowed, then thousands of ghostwriters all over the world are about to go to jail for a long time."

He laughed. "I take your point. But what about the company? How does that feature in the story?"

I looked at Marina again. As always, she rose to the occasion. "It's quite simple. Ghostwriters are paid for their services. In the case of *She Loved the French Captain*, the money didn't come out of my pocket. Instead, for reasons that only make the whole situation infinitely more complicated, I set up a company named Contrapuntal Howitzer Limited in the Cayman Islands, and the company employed Quentin to write the book."

He winked again. "I understand. I also use the Cayman Islands."

The implication was clear: Adrien was accusing us of tax evasion. Marina quickly set him straight. "It so happens that we've provided full details of the company—and every penny of its income—to the British tax authorities."

"Then why, if I may ask, did you incorporate the company in the Cayman Islands?"

"Because the shareholders wanted to be anonymous. And they still do."

Her answer seemed to satisfy him. He didn't press her as to who the shareholders were, so she didn't have to refuse to tell him. Now that it's all over and everything has been settled, I can't think of a reason why I shouldn't tell you that Marina held 100 percent of the shares from the time that the company was set up, and she still does.

One thing was unambiguously clear to me. For all his talk about not comprehending what his lawyer had said, Adrien undoubtedly had a detailed grasp of the highly involved legal situation, notwithstanding the fact that we were witnessing his brilliant portrayal of the role of a French fool who understood nothing about contracts or companies. I quickly realized why film studios all over the world had paid the great actor Adrien Legendre millions of dollars to play the leading role in so many movies: romantic dramas, romantic comedies, even a romantic musical.

I decided to go along with his deception. I asked him, "Is the situation a little clearer now?"

"Yes and no," Adrien replied. "Now I understand that you wrote the book; Marina's name appears on the cover as author, which is standard practice with a ghostwritten book; and your employer was this company. But why is all this relevant?"

Now he was skating on extremely thin ice. His earlier remarks had revealed a detailed grasp of many of the complex aspects of the case, whereas his last question was so basic that it was laughable. It was now unquestionably obvious that his ignorance was no more than a ploy. But I decided to play along and pretend that he had no idea of why we were going to court.

"Megalodeon," I explained somewhat pedantically, "wants to make a movie of the book, with you starring as Captain Philippe le Sabre of the French Imperial Guard. To do that, they have to buy the film rights from the copyright holder. And the lawyers can't decide who that is."

"Does it really matter?" he asked.

I nearly lost it at that point. He was clearly toying with us, asking questions for which he knew the answers in detail, all the while charming us with his impeccable manners and over-the-top French accent. More correctly, he was enchanting my wife with that false accent and driving me crazy to the point of exploding. I was just about to detonate my temper when he went on.

"No, I'm quite serious. The copyright holder can only be Quentin,"—he smiled at me—"beautiful Marina,"—giving an even more dazzling smile to enchant her even further, if that were possible—"or the shareholders of the company. No one else. And that means," he continued, "that the three of you can sell the film rights to Megalodeon Studios."

His voice dropped to little more than a whisper, his French accent all but disappearing. "Why don't the three of you," he said at a slow pace, "sign an agreement that states that each of the three parties sells to Megalodeon Studios such film rights as each of you possess, and you all agree that, in return, Megalodeon Studios should pay half the money to Quentin and half to Marina?"

A total silence lasted for nearly a minute as Marina and I digested his suggestion. It was absolutely masterful. Only three parties could possibly own the film rights, so if all three of the parties individually and collectively sold their rights to Megalodeon, that would be the end of the problem. Also, the contract that our lawyer had drawn up some weeks ago and that was giving Megalodeon Studios severe legal indigestion stated that the two of us would each receive half the largesse, so that part of Adrien's proposal was also fine.

Then Marina said, "That's brilliant!" at the same time as I asked, "Why didn't the lawyers come up with this weeks ago?"

Adrien flashed his blindingly ultra-white teeth at Marina for a few seconds and then turned to me. "Quentin," he said, his voice resuming its normal pace and volume, accompanied by the return of his truly annoying and now undeniably artificial French accent, "do you know how much in fees the lawyers have accumulated in the past few weeks? And have you any idea how much more money they could garner in the forthcoming totally unnecessary lengthy court case?"

Before I could say anything, he went on. "I'm about to phone my agent right now, and we're going to sort the whole matter out in the next hour. He's going to phone my lawyer, my lawyer will phone your lawyer, and we'll soon receive the first draft of the agreement. As you'll soon hear, I'll make it crystal clear that on this occasion the first draft is also going to be the final draft. I've had quite enough of this nonsense, and I'm sure you have too.

"And another thing. They need to know that, if they try to bill us for the last few weeks of totally superfluous legal work, we're going to sue them for negligence. A child of three could've come up with the correct answer in a few seconds, never mind any of those so-called 'top lawyers.'"

55

He took his mobile out of his pocket. "Marina, do you permit me to use the telephone at your dinner table?"

By this time, my wife would've forbidden him nothing, so much so that I was seriously starting to worry that she might go home with Adrien at the end of the evening. She nodded enthusiastically and he got to work. Every few minutes I refilled his glass with mineral water; doing business over the phone seemed to dehydrate the actor.

It turned out that he was better than his word. He'd promised to settle the matter in an hour, but it took him less than twenty-five minutes and two conference calls. It seemed to me that the lawyers had quickly realized that the game was up and they would gain nothing by shillyshallying. Interestingly, I noticed that on the phone he'd again spoken in his nearly accent-free English, softly and exceedingly slowly. Marina, however, seemed oblivious to this.

Adrien put his phone away and rose to his feet. "Marina, it's been a wonderful evening, but I have to go home now."

"But we haven't had dessert yet, and what about coffee, and I bought some delicious petit fours, and—"

"I never have dessert or coffee, and I don't touch petit fours, but I'm truly flattered that you've gone to so much trouble on my behalf. Let's all get together again soon."

We both got up from the table.

"Can I call you a taxi?" Marina asked.

"That's most kind of you," Adrien said, "but my driver is waiting downstairs."

We started to escort him to the door. Halfway there he turned, put his hands on Marina's shoulders, and kissed her gently on her right cheek. I think that she and I were equally stunned. "Thank you for a wonderful evening, Marina. Quentin, would you mind accompanying me to my car?"

Totally mystified, I walked with him to the corridor. Adrien had a cheerful expression on his face as we rode down together in the lift, but he didn't say anything. We walked outside. He suddenly stopped and looked me straight in the eye. Yet again his voice dropped to nearly a whisper, he spoke excruciatingly slowly, and I detected only the merest hint of a French accent.

"Quentin, you don't have to worry. All three of my wives were beards. I paid them in full up front, with a watertight contract. It's up to you what you decide to tell Marina. What matters is that you stop worrying and concentrate on the wonderful film that the three of us are going to make together. Thank you again for a marvelous evening. Good night!"

He climbed into the back of the large black limousine waiting outside the door of our apartment building. The uniformed driver closed the door politely and drove off. I stood stunned on the sidewalk, not understanding anything that Adrien had tried to convey.

A few minutes later I heard a voice calling from a third-floor window.

"Quentin, what's going on?"

I rushed back to our apartment.

"Quentin, why did he want you to accompany him downstairs? And I heard the car driving off a while ago. Why didn't you come upstairs?"

"Marina, you know about these things. What's a beard?"

"Are you drunk? I'm well aware that you polished off the entire bottle of wine before dinner, but I didn't think you'd had anything to drink since then other than mineral water."

"No, I've had only that one bottle."

"Then what's the matter with you? You know exactly what a beard is. Why are you asking me such a stupid question?"

"Marina, as he was getting into the car, Adrien told me that all three of his wives were beards. What did he mean? He also mentioned he'd paid them in full up front and that the contracts were watertight. And he doesn't want me to worry. I simply stood there, flabbergasted, trying to make sense of it all. Then you shouted down, 'What's going on?' Well, that's exactly what *I* want to know."

Marina started to blush. And then she began to laugh until the tears ran down her cheeks. No, she wasn't hysterical or anything like that. It was clear to me that, unlike her naïve husband, she'd understood every single word Adrien had uttered.

"Quentin, let's sit down in the living room. I'm going to pour us both a stiff armagnac. You're going to need it by the time I've explained everything to you."

I obediently sat on the sofa. Marina poured the drinks, placed the snifters on the coffee table in front of us, and sat down next to me.

"My poor dear unworldly Quentin, what Adrien was trying to tell you is that you don't have to worry that I'm about to leave you and become his fourth wife. The reason is that he's gay."

"What nonsense is this? He never used the word *gay* or anything remotely like it."

"Oh yes, he did. You informed me that he told you his three wives were beards."

"I still don't understand."

"A *beard* is a slang term for someone you marry to conceal your sexual orientation. It's sad but true: if the world were to learn Adrien is gay, he'd be out of a job as a romantic film star. He was forced to let you into the secret because he desperately wants to make this film, and he therefore needs to have you on his side."

I grabbed my snifter and downed half the brandy. I was stunned. "What you're saying is that to hide the fact that he's homosexually inclined he married three different women."

"Right."

"He told me that the contracts were watertight. I assume the women were paid a large sum of money up front on condition they never revealed the truth."

"Correct," Marina replied. "And his lawyers must've included a clause stating the women would agree to a divorce when Adrien's agent felt it was time to change wives and that they wouldn't be entitled to any alimony. They'd have to agree in advance as to the grounds of the divorce. Fortunately for him, California was the first American state to permit no-fault divorces. That way, no one would ever know the real reason."

"Which was what?" I asked.

"The marriage was a charade. Do try to keep up, darling."

Then another question came into my mind. "Never mind watertight, would those contracts with the beards even be legally enforceable?"

"Probably not. I suspect that the judge would rule that the whole scheme was contrary to national policy or against the public interest or something like that. However, I'm not a lawyer, so you shouldn't be asking me legal questions. Anyhow, I'm sure the three women have no intention of taking Adrien to court. They have fame—as ex-wives of the great Adrien Legendre—and fortune. And admitting they were beards is likely to cost them dearly in both respects. I'm sure they're all going to keep their mouths tightly shut.

"The main thing, darling, is that I love you. Yes, I was infatuated with Adrien, and I'm probably even more captivated now. But you're the person I love. The only person."

CHAPTER SEVEN

At breakfast the next morning, Marina had a mischievous grin on her face.

"Two days ago, you almost convinced me that Adrien was the letter writer. You claimed that he had financial woes, what with alimony payments to his three ex-wives. According to you, Adrien sent me the letter to get the lawsuit settled as quickly as possible so filming could start without further delay and he could get his salary; later he'd receive his share of the gross box-office earnings."

"Yes, that's correct."

"But now it seems that his ex-wives aren't a financial burden after all."

"That's what he told me," I answered, "but we have only his word for it."

"And as for scaring me into settling the lawsuit at all costs, he sorted everything out in less than half an hour last night."

"True, but if you hadn't invited him to dinner, the matter would still be unresolved."

"I'm pleased you raised that point," Marina responded. "I was wondering about that myself. Why didn't Adrien tell us about his solution before?"

"I've no idea. The only thing I can think of is that he's not a party to the lawsuit between us and Megalodeon Studios, so it would've been hard for him to approach either side."

"He could've phoned his agent, the way he did last night," Marina replied. "And his agent could've contacted the various lawyers, exactly as he did last night. That's the sort of thing that agents do—they're basically fixers. Why did Adrien wait for an invitation that we might never have extended? It would've been so easy for him to invite us to dinner and tell us about his clever idea. The outcome would be the same, but the matter would've been settled much sooner."

"You know, I haven't the faintest idea why he didn't do anything until he came here last night. Wait a minute, perhaps he did do something. Like send you a threatening letter."

"Quentin, now you're being silly. And you've overlooked something, an important fact that I should've pointed out to you two days ago when you first accused Adrien of being the villain of the piece."

"And what's that?"

"How did Adrien discover the ten generations of le Sabres?"

"That's easy," I replied. "He read the book. Either in English when it first came out or perhaps the

French edition. In fact, maybe he read the English version but waited until the French translation was published before sending the letter, to try and trick the police into focusing on suspects who speak only French."

"You're saying he read the book. So did thousands of other people. And?"

"And he found that the hero was named Philippe le Sabre."

"As did everyone else who read *She Loved the French Captain*. Go on."

"And that's the reason why he decided to find out more about the le Sabre family."

"Why would he do that?"

"That's obvious," I replied.

"Is it?"

"Yes, it certainly is. He investigated the le Sabres because he knew that a letter about ten fathers and sons, all bearing the same name, all French military officers, would certainly grab our attention."

"Wait a minute," Marina said. "How did he know about the ten generations of Philippe le Sabres, all officers, *before* he started researching the family?"

"That's an uncommonly good question. How did he know?"

"He couldn't possibly have known, you big nitwit! That's the whole point. And you've overlooked something else. The only place where he could've found out about the first seven of them was the Army

Lists. But why would he check French military records? After all, the internet has no information about multiple generations of Philippe le Sabres."

"I'm not too sure," I said uncertainly.

Marina rolled her eyes. "No one could've known about it unless he or she knew the le Sabre family."

I had a light-bulb moment. "That's it! You've got it! Adrien knew the le Sabres, so he knew all about the family history."

"Quentin, are you saying that he knew Philippe the Tenth? Have you forgotten that Philippe disappeared more than thirty years ago, when Adrien was about ten years old?"

"Well, er, maybe he knew Nicole, his mother."

"Nicole le Sabre had her only child in 1969, so she must be seventy or thereabouts. You're claiming that Adrien Legendre somehow knows Nicole, who's about thirty years older than he is, and he learnt the family history from her."

"Yes, you've hit the nail on the head, as you always do. That's how Adrien knew everything about the le Sabres."

"Quentin, darling, let's look at the facts a little more closely. You wrote a book about an imaginary person named Philippe le Sabre. You checked the internet and you couldn't find anyone with that name."

"Correct."

"By a truly weird coincidence, it turns out that a person named Philippe le Sabre really lived. He happened to be an officer in the French Imperial Guard and was one of the 10 percent of Napoleon's *Grande Armée* who managed to survive the retreat from Moscow in 1812. Exactly as in *She Loved the French Captain*. That's quite a coincidence, wouldn't you say?"

"Yes, but that really happened," I replied. "Doudou's cousin, Gaspard the General, looked it up in the French Army List. And two French police researchers found it too. Independently of one another. That means it's all true."

"It may be true, but you have to admit that it's quite a coincidence."

"Yes, I'll concede that. So what?"

"Well, darling, according to you we have a second huge coincidence."

"And what's that?" I asked.

"You're assuming that the man whom Megalodeon Studios chose to star as the fictitious Philippe le Sabre coincidentally happens to be acquainted with the wife—or, more likely, the widow—of the real Philippe the Ninth. And that Adrien Legendre knows her well enough for her to tell him all about the ten generations of le Sabres, notwithstanding the fact that her father-in-law, her husband, and her son have all disappeared into thin air, a somewhat embarrassing fact that she's unlikely to have shared with anyone other than an extremely close confidant."

I thought long and hard about it. Eventually I replied, "Yes, it certainly is a huge coincidence, but it's no huger than the first coincidence, which three people have verified. One of them is Doudou's cousin, and no general could possibly lie about a thing like that, I can assure you."

"In other words, you're sticking to your story that Adrien wrote the letter?"

"Can you prove he didn't? And before you answer, let me remind you that someone informed me yesterday in no uncertain terms that it's impossible to prove a negative."

CHAPTER EIGHT

"Please sit down," Major Gilles Despoir said.

We were in his office in the building that houses the Regional Directorate of the Paris Judicial Police at 36 Quai des Orfèvres. From the pictures crowding the walls, it appeared that Major Despoir was obsessed with sailing ships of bygone days. I was surprised that he'd made a career as a detective in the French National Police; joining the navy would've seemed a far more appropriate choice.

Major Despoir appeared to be a cheerful man despite his family name, which means *despair* in French. His moon-shaped face was covered with laugh lines, especially around his eyes. But he wasn't laughing now.

He carefully studied the passports he'd asked us to bring along. "Mr. and Mrs. Pakenham, we do not consider the letter you received to be some sort of bizarre joke. On the contrary, we're treating the incident very seriously indeed. We believe that someone has made a genuine threat against your life,

Mrs. Pakenham, and we're doing everything we can to unmask the perpetrator.

"My superiors assigned me to this case because I speak English. In fact, I was born in St. Thomas' Hospital in Lambeth to French parents who were seconded to Britain for some fifteen years. But, as you will learn, by a weird coincidence I have a personal interest in this."

Marina and I looked at one another. We'd already encountered too many coincidences; this did not bode well.

"I don't want to bore you, but I have to start at the beginning; otherwise, nothing will make any sense at all. As you probably know, the victorious German army occupied France from June 1940 until the Allies reconquered France in August 1944. Most Frenchmen and Frenchwomen simply tried to live through the occupation as best they could.

"Our great actor, singer, and cabaret artist Maurice Chevalier was a case in point. Even though he could easily have escaped and become a star on Broadway or in the London Theatre District, he chose to stay in France and continue to perform. He appeared in a successful revue, *Bonjour Paris*. The show was largely propaganda, reassuring the public that nothing had basically changed under the occupation. Subsequently, the Nazis learned that Chevalier was sheltering a Jewish family in the south of France and tried to use that information to pressure him into performing in Berlin and singing for the collaborationist radio station Radio Paris. He refused. On the contrary, to demonstrate his patriotism, he performed for prisoners of war in Germany at the same camp where he'd been held captive during World War I; he succeeded in getting ten French soldiers freed in exchange. After the liberation, the authorities accused Chevalier of collaborationism, but a French court correctly acquitted him. The fact of the matter is that Maurice Chevalier, like the vast majority of the citizens of France, did what he had to do in order to survive.

"Far too few Frenchmen and women actively opposed the Germans by joining Resistance groups and conducting guerrilla warfare. And far too many citizens of France became collaborators, actively working for the Vichy regime or joining the Waffen-SS. But bad as the actual collaborationists were, one group of Frenchmen were even worse. These were the men who pretended to be French patriots but in reality were spies for the Nazis. One of the very worst was a traitor named Philippe le Sabre."

Marina and I looked exchanged glances again.

"In 1940, le Sabre fought against the German invaders at the Battle of Sedan. After France surrendered, he came to Paris and founded a French Resistance group with the sole purpose of attracting fellow countrymen who were opposed to the occupiers so he could betray them to the Nazis. His plan was particularly ingenious. He carried out a series of spectacular attacks against the German authorities. We French assumed that le Sabre's successes were a consequence of the skills he'd learned as he rose to the rank of colonel in our army. However, the truth was the *Gestapo* had planned every detail of his marvelous feats in advance to ensure that le Sabre would be able to carry out his raids without being injured or captured.

"Appointed to ever higher positions in the Resistance movement, he acquired more and more information about the activities, plans, and members of that organization, all of which he passed on to his Nazi spymasters. Then one day, the Germans struck, arresting hundreds of partisans all over France. The remaining Resistance leaders correctly deduced that they had a traitor in their ranks. But Philippe le Sabre was extremely clever, and he'd planned ahead. He knew questions would be asked at some future time, so he made sure in advance that the Nazis would be able to provide the answers.

"One of the founders of the French Resistance in Paris chose 'La Mouche' as his *nom de guerre. La Mouche* means 'The Fly.' I've no idea why he chose that name. Le Sabre encountered La Mouche soon after he started to infiltrate the Resistance and immediately recognized him because they'd been at high school together. As you know, the Nazis had a fetish for paperwork. For example, they kept minutes of every meeting and carefully filed them away. Philippe le

Sabre was understandably concerned that his name might be found on an incriminating document at some future date. To protect himself, le Sabre persuaded his spymasters to use La Mouche's name instead of his on every piece of paper. La Mouche's real name, I mean.

"Soon after the widespread arrests, le Sabre organized a raid on a *Gestapo* office. Ostensibly he carried out the operation to defiantly let the occupiers know the Resistance was still in business. But the real reason for the raid was to ensure that a number of files fell into the hands of the partisans. Almost all the files contained irrelevant information, such as excruciating details of every single case of French wine the Nazis confiscated and sent to Germany in 1941. But one file contained copies of minutes of several meetings le Sabre had held with his spymasters.

"Le Sabre made sure that the documents reached the few leaders of the Resistance who'd managed to escape being arrested. They convened in a cellar and confronted La Mouche with the overwhelming body of evidence against him. He protested, of course, but he could do nothing. They unanimously came to the inescapable but wrong conclusion. The sentence was death by shooting, to be carried out immediately, and was followed by burial in an unmarked grave. His real name was Gilles Despoir."

"But that's *your* name," I said.

"Precisely. I was named after my grandfather."

I was quicker on the uptake than I usually am. "So that's the coincidence you told us about."

Major Despoir nodded.

"And what happened after that?" Marina asked.

"It became obvious to the German High Command that the Allies would soon invade Europe. They knew from le Sabre that the British had been supplying Resistance groups with explosives via air drops. The intention was that immediately before D-Day, June 6th, 1944, the French partisans would destroy critical components of the railroad system, key road intersections and telephone exchanges, and especially German ammunition dumps and fuel depots, making it hard for the German military to rush reinforcements to where they were needed to repel the invasion forces.

"A major difficulty for the Allies was communicating with the Resistance. For example, the main bridge over the Canal de Charentan was only a few miles from the landing beach in Normandy code-named *Utah,* where twenty-one thousand American troops were due to land on D-Day. How could they inform the partisans in Charentan when the time came for them to blow up the bridge to prevent German reinforcements rushing to the area and wiping out the U.S. troops massing on the exposed beachhead?

"The solution they found was to provide each group with a unique sentence that would be broadcast at a specific time on Radio Londres, the radio service of the Free French in London. For example, before reading the ten o'clock news, the announcer might say, '*Madame* Berthe Perigaud wore a pink dress and brown shoes to church last week,' or 'The navel oranges grown east of Avignon are much sweeter this year.' The latter might have been the order to the Charentan group to blow up the bridge over the canal.

"The question facing the German High Command was, How could they prevent the Resistance from receiving those coded messages and carrying out crippling acts of sabotage? They soon realized that it was impossible to block either the transmission or the reception of the signals. After much discussion, an intelligence officer finally came up with the brilliant idea of sending le Sabre, a gilded hero of the Resistance, from group to group to inform them that the code sentences had changed. They were to respond to only the new code sentence he would give them.

"The primary objective of the plan was to prevent the partisans from carrying out sabotage in the hours before the Allied invasion. But the German stratagem went further than that. The occupiers intended to broadcast the new code sentences at the rate of three or four a day, purportedly coming from Radio Londres. When the members of a Resistance group responded to a fake order and headed for their assigned target, they would find large numbers of German soldiers lying in wait to kill the saboteurs."

"What reason did le Sabre give the Resistance groups for the change?" Marina asked.

"He was to tell them that a traitor had turned over all the code sentences to the Germans."

"And did they believe him?" I asked.

"The issue never arose. The Germans sent le Sabre by passenger train to the Calais area because they were convinced that the D-Day invaders would land in that part of France. About twenty miles north of Paris, the track controller ordered the train driver into a siding to allow a top-priority German ammunition train to pass. A Royal Air Force Avro Lancaster pilot spotted the ammunition train, its wagons crammed full of high explosives, and dropped a bomb on it as it sped past the passenger train waiting on the siding. The cataclysmic explosion and resulting conflagration totally destroyed both trains. All that was left was twisted metal at the bottom of a crater."

Marina looked puzzled. "Major Despoir, I'm afraid I don't understand something. If Philippe le Sabre was killed before he was unmasked, how did the truth ever emerge?"

"Now that's a wonderful question. After the initial euphoria of the Liberation, morale in France plummeted to an all-time low. Virtually the sole source of pride for the people of France was the Resistance, so the government commissioned several young historians to write detailed accounts of the members of the partisan groups and what they'd achieved. The researchers were given unrestricted access to a wide variety of documents, including materials that the Germans had failed to destroy when they hurriedly retreated from Paris.

"My grandmother never believed for a second that her husband was a traitor, so she asked one of the researchers, Coralie Vire, to look more closely into what had happened to him. Coralie found the originals of the 'incriminating' minutes. Being a meticulous researcher, she then looked for other documents in which my grandfather's name was mentioned. And in the archives of the Free French in Britain, she found that he'd been in London during three of the meetings he'd supposedly attended at *Gestapo* Headquarters in Paris.

"Shortly after the war, countless suspected collaborationists were brought before the courts. In Paris alone, ten thousand Parisians who allegedly had collaborated with the Nazis were arrested and tried, including Maurice Chevalier. The courts convicted eight thousand, and a hundred and sixteen were executed. The mood of the country was strongly tilted against the collaborators, so when Coralie brought the facts exonerating my grandfather to the attention of the government, they immediately instigated a thorough legal investigation to try to find the actual traitor. The inquiry went on for weeks. The panel was headed by a leading lawyer, and Coralie served as a member. She entered into evidence the many damning documents she'd found in Berlin that stated Philippe was a participant at meetings of the Nazi occupiers in Paris. You see, someone had slipped up; the order to substitute my grandfather's name for Philippe's had not been forwarded to Germany. My grandfather was posthumously decorated, and the name of Philippe le Sabre was added to the growing list of French traitors."

"When was the matter made public?" I asked.

"In 1947," Major Despoir replied. "Why do you ask?"

"If I recall correctly, Philippe the Eighth was born in 1925. He married Odile soon after the end of the war in 1945, and they had a son, Philippe the Ninth, in 1947. Then Philippe the Eighth disappeared."

"Yes, that's all correct. But what are you getting at?"

"Until the facts became known," I replied, "Philippe the Eighth had proudly borne the name le Sabre. He was the scion of a long line of French military officers. His father was an acclaimed hero of the Resistance, with numerous daring deeds to his credit, all meticulously documented after the war by the young historians. Suddenly the son's life was turned around; the legal enquiry had revealed his father to be a traitor of monstrous proportions. As you pointed out, the evidence was voluminous, overwhelming, and incontrovertible. It was one thing for the remnants of the leadership of the Resistance, reeling from the country-wide raids and hiding in a cellar while on the run from the German authorities, to hurriedly condemn your grandfather to death, despite his vehement denials, on the basis of official documents snatched from the *Gestapo*. But the subsequent exoneration of your grandfather and vilification of Philippe the Seventh was, as you described, the outcome of months of scrupulous research and careful analysis of disparate documents that Coralie Vire had located in the three different countries you mentioned: France, Germany, and Britain."

"I agree. The impact on the son must've been life-changing. In your opinion, Mr. Pakenham, what do you think he did?"

"If it'd happened to me, my initial reaction would've been to change my name, as well as the name of my wife and infant son. But my guess is that the stigma would nevertheless remain; people tend to remember former names. And acts of treason carried out on a vast scale are not easily forgotten."

"And your second reaction?"

"I'm not sure. Philippe the Eighth seemed to have solved the problem by disappearing, leaving Odile and Philippe the Ninth to continue to bear the le Sabre name. But how can someone disappear into thin air?"

Marina had an idea. "One possibility is that he killed himself, despite the fact that his body has never been found."

"Yes, Mrs. Pakenham, that certainly may have happened. But we are still faced with the disappearance of Philippe the Ninth and Philippe the Tenth. Did they also commit suicide in some secret place at the age of twenty or so? Perhaps. It's hard to know. And if they did, how could Philippe the Tenth have written the letter?"

He shrugged.

Now it was my turn to ask a question. "Major, one thing still bothers me."

"Yes?"

"The letter states that there have been ten generations of Philippe le Sabres, which we know to be true, from the Army Lists and then from birth records. But then it goes on to say that all ten were officers in the French army. We know that's *not* true."

"Unless they changed their names," Marina said. "Which is quite possible in the light of Coralie Vire's discoveries."

"But if the family name is no longer le Sabre," I said, "then there haven't been ten generations of le Sabres."

"Yes, Mr. Pakenham, that's something that's also been puzzling us. And no one has managed to come up with even a halfway reasonable answer."

Gilles rose to his feet and smiled politely, accentuating the laugh lines on his face. "Well, unless you have something else on your mind, perhaps I should let you two get on with your lives. I'll get back to you when we have a breakthrough, and don't hesitate to contact me right away if anything comes up. Here's my card. And one other thing: Mrs. Pakenham, would you please be so kind as to sign this copy of your book for my wife?"

CHAPTER NINE

Elias Howe tried to design a sewing machine, struggling for years to find a way to pass thread through fabric. He didn't realize that the eye of a sewing machine needle needs to be near the point, not at the heel as with an ordinary needle. Then, one night in 1846, he dreamed that cannibals had captured him and put him in a large cooking pot over a wood fire. The warriors dancing around the pot carried spears pierced near the tip and threaded with a piece of straw. He awoke, immediately realized the meaning of his dream, and within a few hours he'd built the world's first successful sewing machine. He died a multi-millionaire.

My tutor at Oxford frequently repeated this story to support the idea that our subconscious mind is more intelligent than our conscious mind and also that dreams provide a pathway for our subconscious ideas to reach the surface. I'd always wondered whether the story of Elias Howe's dream was apocryphal—until that night.

I dreamed that I was trying to enlist in the French Foreign Legion and the sergeant behind the desk asked me my name. I replied, "Quentin Pakenham."

"No, no!" the sergeant shouted. "What's your name?"

The more I repeated, "Quentin Pakenham," the louder he screamed.

Finally, he drew his pistol and pointed it at my head. I heard him disengage the safety. "You have three seconds to answer. One . . . two . . . three . . ."

I woke in a sweat. My heart was pounding relentlessly. I switched on the bedside light, inadvertently waking Marina.

"What is it? Is the building on fire?" she asked in a blurry voice. "What time is it?"

"Half past three. I've just had the most awful nightmare. The recruiting sergeant at the French Foreign Legion kept asking my name, and he got more and more angry when I told him. Then he threatened to shoot me if I didn't reply within three seconds."

"Eureka!" she shouted, suddenly fully awake. "You've got it! That's how the le Sabre men served as French Army officers."

"What on earth are you talking about?"

"When you enlist in the Legion, you are required to give a false name. That makes sense: people enlist in the Legion to start their lives over. And because it's the *Foreign* Legion, if you happen to be French you also need to come up with a fictitious citizenship, probably something like Canadian or Belgian to explain why you speak French so fluently."

"Are you saying that at the time of their disappearances the le Sabre men enlisted in the French Foreign Legion under assumed names and nationalities?"

"Yes, yes, and yes. That's one yes for each of the three le Sabres who 'disappeared' so mysteriously. And it's also for the role played by the number three in your dream."

"But I was under the impression that the officers in the Legion were Frenchmen from the regular Army."

"Not all of them, Quentin. About 10 percent rise through the ranks."

"How come you're so knowledgeable about the French Foreign Legion?"

"As you know, after the skiing accident in which my parents died, my maternal grandparents, the Earl and Countess of Dover, brought me up. The Earl had been a major in Her Majesty's 1st The Queen's Dragoon Guards—yes, that's really the name of the senior regiment of the line of the British Army. Soldiers of the QDG were deployed in Lebanon in 1983 in support of the United Nations Multinational Force during the Lebanese Civil War, along with the 2nd Parachute Regiment of the French Foreign Legion. For some reason, his contact with the Legion resulted in a total obsession with that branch of the French Army; hardly a day went by without some reference to *le Légion Étrangère*. And one of his many annoying habits was singing *Le Boudin* at the top of his voice while marching around the house at exactly 88 paces per minute, the parade cadence of the Legionnaires."

"What's *Le Boudin*?"

"It's the official marching song of the Legion. I've no idea what the name means, and I certainly don't know the meaning of the words either, because it's a French song, naturally. Anyhow, as I was saying, about a tenth of the officers of the Legion are promoted from the ranks. That would explain what happened to the three 'missing' le Sabres. I'm sure of it."

"Hold on, your argument has a flaw somewhere. To be an officer in the Legion, you must be a French citizen, not a Belgian or a Canadian."

"That's not a problem. Once you're in the Legion, you have the possibility of acquiring French citizenship. After three years of outstanding service, you can apply to become a Frenchman. You have to give your real name and provide proof that the authorities are no longer after you."

I smiled wryly. "That wouldn't have worked. The three le Sabres would never ever have divulged their real names under any circumstances whatsoever."

"True. But the regulations also include a second route to citizenship. Any soldier who becomes injured during a battle for France immediately becomes a French citizen."

"Yes, I've heard of that," I said. "They call it *Français par le sang versé*, or French by spilled blood. If that's how they acquired French citizenship, they wouldn't have to give their real names; they could retain their *noms de geurre*. But how could they guarantee that they'd become wounded?"

"If you volunteer for enough dangerous duty in wartime—and the Legion has been involved in dozens of wars since 1945—and you insist on playing the hero, sooner or later you're going to get wounded."

"Or, more likely, killed," I observed.

"True. But clearly all three of them were lucky, and they survived their injuries and became French Army officers. And in the case of Philippe the Eighth and Philippe the Ninth, they informed their sons at the appropriate time as to what they'd done and instructed them to follow in the footsteps of their respective fathers."

"That's a good point, Marina. I was wondering how the next generation would know what to do."

"That means the only thing we have to do is get a list of all the legionnaires promoted from the ranks who kept their names and we'll find our men."

"I doubt if we can do that right now. Why don't we go back to sleep until morning?"

Marina scoffed. "Sleep? Who wants to sleep? We've solved the mystery!"

"I'm not sure how to put this tactfully, but all we've managed is a preliminary step. Tomorrow—"

"You mean today. It's four o'clock in the morning—"

"Which is precisely why we need to go back to sleep. We can't do a thing about finding the perpetrator until people get to work, which usually means about nine o'clock."

"Who are we going to talk to?" Marina asked. "Major Gilles Despoir?"

"No. We're going to visit Doudou, the police lieutenant."

"Why Doudou?"

"I want him to phone his cousin, Gaspard the General, at the Army Human Resources Directorate and ask him to put us in touch with his opposite number at the Foreign Legion, whoever he or she might be. That person will have access to the files of the officers of the Legion. It should be straightforward enough from there."

CHAPTER TEN

"Bonjour, *madame!*" the lieutenant enthused, completely ignoring me.

I wondered what would've happened if I'd followed in the footsteps of the last three Philippe le Sabres and disappeared off the face of the earth. When Marina rushed to the police station to report me missing, Doudou would undoubtedly reply, "I'm sorry, *madame*, but no such person exists."

Forgetting that my wife can't speak a word of French, Doudou tried to charm her; I assumed that having a wife and only two mistresses wasn't enough for him. He eventually realized that she hadn't understood a word he'd spoken to her, so he turned to me and asked, "Would you please translate what I told your wife?"

I was strongly tempted to say something along the lines of *Darling, the lieutenant says that you look like a baboon's backside and you have the morals of a sewer rat*, but I knew that Marina wouldn't believe me. Instead I decided to tell her what I knew she'd be pleased to hear. "The lieutenant says that his wife and one of his mistresses loved your book, exactly like everyone else in France."

Marina looked gratified and smiled appreciatively at Doudou. Before he could continue to try to seduce her, I quickly jumped in. "Lieutenant, we need your help. My wife has come up with a truly brilliant idea."

I'll say this for Doudou, he caught on after only two or three sentences. So I said, "Would you please phone Gaspard the General, your cousin, and ask him if we could meet with him?"

"No, no," the lieutenant replied. "Gaspard isn't the right person. You need to talk to Valérie. She's in charge of information technology in the Legion."

"Don't tell, let me guess: she's your cousin, and she's also a general. Am I right? Aren't all your cousins generals?"

"*Monsieur*," Doudou replied, "Valérie is my aunt, not my cousin. And she's only a colonel. And only some of my cousins are generals. Gaspard you already know, and Jean-Luc, Auguste, Clément, and Daphné are all Army generals. And so is Jérôme; I forgot about him. And I mustn't overlook Aline, but she's not on speaking terms with anyone in the family—she's a truly nasty piece of work, and paranoid to boot. In the navy, Jules and Raphaël are admirals, and Ségolène is an air force general."

"If almost everyone in your family has flag rank, why haven't they ordered your superiors to promote you well above the rank of lieutenant?"

Doudou gave a Gallic shrug. "*Monsieur*, I am the *brebis galeuse* of the family."

"The black sheep? Why? What did you do?"

"Soon after I left school, I became a pacifist. Even though it was only for a few months, it wasn't a particularly smart move."

"No, I can see that. As a matter of interest, is your father also a general?"

"No, *monsieur*. He's the Deputy Minister of Defense."

I realized that Marina and I had come to the right person. "Lieutenant, could you please have a word with your Aunt Valérie and ask her if she'll meet with us?"

"Certainly. Let me see if I can find her number. Excuse me, please." And Doudou disappeared into the room behind the charge-office.

A few minutes later he returned. "You have an appointment with Valérie at half past nine tomorrow morning in Aubagne."

"Aubagne?"

"It's an outlying suburb on the east side of Marseille. Around 1960, when Algeria became independent, they moved the headquarters of the Legion from Sidi Bel Abbès to Aubagne. Why

Aubagne? I'm afraid have no idea." He shrugged again and then continued.

"My suggestion would be to fly to Marseille this afternoon, rent a car, sleep at a hotel at the airport, and drive to Aubagne in the morning. Two other things. The rule about *noms de guerre* has changed recently, but I'm sure Valérie will explain all that to you. And when you arrive at Aubagne, tell them you have an appointment with Colonel Demoiseaux. You'll have to bring your passports, of course."

I immediately realized that we had a complication on our hands, because our passports were in the names of Quentin and Marina Pakenham. I started to explain to Doudou that Marina's passport is in her married name.

The lieutenant seemed stunned. "You're not *Monsieur* and *Madame* Aver-smeet?"

"No. My wife's *nom de jeune fille* was Haversmith, and she wrote *She Loved the French Captain* before we were married. Darling, do you happen to have your passport with you to show the Lieutenant?"

Fortunately, Marina had her travel document in her handbag, and once again, Doudou caught on immediately. He promised to call back immediately and leave a corrected message for his aunt. We left the police station and headed for our usual café.

"What do you think?" I asked.

"I'm certain the le Sabres have been hiding in the Legion. And I'm extremely hopeful that Aunt Valérie will be able to help us."

"I'm sure she will. I have the utmost faith in Doudou and his military kin."

And then I had a sudden flashback from nearly thirty years back. "Marina, I've just had an idea, and it's an absolute humdinger. Are you familiar with the books by P. C. Wren? As a boy, I greatly enjoyed reading *Beau Geste* and *Beau Sabreur*. They're both adventure stories about the French Foreign Legion in Africa. Do you know the English bookshop on Rue Balmain? It's a wonderful emporium—they even stock all my bodice rippers. It's only a couple of blocks from here. Before we go to the café, why don't we go to the shop and try and buy those two books? I'm sure they're both still in print. We can read them before we meet with the colonel tomorrow morning."

"That's fine by me. Reading adventure stories for boys has been the second most pressing item on my bucket list for years and years."

"What's the first item?"

"Reading a good bodice ripper," Marina replied, with a wicked grin. I tried to maintain my dignity, but to no effect.

We entered the bookshop and almost immediately found a copy of *Beau Geste*, as well as a paperback entitled *Beau Trilogy* that comprised *Beau Geste*, *Beau Sabreur*, and *Beau Ideal*. The cover of each book

91

depicted an exciting moment in the life of a legionnaire. The flamboyant style revealed that they were unmistakably the work of Charles J. Conway, the third-rate artist who designed the covers of all thirteen of my books.

I noticed that the legionnaire who was ramming the bayonet fixed to the end of his rifle into the body of a turbaned Arab lying on the ground looked identical to the dark, exceptionally handsome man who graced the dust jackets of every one my books and, at the end of the novel, always turned out to be an exceptionally wealthy aristocrat. Perhaps I'm being unfair. I must admit that all my books have essentially the same plot, so that probably justifies having essentially the same man on the cover. However, I quickly noted one significant difference between Conway's artwork for my books and for Wren's adventure stories. In addition to the noble hero, the covers of my bodice rippers also always depict the same exceptionally scantily clad woman with an exceptionally long neck, exceptionally large heaving breasts, and exceptionally long flowing auburn hair arranged in an exceptional way. Surprisingly, the otherwise enterprising Charles J. Conway couldn't find a way to include her on the covers of the P. C. Wren books. Thank heavens.

We reached the café later than usual and were delighted to find that our usual table was still vacant. Claude, the only waiter on duty before eleven o'clock, came bustling up. I nodded to him to indicate that we wanted our usual order, and he hastened to the kitchen. We sat back and waited for our coffees.

After enjoying another dose of the weak early summer sun for a while, I took the two books out of the bag and laid them on the table side by side. At that moment, Claude arrived with our order. He carefully placed Marina's *double café espresso noisette* on the marble-topped table. He turned towards me, then dropped my coffee cup onto the pavement. Without saying a word, he bolted back to the kitchen.

After about five minutes, I began to get worried. The broken cup and saucer still lay where they'd fallen, and Claude seemed to have disappeared. I got up to talk to *Madame* the Proprietress at the cash desk inside the café.

"What's happened to Claude?" I asked.

"What do you mean?"

I told her what had happened.

"I'll go and see."

She returned shortly. "Claude has left the café. The chef says he tore off his apron, waistcoat, and black bow tie. He stuffed them into his locker, grabbed his jacket, and ran out the back door. It's unbelievable. He's worked here for more than twelve years, and nothing like this has ever happened before. He's been the perfect employee in every way."

"Maybe he's embarrassed that he let my coffee fall onto the pavement."

"And that's another thing. Claude never ever drops even the tiniest sugar cube, much less a full cup of coffee. No, *monsieur*, something is seriously wrong."

"Maybe he's been taken ill. Do you know where Claude lives? I'd like to make sure that he's okay."

She pulled a face. "Claude is a secretive person. The only address he's ever given me is a post office box. The tax authorities are quite happy with that, so I never saw the need to press the point. Now that I come to think of it, I wonder why he's never told me where he lives."

I thought for a second or two. "Could it be that he's living with someone and doesn't want her to be embarrassed?"

"It's undoubtedly possible. But in my experience, the woman soon turns up at the café for some reason or other. And no one has ever come here looking for her boyfriend. Not once in all the twelve years he's worked here."

Suddenly, I had an idea. "*Madame*, can you please tell me Claude's family name?"

"May I ask why?"

I understood the reason behind her question. The French are extraordinarily protective of personal information: confidentiality—and conspiracy—runs in their blood.

I decided to lie. "*Madame*, I am most concerned about Claude and I want to check the hospitals in the vicinity. I can't ask a triage nurse, 'Do you have a slightly overweight patient called Claude?' I need to know his last name."

She considered my request for a long while before answering. "Claude Malmaison. But don't tell him that I told you."

I thanked her, paid her for the two coffees, and returned to Marina, who was still sitting at the table. I spoke loudly enough to ensure that *Madame* the Proprietress could hear every word. "Claude seems to have been taken ill. Let's go home. I need to check hospitals and clinics."

I put the two books back in the packet and we left the café.

When we were out of earshot, I said to Marina as quietly as I could manage, "I'll explain everything when we get back to the apartment."

We took the lift to the third floor. In my excitement, I fumbled with the lock, but eventually we got inside. I invited a mystified Marina to sit down on the sofa. I sat on my usual armchair.

"What's going on?" Marina asked. "Claude's behavior is mystifying, but it's nothing compared to the way you're carrying on."

"I don't think Claude has anything wrong with him."

"Then why did you say what you did? And why were you talking so loudly?"

"I lied to *Madame* the Proprietress," I said. "I informed her that the reason that I needed to know

Claude's family name was to be able contact the local hospitals."

"And the real reason?"

"To be able to give Claude's name to Colonel Valérie Demoiseaux tomorrow morning."

"Are you out of your mind?"

"No, I'm not. Claude saw the covers of the two books when he served you your coffee, and he realized the game was up."

"'The game was up?' What 'game' is this? What on earth are you talking about?"

"Claude is the author of the letter. He's Philippe le Sabre the Tenth."

"You're crazy. My grandfather, the Earl of Dover, was certifiably insane. After all, he sliced my grandmother's head off with a samurai sword and then committed *hara-kiri*. But you're even crazier than he was."

"I'm not. Look at the facts. Claude is about fifty. He's been working at the café for some twelve years. That would tie in with his leaving the army at the age of about thirty-eight."

"What does age have to do with it? Quentin, did you have a few drinks when you went to talk to *Madame* the Proprietress? An armagnac or two? Or more?"

I ignored the slight. "He's never given *Madame* the Proprietress his home address. And why? Because he has a wife, and her married name is le Sabre. And when Claude saw those truly awful French Foreign Legion illustrations on the covers of the two books lying on the café table, he realized I was onto him. He dropped the cup, something he never does, rushed out of the café, and is surely on his way out of France."

Marina shook her head. "I still think you're crazy. And when we meet with Aunt Valérie tomorrow morning, I don't have the slightest doubt that she'll tell you exactly the same thing."

CHAPTER ELEVEN

Susan Travers is the only woman who has ever served in the French Foreign Legion. Born in England, she was a nurse and ambulance driver with the French Red Cross during World War II. After the war, she enlisted in the Legion and served in Vietnam during the First Indochina War. Her many acts of heroism resulted in the French government awarding her three medals: the Légion d'Honneur, the Croix de Guerre, and the Médaille Militaire.

Accordingly, I certainly didn't expect Colonel Valérie Demoiseaux to be dressed in the light khaki uniform that legionnaire officers wear for day-to-day duties. On the other hand, when the elderly legionnaire sergeant with grizzled hair escorted us into her office, I was most surprised to see that the information technology specialist sported both paratrooper's wings and a commando badge on the blouse of her blue air force uniform. I had a vision of a battalion of air force commandos descending from the skies, with the colonel brandishing a fearsome automatic weapon in one hand and a laptop computer in the other.

As we walked into her office, I realized with a start that we'd forgotten to bring along a copy of *She Loved the French Captain.* I needn't have worried. Lying on her desk was the French translation.

Valérie Demoiseaux ordered her sergeant to bring us coffee. As he left the room, she shouted, "Grind the good beans that we serve to visitors. We certainly don't want guests from Paris to think that we're country bumpkins!"

Turning to us with a broad grin, she asked in perfect English, "What brings you to Aubagne? The cryptic message that my nefarious nephew Doudou left with the sergeant wasn't terribly enlightening."

I left out details like my dream and got straight to the point. "My wife's life has been threatened. Perhaps you would like to read the letter."

The colonel's eyebrows slowly rose as she read it. "Interesting. What did the police say?"

"They're undoubtedly doing their best, but they've encountered what appears to be an insurmountable obstacle: they can't find a record of anyone named Philippe le Sabre serving in the French Army in any capacity, let alone as an officer, since 1944. They've been able to use Army Lists to trace seven generations, starting with Philippe the First, who fought in Russia with Napoleon Bonaparte. But the line of officers stops near the end of the Second

World War. However, Marina has come up with an interesting idea; she thinks that the letter writer is a former officer in the Legion."

"Indeed? And what makes you say that, Mrs. Pakenham?"

"We have an obvious disconnect between the ten generations of French army officers as stated in the letter you've just read and the seven generations found in the Army Lists. One way to resolve the contradiction would be if the last three Philippe le Sabres enlisted in the Foreign Legion. As Frenchmen, they would've had to change their names and declare a foreign nationality, but they could reacquire French citizenship without resuming their original names if they were wounded in battle. We're here to ask you if any legionnaires who rose in the ranks happen to fit the bill. If Philippe the Eighth joined the Legion, it would probably have been in 1947. His son, Philippe the Ninth, would've enlisted around 1969, and Philippe the Tenth in 1990."

The colonel said to Marina, "I understand. But before I answer your question, I need to clarify something. Nowadays, the Legion is extremely selective. Volunteers must pass physical, medical, and intelligence tests. Furthermore, before anything else, they have to produce their passports or European Union identity cards. And we check their financial, criminal, family, medical, and employment history. Also, we assign a new name to each recruit, the next on a list based on his actual initials. A volunteer can no longer choose his own name.

"What I'm saying is that today it would be possible for someone named Philippe le Sabre to join the Legion. But irrespective of the new identity we assigned to him, we'd have a record of the name he held when he enlisted. As a result, I could answer your question in seconds by searching the database for anyone with the family name le Sabre. Unfortunately, I gather that the three missing le Sabres enlisted in the Legion before we changed the rules in the last few years."

I heard a polite knock on the open door, and the sergeant entered bearing a tray with our coffee.

The colonel ignored the interruption. "As I understand it, you want me to start with all the individuals who enlisted in the Legion since 1945. Within that set, you want a list of men who satisfy three criteria. First, they acquired French citizenship by virtue of being wounded in battle for France. Second, they didn't revert to their birth names when they became Frenchmen. And third, they were promoted to officers from the ranks. Is that correct?"

We both nodded.

"I would very much like to help you, not least because I think that your life is in danger. Unfortunately, my hands are tied for two different reasons. We don't have the personnel to computerize our old records, so compiling a complete list would entail a lengthy manual search of every file since 1945. Our database goes back to only 1972. If your theory is correct, we could quickly come up with a list that definitely would include Philippe the Tenth, and almost certainly Philippe the Ninth. But if Philippe the Eighth served in the Legion for less than twenty years, he's not going to be in our computers, and it could take weeks of work to find him. I realize the one you want most is Philippe the Tenth, the man who has threatened to kill you, but even with him we have an obstacle. Giving you the information would violate French and European Union confidentiality regulations. My advice would be to go back to the police, tell them your theory, and convince them to request such a list from me. Not only would that solve the personal privacy issue, but police personnel would do the work of searching our files for Philippe the Eighth."

She added politely, "Can I do anything else for you?"

Marina spoke up. "My husband suspects that the writer of the letter is a man who calls himself Claude Malmaison. He was born around 1970. If he's indeed Philippe le Sabre the Tenth then he would've enlisted around 1990 and left the army around 2008, which means he's on your computers. I understand about confidentiality, but as you correctly pointed out, my life is in danger. Is it possible for you to interrogate your computer and tell us if he satisfies the three criteria?"

"Your husband would first have to tell me why he thinks this man wrote the letter. Mr. Pakenham, what are the grounds for your suspicion?"

I told the colonel about the incident in the café with the P. C. Wren books.

She looked at me quizzically. "You've made an awful lot of assumptions and unsupported suppositions, haven't you?"

"That's true, Colonel Demoiseaux. On the other hand, can you come up with any other explanation that fits the facts?"

She laughed. "Okay, you win. I'm entering my password so that I can interrogate the database. Now I'll type in the name Malmaison and see what comes up. The system is user-friendly and it's quite easy to . . . one moment. *Qu'est-ce que c'est que ça?*"

I wondered what she could've seen that was so astonishing that it caused her to return to her mother tongue and ask herself, *What on earth is this?* But she didn't say anything more. Instead, she alternately studied the monitor and typed furiously. The tick-tack sound went on and on until I was almost ready to scream. At long last, she looked away from her screen.

"Mr. Pakenham, confidentiality be damned—I'm sure that your wife's life is in danger. I have two things to tell you. First, a man who called himself Claude Malmaison enlisted in 1990 and—"

"That's the year in which Philippe the Tenth disappeared!" Marina shouted.

Colonel Demoiseaux smiled encouragingly. "Yes, it is. And about a year after he enlisted, he was involved in the evacuation of French citizens and other foreigners in the Republic of Zaire, formerly the Belgian Congo and now the Democratic Republic of the Congo. I've just looked up the details; that's one reason why it took me so long. In September 1991, Zairian soldiers looted Kinshasa, the capital of Zaire, to protest unpaid wages. Two thousand French and Belgian troops, including Malmaison's battalion, flew in to rescue the twenty thousand endangered foreign nationals. Malmaison was shot in the groin while carrying two small children to an evacuation plane at an airstrip near Kinshasa. Despite the seriousness of his wound, he somehow managed to stagger to the aircraft without dropping the children. He even managed to continue to shield them from gunfire with his body. He made a full recovery, after which he acquired French citizenship 'by spilled blood' without revealing his birth name, let alone adopting it. His performance after he returned to duty was outstanding in every way, and three years later he was promoted from the ranks. Yes, Mr. Pakenham, you were quite right. Claude Malmaison satisfies all three criteria.

"But I've found something more. The other reason I took so long was that I wanted to check if

104

any other legionnaires in the computer system also satisfied the same three criteria. The answer surprised me: I found exactly one other person. His name is Bertrand Malmaison, and he enlisted in 1969."

Marina and I grinned triumphantly at one another.

Then Marina asked, "Colonel Demoiseaux, I assume you found a photograph of Claude Malmaison in your files. May we please see it?"

She tapped a few keys, then turned the monitor around. A younger version of Claude was staring straight at us. He was a lot thinner and the pencil moustache was missing, but it was unquestionable that this was our waiter from our favorite café.

"That's definitely and unmistakably him," I said, revealing that the many weeks I'd spent in the company of Lancelot Aylesworth, millionaire newspaper proprietor and punctilious grammarian, had done nothing to convince me of the value of speaking pedantically correct English.

"Let me be quite clear," the colonel said. "If your theory is correct, Mrs. Pakenham, then Claude Malmaison is Philippe the Tenth, the author of the threatening document. But maybe we can uncover another mechanism whereby someone can serve in our military under an assumed name. I can't think of one, but it may be possible. The important thing is for me to contact the police right away with what I've found out so they can start looking for Malmaison to interrogate him. Who's handling the case?"

"Major Gilles Despoir, at the Regional Directorate of the Paris Judicial Police."

"Yes, at 36 Quai des Orfèvres. Well, he's only a major. We'll need to go higher than that. The PJP falls under the Paris Police Prefecture, and the current *Prevote*—that's the senior police officer in the prefecture—is my brother-in-law. I'll call JoJo and have this sorted out right now. But before you go, Mrs. Pakenham, could you please sign my copy of your masterpiece?"

* * *

"That was a most successful trip to Marseilles," Marina said as we walked into our third-floor apartment. "I'm convinced that Claude is our man."

"So am I, but perhaps for a different reason."

"Oh? And why are you so certain he's the perpetrator?"

"Chekhov's Gun, of course. I wrote about Claude in Chapter One. I originally believed that I included him because he served our coffee, but now I realize that he's there because he wrote the letter."

"So you've changed your mind, have you?" Marina replied. "You decided it was Adrien Legendre simply because of Chekhov's Gun. Now it's Claude, for the same reason. And women are supposed to be flighty! Does that mean that you now have to remove Adrien from Chapter One and therefore from the book?"

106

"I don't think so. I thought Chapter Five was quite interesting, and I managed to include some amusing bits."

Marina pulled a face. "I didn't find the exorbitant price of the wine you bought to impress a teetotaler to be particularly amusing."

"No, that's true. But my confusion over the word *beard* made up for it."

"I don't think so. When you receive our credit card account this month, I doubt you'll see anything even remotely funny in the events of that evening."

CHAPTER TWELVE

"We have a problem," Major Gilles Despoir said.

We were back in his sailing ship-themed office at 36 Quai des Orfèvres at the request of JoJo, Aunt Valérie's brother-in-law and the *Prevote* of the Paris Police Prefecture. It seemed that JoJo's English was essentially nonexistent, and accordingly, he'd decided that Major Despoir should continue to be our contact person.

"More precisely," the major continued, "we have three problems. We can't locate Claude Malmaison. The chef at the café saw him run out the back door, and we've yet to find anyone who claims to have seen him since."

I nodded.

"The second problem is worse. Suppose we were to find Claude. We couldn't charge him with any crime."

"But what about the letter?" Marina asked.

"We can't prove that he wrote it. No physical evidence links him to it."

"But what about the signature?" I asked. "Surely a handwriting expert can use that to tie Claude to the document?"

"Unfortunately not. The signature was computer-generated. Worse, our people can't even determine which of the many programs available on the internet the perpetrator used to produce the 'handwritten' signature."

Marina started to get flustered. "What about DNA evidence? Use that."

Despoir smiled sadly. "Suppose we arrest Claude and suppose further that both he and Nicole, the wife of Philippe the Ninth, agree to give DNA samples, which is by no means a given. And suppose still further that the genetics experts tell us that Nicole is indeed Claude's mother. What then?"

"That would prove Claude is Philippe the Tenth," I said.

"Not exactly," Major Despoir replied. "If you want to want prove that, you'd have to show that Claude's father is Philippe the Ninth. But we can't find Bertrand Malmaison either. And even if we could locate him, how would we verify that Bertrand is actually Philippe the Ninth? His parents are dead. In addition, we've found a newspaper article that suggests Bertrand himself died some years ago. He was apparently swept away when his small fishing boat encountered an incoming tidal surge in the Bay of St. Malo; his body was never found. In that area, the tide raises the water level by more than thirty feet, but this was a spring tide and the surge was over forty feet. If it proves to be true that Bertrand drowned at sea, the only living descendants of Philippe the Seventh are Claude and his mother."

I had an idea. "Can't you dig up the body of Philippe the Eighth and compare his DNA with that of his grandson, Claude?"

"We thought of that," Despoir replied, "but we've found records that show that a man named Alphonse Malmaison was cremated. But even if that information is erroneous and we could lay our hands on the body of Alphonse Malmaison, we couldn't prove that he was Philippe the Eighth.

"That led one of my colleagues to suggest that the way to be certain beyond all doubt that Claude is the great-grandson of Philippe the Seventh would be to exhume the body of the traitor and test his DNA. That's obviously impossible to do, given that the explosion of the ammunition train reduced Philippe the Seventh to atoms.

"And it's even more convoluted than that. Merely for the sake of argument, let's imagine that we somehow manage to locate Claude and he freely admits under oath that he's Philippe the Tenth. What then? Our third problem is that we can't prove Claude wrote the letter. After all, anyone can compose a document on a word processor and add a computer-generated signature at the bottom. I'm sure Claude would deny that he had anything to do with the threatening letter, and that'll be the end of it."

"Not so," Marina interjected. "Claude took one look at the French Foreign Legion adventure books lying on the table in the café, dropped the coffee cup, and fled."

"I'm afraid that that's not really evidence of anything," the policeman replied, as gently as he could. "Claude could come up with any number of likely explanations. Or, more likely, he'll simply say nothing at all. The onus is on the police to establish that Claude's actions prove he wrote the letter. And that would be extremely hard to do."

"But he was in the Foreign Legion," Marina insisted. "We saw his photograph in Colonel Demoiseaux's office. It was definitely Claude."

"I understand. But what if he says the lurid covers of the books brought back the horrific memory of the wound he received while saving the lives of those two children and that was why he dropped the coffee and rushed out? After all, graphic flashbacks are a common consequence of post-traumatic stress disorder."

Neither Marina nor I could think of an answer.

Major Gilles Despoir looked Marina straight in the eye. "Mrs. Pakenham, I can assure you that everyone involved in this case is 120 percent certain that Claude Malmaison is Philippe the Tenth and that he was responsible for the letter you received. But not even the finest legal brains attached to the French police

111

forces have been able to come up with a valid reason for arresting him.

"As you probably already know, he's a highly trained commando. Also, he has the financial resources, in the form of extensive tips he's never declared to the tax authorities, to live underground for a long period. He's probably armed, and unquestionably he's dangerous. So until we find him, we're providing you with twenty-four-hour armed police protection."

"Before you do that," I said, "I think we need to discuss something. I'm sure the paper files of the Legion will reflect that a man who called himself Alphonse Malmaison enlisted in 1947, and I strongly suspect you'll be able to demonstrate that his real name was Philippe le Sabre the Eighth. It's virtually certain that the man calling himself Bertrand Malmaison who enlisted in 1969 was Philippe the Ninth and that our Claude Malmaison was Philippe the Tenth."

The other two nodded their agreement.

I persevered. "Philippe the Eighth, Philippe the Ninth, and Philippe the Tenth went to extraordinary lengths to disguise the fact that they're descendants of Philippe the Seventh, a traitor of the very worst kind. For example, they cut themselves off from their wives and their infant sons. And all three of them must've chosen to put themselves in extreme danger in order to deliberately shed blood for France. In short, it's not too much of an exaggeration to claim that they all devoted a considerable portion of their lives to disguising their origins."

They both nodded again.

"It therefore makes no sense to me," I went on, "that Claude would jeopardize his false identity in any way at all. The letter couldn't possibly have been from him and—"

"I disagree," Marina interrupted. "The name 'Philippe le Sabre' was sacred to him, irrespective of what his great-grandfather did. Inadvertently, I brought his ancestor into disrepute—"

"No, you didn't," I interrupted in turn. "That's the second contention that suddenly came to me. The letter stated that you 'despoiled and desecrated the family name by writing a scurrilous novel about his gallant and fearless ancestor.' But you didn't. What you wrote regarding that captain in the French Imperial Guards wasn't the least bit scurrilous. On the contrary, you painted him as a most heroic figure.

"And I have to tell you about a third contention."

I paused for a few seconds to gather my thoughts. "Major Despoir, you've told us Claude Malmaison is a killer. Your actual words were, if I recollect correctly, 'a highly trained commando,' but that's nothing more than a polite way of putting it. If Claude wanted to murder my wife, he'd simply go ahead and kill her. He wouldn't have sent a warning letter.

"In short, that letter is a load of nonsense. No way could Claude Malmaison possibly have written it, despite the fact that it was signed 'Philippe le Sabre.' Someone else sent it, someone who isn't from the line of French officers bearing that name."

"Could it have been Philippe the Ninth, otherwise known as Bertrand Malmaison?" Despoir asked. But I could hear a strong note of doubt in his voice.

"No. My first two contentions apply equally to father and son. And for all I know, Bertrand may also be a highly trained commando. As a matter of fact, he probably is."

"I strongly agree," my wife said. "But then who wrote the letter? And why?"

The phone on Despoir's desk rang. "I ordered you to hold all calls. How dare you interrupt this meeting . . . Oh, I see . . . Thank you for telling me."

He smiled faintly. "They've found Claude Malmaison. He's suffering from severe post-traumatic stress disorder, manifested primarily as an extreme form of fight-or-flight response and secondarily by confusion and partial amnesia. He's being transferred to the psychiatric ward in a military hospital. My guess would be that they'll send him to Druny Military Hospital in Bagnolet, no more than five miles from here."

I stared at him. "Isn't PTSD exactly what you suggested as a possible explanation of why he fled from the café after seeing the covers of the two books?"

Major Despoir nodded. Then he added, "Obviously, we can call off the twenty-four-hour police guard. That's the good news. The bad news is that, thanks to your analysis, we're right back to square one. We've no idea who wrote that letter. And we don't know why he sent it to you."

As he rose from his seat to usher us out, Marina asked, "Where did they find Claude?"

"I'll find out for you in a moment."

Resuming his seat, he pushed a few buttons on his phone. The person at the other end didn't seem to have that information, nor did the next one, but eventually the major smiled at Marina and replaced the handset.

"I'm amazed none of my subordinates bothered to ask that question. However, they finally put me through to the policeman who found Malmaison. He was cowering under a bush in a fetal position right next to Monet's garden in Giverny."

CHAPTER THIRTEEN

When we returned to our apartment, Marina headed for the big bookcase in the living room, pulled out a few books, and laid them on the coffee table.

I was totally mystified. "Interior decorators usually suggest that you put art books on coffee tables, not paperback novels. Is this some new fashion trend?"

Marina wisely ignored my sarcasm. "On the left are the two P. C. Wren books that you bought. On the right is the French translation of *She Loved the French Captain.*"

"Yes, I can see that."

"Do you notice any sort of resemblance between the male figures?" she asked.

"Darling, we've discussed this ad nauseam. All three covers were incontrovertibly created by the inimitable Charles J. Conway, notwithstanding my pathetic pleas to my publisher humbly begging that the covers of my books be designed by an artist with even a modicum of talent.

"I assume," I went on, "that you're trying to send me some sort of message. I'm sorry to say that the communication is as clear as mud."

Marina raised her eyebrows. "Is nothing getting through to you?"

"Not a jot. Not even an iota."

"Here's a clue: Claude fled to Monet's garden at Giverny."

"If you're trying to suggest that Charles J. Conway is the new Monet, then I have to ask you what you've been smoking."

"Darling, believe it or not you're starting to think along the correct lines. Sort of. Maybe. In a way. So let me ask you this: What do Charles J. Conway and Monet have in common?"

That one was easy to answer. "Nothing. Absolutely nothing. Monet was an artist, but Charles J. Conway probably can't even spell the word *art*."

"Now you're being unkind."

"No, Marina, I'm being realistic. Which is something Charles J. Conway tries to achieve in his so-called art but fails miserably every time. Just look at the woman on the cover of *She Loved the French Captain*. I'm surprised you approved it."

"As you know very well, Quentin, Lane Hookham Press brooks no interference from authors when it comes to cover design."

"I'll concede that small point, grudgingly, but I won't budge an inch in my relentless criticism of

Charles J. Conway. Anyhow, why don't you tell me what that miserable worm of a would-be artist has in common with Monet?"

Marina looked amused. "Their work is instantly recognizable. When you see a glorious masterpiece depicting water lilies or haystacks or Rouen Cathedral, you immediately say, 'Monet.'"

"And when you see a cover by Charles J. Conway, you immediately say, 'Oh—!'"

"Quentin! Mind your language! Whatever would your readers think? Profanities are absolutely forbidden in historical romance fiction. As you're well aware, even the mildest of the mild imprecations and execrations are totally taboo when it comes to bodice rippers. By the way, what's the difference between an imprecation and an execration?"

"Let's stick to the topic under discussion, if you don't mind. Are you trying to tell me that the cause of the outbreak of PSTD in Claude was the cover art on the two P. C. Wren books and not the association with the French Foreign Legion?"

"First and foremost, it's PTSD, not PSTD. And secondly—"

"Correcting acronyms," I said, "invariably induces post-traumatic stress disorder in authors, including your dearly beloved husband, so don't do it again. Ever. And your second point?"

"In my opinion, the most traumatic event in Claude's life was suddenly learning what his great-grandfather did in World War II, not Claude's rescue of the children in Zaire when he received that bullet in the groin. On seeing the covers of the two P. C. Wren books on the marble table top, he immediately thought of the cover of *She Loved the French Captain*, and that naturally made him think of Captain Philippe le Sabre. And that, in turn, triggered his PSTD."

"You mean PTSD," I said as maliciously as I could.

Marina stuck out her tongue. "You're impossible."

"True. And that's why you married me."

She rolled her eyes. "Anyhow, that's why he fled. As to why he chose Giverny as his bolt hole, I'm still not clear. I grudgingly admit that in one respect you were quite right: It's impossible to find any connection, no matter how tenuous, between Monet and Charles J. Conway."

"And I don't understand one thing," I said. "Why is it so important that Claude's PTSD was triggered by the memory of Philippe the Seventh, rather than by recalling the Zaire incident that occurred while he was serving in the Foreign Legion?"

"If the covers of the P. C. Wren books reminded him of his great-grandfather, then he must've seen the cover of *She Loved the French Captain*. And that means that he might well have written the letter."

I wasn't happy with Marina's answer. "But we've just met with Major Gilles Despoir, and I gave him three excellent reasons why Claude couldn't possibly have penned it. Why didn't you speak up then?"

"What you explained in his office sounded so plausible. But after thinking about it for a while, I realized that it might be possible to look at Claude's PTSD in another way. If I'm right, and I think I am, then we'll also have to look at the letter in a different light."

I thought about that for a while. "Darling, the reason we were so worried that Claude wrote the letter was because the man is a trained killer; threats from someone with his background can never be taken lightly. But now he's safely ensconced in a psychiatric ward, and I'm sure the police will ensure he'll stay locked away until they find the culprit."

"Surely you mean Claude will stay in the hospital until he gets better?"

"In a perfect world, that's what would happen. That said, I strongly suspect that, even though I think I can convince Despoir to release Claude when the doctors pronounce him cured, Gilles's superiors will keep Claude locked up until his name can be cleared by finding the actual perpetrator. After all, the powerful Frenchmen who make the genuinely important decisions in this country aren't going to take any risks. They're well aware that if anything were to happen to *Madame* Aver-smeet their wives would make their lives utterly unendurable. And so would their mistresses."

"That certainly makes me feel a lot safer," Marina said, "but only if Claude really is the perpetrator. In the unlikely event that you're right and someone else wrote the letter, then locking Claude up and throwing away the key won't help me a bit."

"Don't worry," I said as brightly as I could. "I have an idea."

Marina chose to ignore my attempt at cheerfulness and proceeded to replace the three Conway-covered paperbacks in the bookcase. Her action greatly improved the appearance of our coffee table, but her attitude did nothing for my self-esteem. So I tried again.

"Ahem. Author to dearly beloved wife. I have an idea."

This time she looked in my direction, but she still didn't respond.

"You don't especially like my ideas, do you?" I asked, perhaps just fractionally too aggressively.

"Darling, you've been wrong on virtually everything else so far, but let's hear your latest suggestion. I could do with a good laugh."

"Why don't we go and talk to Claude?"

"In the psychiatric ward in that military hospital?"

"Exactly," I said. "That's where he is, and that's where we'll visit him."

"You're crazy."

"No, Claude is the one in the psychiatric ward. I'm sane. Well, saner than Claude. I think."

"No, darling, you're out of your mind. What makes you think they'll let you into a French military hospital?"

"Because I'm married to *Madame* Aver-smeet, that's why. You'll phone Gilles Despoir. You'll tell him you'd like to thank him for his help by sending his wife a signed copy of the French translation of *She Loved the French Captain*. And then you'll ask him if you can visit Claude Malmaison. Unquestionably, he'll say yes."

"Unquestionably, he'll say no. Maybe, just maybe, he'll be polite. He'll claim he has to consult the military authorities, and that will be the end of it. But in any event, he'll tell me that I already signed a copy of the book for his wife. If you had a memory slightly more retentive than that of an average goldfish, you'd remember that happened in Chapter Eight, on the day of our first meeting in his office."

"You're quite right, Marina. I'd completely forgotten. That means we need to try Plan B."

"Plan B?"

"Doudou."

"Forget it. We've already used him to get to Aunt Valérie. We can't use him again."

"What if we invite him to dinner to thank him?"

"With whom? His wife? His mistress who loved the book? His other mistress, the one with an utterly abysmal taste in literature? The whole ménage?"

"I take your point," I conceded. "So now we go to Plan C: you invite his wife or his mistress—the one who loved the book, naturally—for afternoon tea this weekend."

"Afternoon tea, Quentin? Do you think you're living in London? This is Paris. Paris is in France, and French people don't indulge in afternoon tea."

"Is that so? So why did Marie Antoinette say, 'Let them eat cake'?"

"She never said that," Marina insisted.

"Is that a fact? What did she say, then? Something along the lines of, 'Let them eat cucumber sandwiches on super-thinly-sliced bread'?"

"I thought everyone knew that the phrase 'Let them eat cake' first appeared in Jean-Jacques Rousseau's *Confessions*, written at least twenty-five years before the French Revolution."

"Everyone with a Cambridge degree believes that," I said. "Those of us who received the superior education offered at Oxford University know that Rousseau wrote about a princess who, when informed that the peasants had no bread, replied, 'Let them eat brioche.'"

Marina stuck her tongue out at me. And I retorted by thumbing my nose.

Honor having been satisfied, I returned to Plan C.

"As I was saying, Marina, I'll phone Doudou and tell him—"

"Wait a second. Doudou doesn't speak much English."

"True. Do you know, that's rather surprising. Most French people of his age are fluent English speakers, but that's how it is," I said.

"And what makes you think that his wife and mistresses speak sufficient English to be comfortable having tea with *Madame* Aver-smeet, an otherwise delightful woman who regrettably cannot understand a word of French?"

"Fine. Plan D, then. Any ideas?" I asked.

"Oddly enough, yes. Why don't we invite Major Despoir and his wife for tea? Gilles is totally fluent in English; you might not have been at Cambridge, but your English isn't too bad for someone educated at 'the other place.' So, even if *Madame* Despoir's English is as limited as my French, our respective husbands will be able to translate for us."

"Now that's an excellent plan. Once *Madame* Despoir has spent an hour or two in your company, her husband will be putty in her hands. Your request to Gilles to authorize us to visit poor Claude will result in Mr. Gilles receiving a short, sharp kick under the table from Mrs. Gilles, and that will be that. How clever you are, my dear, notwithstanding the three years you spent as a student at—"

The short, sharp kick I received brought that conversation to a painful end.

CHAPTER FOURTEEN

"Good afternoon, Mr. Pakenham. How kind of you to invite us over for tea. I'd like you to meet my wife. Priscilla, this is Mr. Pakenham."

They say that first impressions matter. My first impression of *Madame* Despoir was of a statuesque blonde with an hourglass figure. She walked towards me, right hand extended precisely as specified in those etiquette books I've never read.

"How do you do, Mr. Pakenham? We're delighted that—"

She stopped talking the instant she saw Marina. Then she yelled, "Bubbles!" at the top of her voice.

Not to be outdone, my wife screamed, "Chunky Monkey!" loudly enough to be heard back in London. The two women rushed towards one other and embraced enthusiastically, while Gilles and I stood wordlessly, utterly bewildered.

I looked at Gilles. He looked at me. We simultaneously gave a Gallic shrug.

The clinch lasted considerably longer than most boxing referees would've allowed. Eventually, Marina spoke. "Priscilla and I were in the same class at school."

"Gilles," his wife said, "why didn't you tell me that we were having tea with Marina Haversmith and her husband? You're impossible. Marina and I were at boarding school together for twelve years, and you didn't think that fact was important enough to share the good news with me? And even if you had no idea we were best friends for twelve years, don't you think I'd have liked to know that we were going to visit the author of *She Loved the French Captain*, my favorite book of all time?"

"Well, dear, I thought, er, I thought—"

"Men!" Priscilla declaimed in a voice that made it unmistakably clear that one gender was infinitely superior to the other, and it wasn't the one with the Y-chromosomes. "Come on, Bubbles, let's go to your room and catch up."

I turned to Gilles Despoir. "Have a seat. Better still, have a seat and have a drink. How about a stiff whisky? I have a bottle of eighteen-year-old Lochervan, the finest single-malt Scotland ever produced, in my opinion."

Despoir nodded and sat on the sofa. I poured two triple whiskies and handed one to Gilles. He nodded again. We sat in companionable silence for a while.

"By the way," I said, "my wife has never mentioned Priscilla to me. And I gather that your wife hasn't mentioned Marina to you."

Gilles nodded gloomily.

"Not only do they expect us to live up to their expectations in every way," I continued, "but we're also supposed to be mind readers."

Another silent nod.

"And where do they come up with those nicknames? No way could your gorgeous wife ever have been 'Chunky' in any way, not even when she was little. And what was all that about 'Bubbles'?"

This time, not even a nod.

Once again we sat without speaking, slowly sipping our *uisge beatha*, as they call it in Scotland. After maybe fifteen minutes, Bubbles and Chunky Monkey returned.

"How about some tea?" Marina asked brightly. "I bought a *tarte Tatin* at that new bakery on the corner of Rue Szolem Mandelbrojt."

"That sounds scrumptious," Priscilla said, joining her husband on the sofa. "I really love that upside-down French apple tart—I can't get enough of it." Her whole manner now was as if the earlier spat with her husband had never happened.

"Tell me, Quentin," she added, "how did you meet Gilles? He mentioned that it was in connection with a case of his, but he told me that the details were confidential."

I looked her husband in the eye. "Can I tell her?"

Precisely as you'd have expected, dear reader, Gilles simply gave another shrug. I decided to interpret this as a reluctant go-ahead, and I accordingly gave a *Reader's Digest* version of what had happened. I won't repeat any of it here, because you already know everything I explained to her and a lot more besides. Priscilla sat wide-eyed during my brief report, occasionally flashing a sympathetic smile at Marina. Sensitivity is hardly my middle name, but on this occasion, I was extremely careful not to say anything negative about the French police in general and, more specifically, her husband. Marina didn't send any dirty looks my way, so I'm confident that, for once, I didn't put my foot in it.

When I'd finished, Priscilla turned to her former school mate with a look of horror on her face. "My dear, what you've only had to endure. Gilles, why haven't you found out yet who sent the letter and locked him up—for good?"

Gilles knew better than to say anything, and even I knew that a Gallic shrug at that point would undoubtedly have ended up in a Parisian divorce court. Now, I forgot to tell you that, while I was busy informing Priscilla about the threatening letter and the ensuing goings-on, Marina had served tea and a large slice of a rather delicious *tarte Tatin* to everyone. So when his wife reprimanded Gilles for the second time, he picked up his cup, took a sip of tea, and replaced the vessel on its saucer. The idea that a cup of tea is the solution to all problems is so ingrained in my fellow countrymen and women that Priscilla calmed down at once.

Not wanting any more friction between husband and wife, I decided to get Priscilla to talk about herself. After all, nothing she herself might say could possibly upset her—or so I thought.

"Priscilla," I said, "I've just told you how I met Gilles. How did you meet your husband?"

"I was doing an M.A. in History at London University. My thesis was to be a survey of the available documentation regarding the activities of the French Resistance during the Second World War. Those heroic Frenchmen and Frenchwomen were far too busy desperately eluding capture by the Nazis to write much down; the Germans were responsible for almost all the contemporaneous documents. As a result, most of what we know about the Resistance from the French side is based on oral histories obtained after the war from the survivors and their relatives and friends. But I knew of one exception: the Free French in London kept detailed written records." She paused to sample the *tarte Tatin*. "Now, do you know about Gilles's grandfather?"

We both nodded.

"Have you heard about Coralie Vire and the research she did?" Priscilla asked.

We both nodded again.

"In the course of working on my thesis I read about her. Something made me wonder if when she was in London she'd had the time to examine anything more than just those specific documents that pertained to La Mouche. I tried to locate the material Coralie had accessed, in the hope that I might uncover some new information regarding the heroes of the French Resistance. After a fruitless search, I learned that, a few years after the legal enquiry had exonerated La Mouche, the French government had arranged for the Free French records in London to be transferred to the archives of the French Ministry of Defense. I started in Vincennes, an eastern suburb of Paris, where they have sixty miles of shelves of military records, and I tried to find the material that Coralie had used to compile her report. No luck there. Then I tried the military archives at Châtellerault, near Poitou, where you can find another thirty-five miles of shelving. Again nothing. In desperation, I tried to locate the people who'd been responsible for the 1947 report more than seventy years ago. Not surprisingly, everyone directly involved was now dead.

"After months of dead ends, I eventually had a stroke of luck. The son of the vice-chairman of the legal panel mentioned to me that one of La Mouche's three sons had survived him; in turn, the son had produced a grandson, named after his grandfather. I had no trouble locating Gilles. And Gilles had no trouble locating the records that Coralie Vire had found in London. It seems that she'd brought nine large boxes of papers from London for the members of the panel to study, and after they'd published their report totally vindicating La Mouche, she was kind enough to deliver the documentation to his widow for her to see. Coralie's intention was that my husband's grandmother would be comforted by examining some of the actual papers that had cleared her husband's name, after which she was to return the papers to the Free French archive in London. Somehow that never happened, and the nine boxes stayed in the possession of Gilles's family. He took me to an outbuilding on a farm in Picardy where an aunt of his had lived, unlocked the door, and pointed to a dusty stack of cardboard boxes in the far corner.

"The material I found on that farm was so significant that it changed the entire direction of my research. I'd intended to spend a year or two setting up a somewhat mundane catalogue of available documentation on the Resistance. However, in those boxes I found a treasure trove of previously unknown documents that reflected the relentless five-year struggle between General Charles de Gaulle, the leader of the Free French in London, and Winston Churchill, the British Prime Minister."

"I'd no idea that they fought so bitterly," I said.

"Oh, yes," Priscilla replied. "At one point during the war, Churchill declared, 'He thinks he's Joan of Arc, but I can't get my bloody bishops to burn him.'

And De Gaulle is on record as saying, 'When I am right, I get angry. Churchill gets angry when he is wrong. We are angry at each other much of the time.'

"Anyhow, the papers I found in those nine boxes enabled me to shed a totally new light on the endless conflict between the two great leaders. My analysis earned me a doctorate from the Sorbonne and was the basis for a favorably received book. And you'll be pleased to know that the papers in those nine boxes now reside on the miles and miles of shelving in Châtellerault.

"And in the course of my research, Gilles and I fell in love."

They smiled sweetly at one another. Seizing the moment, I addressed Gilles by his first name, something no Frenchman would do on such short acquaintance. Usually they wait at least five to ten years before attempting any sort of informality of that kind. Sometimes longer. A lot longer. Like forever. "Gilles," I asked, "would it be possible for Marina and me to visit Claude in the psychiatric ward?"

As I'd hoped, Priscilla jumped in before Gilles could open his mouth. "Darling, of course you must let them see poor Claude. He'll be delighted to see them, and he may provide them with information that will lead to your solving the riddle of who wrote the mysterious missive."

I immediately picked up on Priscilla's clever ploy. She'd suggested to her husband that *our* visit to the hospital might result in *his* solving the case, and no man I know can resist flattery of that kind.

"Dearest one, I'm sure you're quite correct. Right now, the waiter is receiving treatment in Druny Military Hospital. They constructed the original institution in the middle of the nineteenth century to treat military personnel, but lately they've completely rebuilt it. Nowadays, the overwhelming majority of patients are civilians who receive treatment in that hospital via the government national health insurance scheme. That said, Druny is an Armed Forces Health Service hospital, so Marina and Quentin will need permission from the relevant military authorities. I'll phone my contact in the Ministry of Defense in the morning; I'm sure he'll be most cooperative."

"I have a better idea," Priscilla said sweetly. "Why don't you phone his wife and tell her that Marina Haversmith, the author of *She Loved the French Captain*, wants to visit Claude Whatever-His-Last-Name-Happens-To-Be in the Druny Military Hospital? She, in turn, will instruct her husband to organize the visit. And please don't forget to give her Quentin's and Marina's actual names."

After Gilles and "Chunky Monkey" had left, I invited "Bubbles" to sit on the sofa. I occupied my usual armchair. "Darling, I don't understand something. In fact, lots of things don't make any sense to me."

"Oh? Is that so? Do tell."

"For starters, the two of you were best chums at school for twelve years, weren't you?"

Marina nodded.

"And you and Priscilla seemed as close as ever, screaming out your nicknames hysterically and then hugging one another like two bears."

"Yes, that's true."

"But you didn't even invite her to our wedding, let alone make her a bridesmaid or matron of honor or something. I know that only a dozen or so friends and family were at the ceremony, so adding your best friend and her husband to the list wouldn't have overcrowded the registry office in Yarrow-upon-Wey; I noticed enough seating for at least twenty people, maybe more."

"Correct."

"So, why not?"

A lengthy pause followed.

"It's a long story."

"We've got all night."

"Actually, Quentin, I've already told you about her."

"I know you're convinced that I have the three-second memory span of an average goldfish, but I don't remember your ever telling me about a school friend of yours named Priscilla."

"Well, darling, when I told you about her in that café near the Old Bailey, perhaps I didn't mention her name."

"Perhaps you didn't. And I don't think you said more than a sentence or two about your anonymous friend, either."

"No, I don't believe I did."

Another long pause. Then, hesitantly at first. "As you know, my parents died before I was a year old. My grandparents, the Earl and Countess of Dover, were my guardians—they brought me up. He was certifiably insane; she pretended that his conduct was normal, thereby enabling his dysfunctional behavior. Neither of them ever showed the slightest affection towards me.

"Priscilla and I became friends within days of my grandparents sending me to boarding school at the age of seven. At the end of the term, she asked her mother to invite me to spend part of the school holidays with them. Her mother had heard rumors about my grandparents, and soon after I arrived at their home, she delicately asked me about them.

"Once her suspicions had been confirmed, she took charge of my life. She contacted the parents of my other school friends and arranged for me to spend my school holidays with them, a week or two with each family. If you think that Priscilla is bossy, you should meet her mother; she's the epitome of a control freak. But the fact of the matter is they're both truly kind people, and I'm eternally grateful to Priscilla for her friendship and to her mother for organizing twelve years of visits to the families of my classmates.

135

The warmth and understanding of both mother and daughter far outweighed their occasional imperious attitude, and if I occasionally felt cowed when they ordered me about, merely thinking about spending time with my grandparents was enough to banish any negative emotions I might be experiencing.

"However, once we left school, everything changed. Priscilla decided to go to Princeton. She spent her college vacations with her new American friends in the warmth of the Caribbean in winter and the sunshine of California in summer, whereas I stayed in enduringly cold and rainy England and went up to Cambridge. Imperceptibly, but inevitably, we started to drift apart. Her mother realized that I'd entered a new phase of my life, so I didn't receive any invitations to stay with her and her husband while Priscilla was in America. Instead, about once a term she invited me to afternoon tea at Harrods, and I eagerly took the train down to London to see her again and catch up on the doings of the members of the family.

"The title of Thomas Wolfe's posthumous book says it all: *You Can't Go Home Again.* Our lives had changed to a major extent, and Priscilla and I were moving inexorably along trajectories that didn't intersect. Then came the double tragedy—you know all about that. Soon after I finished my degree, my grandfather snatched the razor-sharp samurai sword and dagger off the wall of his study, sliced off his wife's head with the sword, and committed *hara-kiri* with the dagger.

"I now realize that, paradoxically, that terrible event had the effect of allowing us to slip even further apart. When we first met, we were just two seven-year schoolgirls who enjoyed one another's company. But once her mother started to do so much for me, I believe that my grandparents' aberrant behavior became the glue that cemented the friendship together. Consequently, the force that had bound us together understandably started to weaken after their deaths.

"Inevitably, Priscilla and I continued to drift away from one another. Her mother's invitations to afternoon teas at Harrods ceased. As often seems to occur in such situations, my friend and I both realized what was happening, but neither wanted to be the first to try to re-establish the relationship for fear of being rejected by the other. Consequently, I never told Priscilla about our wedding, and she never informed me that she'd moved to Paris to do the research for her postgraduate studies, met Gilles here, and married him.

"It's strange how unpleasant happenings have brought Priscilla and me together. Initially, it was my grandparents' conduct and now the threatening letter. You'll be pleased to hear that, like all truly close friendships, we've simply resumed our relationship as if no interruption had occurred."

"I'm delighted to hear that," I said. "However, can you think of a way of asking Priscilla to be a little nicer to Gilles when I'm around? I'm sure you felt as uncomfortable as I did."

She pulled a face. "Maybe I misspoke when I stated that things are exactly the way they were when we left school. We've both changed, as people do. I'm convinced that Priscilla realizes that she can't control me the way she did. On the other hand, now she has Gilles to order about. I have to say that I was surprised at her outburst, because public displays of displeasure were never her thing. Maybe we can put it down to the emotion of seeing me again and resuming our friendship. I hope that's what happened.

"Does that answer your question?"

"It answers my first question," I said.

"And what else is bothering you?"

"Without in any way justifying Priscilla's behavior when she first saw you, I can see her point. Why on earth didn't Gilles tell her earlier that Mrs. Quentin Pakenham is actually Marina Haversmith, the immortal author of *She Loved the French Captain*?"

"But which in reality you wrote."

"Yes, which I wrote from beginning to end."

I thought for a second or two, then continued. "Darling, do you remember that at the end of our first interview with Gilles he asked you to sign a copy of the book for his wife?"

"Your memory is in fine fettle today, Quentin. Excellent! Anyhow, when I asked him for her name so that I could personalize the inscription, he said 'Priscilla.' We both know that's a very English name, but then Gilles was born in London and speaks impeccable English, so I thought nothing of it at the time."

"Yes, I can understand that. But I want to know what happened when Gilles handed the book to his wife and she saw the name of her best friend at school at the end of an inscription penned in a familiar hand. Imagine the scene: Gilles comes home proudly bearing a personalized autographed copy of *She Loved the French Captain*. He may even have phoned her directly after we left his office to tell her he has a wonderful surprise for her. He walks into the flat, smiling from ear to ear. He kisses Priscilla fondly, and then presents her with the book.

"What happened next?"

Marina stared out the window into the darkness of a Paris evening. She thought for a long while. Then she got up and drew the curtains. Resuming her seat, she continued to ponder.

Eventually, she put her thoughts into words. "Gilles is a senior police officer, so he certainly understands the need for confidentiality. As he handed the book to Priscilla, he may have mentioned to her that you'd come to see him on a police matter. But once she'd seen my name, she must've told him about our friendship at school and how and why we drifted apart. And at that point, policeman or no policeman, I'm sure he told her that you're now Mrs. Quentin Pakenham and that you're living here in Paris."

"In that case, why the outburst?" I asked.

"Here's how I see it. Priscilla was in a difficult position. She had no idea how I'd react to seeing her again. She's no coward; she wouldn't have dreamed of getting a case of diplomatic flu to avoid coming to tea. And she's highly intelligent. She got a doctorate from the Sorbonne, which is no small achievement in itself, but getting a degree from a French university means she can actually speak French. Fluently. And I'm sure she can understand what they say when people talk to her in that language."

"Get to the point, dammit!"

"As I was saying before the control freak I married started ordering me about, Priscilla is very bright. Once she'd learned from her husband that I was living in Paris, she could've picked up her phone and called me. But what if she received a cold reception? That fear of being rejected that I talked about earlier must've dissuaded her from phoning. Instead, she waited until she was sure our friendship was about to resume where we'd left off—which was about seven nanoseconds into that amaranthine hug—and then she covered up her failure to make contact by yelling at Gilles for not telling her about me."

140

"That makes sense," I said. "It would also explain his bewilderment. They probably talked about nothing else from the time I invited him. Nevertheless, here she was yelling at him, in public—how terribly un-English!—for something he didn't do and that he was fully aware she knew he didn't do. In retrospect, that triple whisky I poured him was an excellent idea. Eighteen-year-old Lochervan is an unfailing soother of perplexed souls."

"And it also explains why she was as sweet as honey when we rejoined you in the living room. If she'd genuinely been that angry with Gilles, she probably wouldn't have spoken to him for a week, but she acted as if nothing at all had happened."

"Because in reality nothing had happened except her unjustified outburst. Did he comment on her behavior while we were out of the room?"

"On the contrary," I replied. "I couldn't get a word out of him. We sat here without saying a word to one another—"

"Because Gilles was trying to work out what had occurred. And I think I know why she didn't warn him in advance as to how she intended to handle the reunion."

"Was it because she couldn't be sure he could play the required role for the whole time?"

"Precisely! Well, now I've answered your second question. Any more?"

141

"Yes. I was thinking about that other outburst. Perhaps describing it as a mini-outburst would be more accurate. Or perhaps a micro-outburst. Or even a nano-outburst."

Marina frowned, and her voice was heavy with doubt. "What are you talking about? I don't recall anything like that."

"Don't you remember that she asked something along the lines of 'Gilles, how come you haven't yet found the perpetrator and locked him up and thrown away the key?' It wasn't delivered in a particularly nice way, in my view."

"Oh, that. Well, having heard what I'd been through, I thought she was doing her level best to be supportive. I interpreted it as a sympathetic remark rather than a nasty dig at her husband."

I had no doubt that Marina was wrong and that what she was doing was defending her newly reinstated best friend. However, having lived in France for twenty years, I knew precisely how to respond.

I shrugged.

CHAPTER FIFTEEN

D runy Military Hospital turned out to be a modern steel-and-glass building situated no more than a ten-minute walk from Gallieni Métro Station. Druny and Gallieni went well together. After all, Marshal Joseph Gallieni was the Military Governor of Paris during the First World War. He played a vital role in the First Battle of the Marne in September 1914, saving Paris by rushing soldiers to the frontline in commandeered Parisian taxicabs. And Olivier Druny was a famous French military surgeon who'd worked with Florence Nightingale during the Crimean War.

A middle-aged buxom woman with her hair in a bun was seated behind the hospital main reception desk. When I gave her my name, she beamed at me. I realized that the wife of Gilles's contact in the Ministry of Defense had thoroughly enjoyed *She Loved the French Captain*. The receptionist picked up her phone, and soon a psychiatrist in a white coat arrived.

She introduced herself as Léonie Falleron and escorted us to a nearby lift.

As the doors closed, I looked closely at her face. "Haven't I met you before?" I asked.

"Probably not. But the receptionist downstairs is my identical twin sister." She grinned impishly. "The two of us have been the cause of immeasurable confusion around here. But we've also been the source of a considerable amount of amusement in the hospital, which specializes in the treatment of tropical diseases, many of which can be most unpleasant. Given that a good laugh is a relatively uncommon occurrence in Druny Hospital, the medical director has encouraged Lucille and me to make every effort to capitalize on the similarity of our appearance."

"But what about your psychiatric patients?" I asked. "Surely many of them are brought to this hospital because they are confused for one reason or another."

"You're right, of course. We try to ensure that my patients don't interact with Lucille in any way, but from time to time . . ." She shrugged. Then she said, "Here's Claude's room. Before we go in, a brief word, please. We're treating him with an antidepressant, the standard first-line treatment for post-traumatic stress disorder. If the drug doesn't work—and, given that the traumatic event that caused his PTSD occurred so long ago, it probably won't, notwithstanding the

144

heavy doses we're injecting into him—we'll try counselling and psychotherapy next.

"I'm so pleased that you're here. Claude is embarrassed beyond all measure by what happened in the café. Dropping that cup of coffee was, for him, the ultimate humiliation. I'd be most grateful if you could explain to him that no harm was done."

I nodded in assent. "Tell me, Dr. Falleron, should we talk to him about the traumatic event to which you alluded, or steer away from it?"

"By all means discuss it. It may surprise you to know that if you hadn't requested this visit I'd have contacted you and asked you to come. Claude needs to know that people whom he respects, like you and your wife, see no shame in having a forebear who acted so disgracefully. The sins of the great-grandfather should never be visited on the great-grandson."

"Just a second," I said. "What does his great-grandfather have to do with what happened in Zaire?"

"Claude was wounded in Zaire, but that wasn't the traumatic event that caused his PTSD. I was informed that you're aware of the connection between Claude Malmaison and the Seventh Philippe le Sabre. Is that correct?"

We both nodded as she continued.

"Claude told me that when he was twenty-one his father visited him one night and laid out all the facts regarding his great-grandfather. That was the traumatic event that I mentioned earlier."

Marina gave me a meaningful look, the meaning of which was crystal clear: yet again, my wife had hit the nail firmly on the head.

Dr. Falleron noticed the look but tactfully ignored it. "The most important thing for him now is to talk to someone about what happened that day when he was twenty-one years old. He won't open up to me, because he views me as a stranger, and family secrets are not to be shared with an outsider like me. Claude lives by himself. He's unmarried and he apparently has no friends of either gender. But he thinks the world of the two of you, and maybe you can help him to unburden himself.

"He read *She Loved the French Captain* and thinks it's the best book he's ever read, so it's possible that he'll speak freely to you.

"I'll call a nurse, then leave you with him."

She walked to the end of the hallway and turned right. While we waited for her to return, I asked Marina, "Doesn't it strike you as odd that Claude read *She Loved the French Captain* and even odder that he loved it?"

"I can't say it does. He must've seen my photograph in the newspaper and bought the book out of loyalty to a staunch customer. And why shouldn't a man enjoy *She Loved the French Captain*? After all, a man wrote it."

I was about to respond when Léonie Falleron reappeared, accompanied by a tall, muscular man in an all-white uniform, whom she introduced as Jules. Then she opened the door and walked in, followed by Marina and me. Jules came in last, effortlessly carrying a chair he'd brought in from the corridor. He placed it next to the existing chair on the side of the bed, and Marina and I sat down. Jules moved to a far corner of the room, where he stood at attention staring intently at the other far corner. I realized that Dr. Falleron didn't want us to be left alone with Claude but had instructed Jules to be as unobtrusive as possible. I leave it to you to judge the extent to which the large nurse was successful in carrying out her order.

I looked around. The colorful curtains and the bold paintings mounted on the walls made it clear that we weren't in a typical hospital room. Claude lay in bed, looking slightly dazed. When he saw us, he seemed embarrassed.

Dr. Falleron spoke warmly to her patient. "I've brought you some visitors. More correctly, I should've said that I've brought you some friends. I'll leave you with them."

Marina handed Claude the large box of chocolates she'd brought him. As brightly as she could manage, she said, "These should cheer you up!"

Claude thanked her in a small voice that didn't sound the least bit cheerful.

"Claude, we're here to apologize," I said.

"For what? I should be the one to apologize."

"Not at all. Inadvertently, we're responsible for your being here."

"I don't understand," Claude replied.

"You see," I said, "after Marina received that threatening letter—"

"What threatening letter?" he asked.

I suddenly realized, far from having written it, Claude hadn't even heard about it. For the second time in less than twenty-four hours, I gave an account of what had happened. This time, however, I included every single detail—with one exception. For obvious reasons, I didn't tell Claude how I'd tricked *Madame* the Proprietress into giving me his family name.

As you know, I've authored thirteen successful bodice rippers, one of them a world bestseller: I refer, naturally, to *She Loved the French Captain*. Accordingly, I can immodestly claim to be able to tell a good story. But never have I had a more rapt audience than Claude. From the beginning to the end of my account, he was entirely engrossed in what I was saying. Better yet, he seemed to come out of his PTSD. I'm prepared to admit, exceedingly reluctantly, that it might have been the antidepressant drug finally working. That said, my personal belief is that my skill as a raconteur was, if you'd allow me to lapse into the pseudohistorical terminology that we bodice-ripper writers are required by law to employ, "the physick that cured what ailed him."

I glanced at Jules. His earlier basilisk-like glare directed at the other far corner of the room had melted into an open-mouthed gaze in my direction. When he saw me looking at him, he gave a disconcerted half-smile then redirected his glower as before.

I turned back to Claude. "Now do you see why I placed those two books on the café table and why they reminded you of the cover of *She Loved the French Captain* and brought about your PTSD?"

"Yes, certainly."

"I'm so sorry to have caused you all that trouble."

"Certainly not," Claude said. "Please don't apologize. It was obviously an accident—something that simply happened."

"Thank you for being so forgiving," I said. "However, I have to say that I still don't understand one thing. You read the whole of *She Loved the French Captain* without reacting to the name 'Philippe le Sabre,' which appears hundreds of times in the book. But merely seeing the covers of those two books by P. C. Wren set you off. How could that be?"

Claude thought for a long while. He started to answer my question, but lapsed back into silence. Another lengthy pause ensued. Eventually, he spoke to Marina. "*Madame*, I'm not trying to flatter you as a writer when I say that I saw the Philippe le Sabre whom you imagined so brilliantly in your masterpiece as a fictional person from the past. You wrote the book so well that at no time did I associate your

149

historical hero with my great-grandfather. Your Philippe is a creation from the Age of Napoleon. On the other hand, my great-grandfather lived in the twentieth century, as did the characters depicted on the covers of the two books I saw on the table top. The best explanation I can come up with is that the covers reminded me of your book, but within a modern-day context, if you know what I mean, and that brought back my father's visit."

Dr. Léonie Falleron had told us that it was important to get Claude to talk about the event that had resulted in his post-traumatic stress disorder. But that was before he came out of the PTSD. In his present state, describing what had occurred might bring back the condition, which was the last thing we wanted. I thought quickly. Then, despite my momentary misgivings, I took the bull by the horns and dragged it across the Rubicon. "Tell me, Claude," I asked as casually as I could manage, "what happened that night?"

CHAPTER SIXTEEN

"Monsieur Pakenham," Claude said, "I have to start at the beginning, or my story won't make any sense at all.

"According to my birth certificate, I was born here in Paris in 1969, but I grew up in a suburb of Lyon. I lived in an apartment with my mother, Nicole. When I was old enough to ask my mother about my father, she told me he was a soldier who'd died defending France in North Africa. That was a source of immense pride to me, so I never ever questioned her about it, or asked for details of when or how he'd been killed. The first internet browser dates from 1990, when I was twenty-one, so it simply wasn't possible for me to investigate the matter, had I been curious—which I wasn't.

"Some aspects of our life in Lyon were odd. The other children had extended families: aunts, uncles, cousins, grandparents, and so on. I had no relatives other than my mother. When I asked her why, she stated that neither she nor my father had any siblings and that all four of my grandparents had died before I was born.

"Another unusual feature of my life became apparent in my early teens. My mother worked half days as a dentist's receptionist, hardly a well-paid occupation even on a full-time basis, but we somehow always had enough money in the house. We didn't live lavishly, but one day I suddenly realized that we lived in a nice rented apartment and had plenty of nice possessions even though my mother's income couldn't possibly have covered our expenses. I asked her about it. She replied that she'd inherited money from her parents.

"The postman used to deliver the mail to our apartment during the mornings, so my mother used to empty the mailbox on her way home from her job. One day, when I was about twelve, she twisted her ankle badly and had to stay in bed to recover. I came home from school and found her fast asleep. I assumed that was a side-effect of the strong painkiller the doctor had prescribed for her. I realized no-one had checked for mail that day, so I took the key, went downstairs, and opened the letterbox.

"Inside I found a long, white reinforced envelope with no return address. I looked again and noticed the stamp was missing; someone had written 'Madame Nicole le Sabre' on the envelope and dropped it into the box. I took the envelope upstairs and—I know I shouldn't have done it—I cut it open with a pair of scissors. A heap of banknotes fell onto the table, including several 500 Franc notes; I'd never seen anything larger than a 100 Franc note before. I tiptoed into the bedroom, placed the money on my mother's bedside table, and laid the remains of the envelope next to the pile. Neither of us ever spoke about it.

"Another feature of our lives wasn't at all unusual for France: when I was about six years old, my mother acquired a lover. He was an army officer, a colleague of my late father. He stayed with us when he was on leave and moved in permanently after he retired from the army some ten or twelve years later. *Monsieur*, you mentioned his name earlier: Bertrand Malmaison."

"But he was your father!"

"Precisely, *monsieur*, but I wasn't aware of it until that fateful night. He always used to say he was proud that he treated me like the son he'd never had, but I never caught on. Then, the evening after my son was born, he knocked on the door of the flat where Marie-André and I were living. He congratulated me on becoming a father, proffered a bottle of excellent cognac, and asked if we could have a talk.

"He began by asking me if I realized I was the tenth in an unbroken line of nine French army officers named Philippe le Sabre. I was surprised. My mother had told me that my father's name was Philippe, and my birth certificate confirmed that fact. But I'd had no idea that his father had also been named Philippe, and his father before him, for ten generations.

"Then he asked me if I'd ever heard of a Philippe le Sabre other than my father and myself. I said no. He smiled. 'Your mother made sure you knew that your father was a hero. But another Philippe le Sabre was an infinitely greater hero: your great-grandfather Philippe le Sabre the Seventh.'

"He then explained to me that in the years leading up to the Second World War a group of patriotic Frenchmen believed that Adolf Hitler was the greatest man who'd ever lived, and they did everything they could to bring France into the Third *Reich*. My great-grandfather was one of the leaders of that movement; during the war, he managed to single-handedly destroy much of the French Resistance.

"My initial reaction was that 'Bertrand' was trying to be funny and that this conversation we were having was a joke in exceedingly bad taste, but I quickly realized he was deadly serious. I decided that the best way to handle the situation was to listen carefully to everything he had to say and then draw up a plan of action on the basis of as much information as I could glean from him. Accordingly, I nodded every so often to show him I was listening carefully to what he was telling me. At times I tried to agree with him, but the words stuck in my throat for obvious reasons.

"Then he asked me if I'd heard about ODESSA. 'Yes,' I replied, 'it's a city in the Ukraine. Odessa is a port on the Black Sea.' He said, 'No, I mean the acronym ODESSA.'

"I had no idea what he was talking about. 'It's German,' he said. 'It stands for *Organization der ehemaligen SS-Angehörigen,* or Organization of Former SS Members. French patriots served in the SS during World War II; the 33rd *Waffen Grenadier* Division of the SS Charlemagne and the Charlemagne Regiment were units of French volunteers, first in the *Wehrmacht* and later in the *Waffen-SS*. I'm proud to say that they were among the last units to surrender during the final days of the Battle of Berlin. And after the war, ODESSA leaders helped former SS members to escape to Argentina, Brazil, Egypt, and Syria under false names, and they provided funds to enable them to live out their lives in those countries. ODESSA has been looking after the le Sabre family all these years.'

"I suddenly realized that the long, white reinforced envelope had contained banknotes that ODESSA had supplied and that I'd been living a comfortable upper-middle-class life courtesy of a group of murderous fascists who still believed in Nazi ideals. Fortunately, my father misinterpreted my gasp of horror as a gasp of admiration, and he continued.

"He started to explain the actions of my grandfather, Philippe le Sabre the Eighth. In 1947, the report came out that exonerated Gilles Despoir—as you said, his *nom de guerre* was La Mouche—and proved beyond all doubt that my great-grandfather was the worst traitor France has ever known. When my grandfather read the report, he came up with a way of protecting the name of the family and continuing the le Sabre line until the time came when Germany would awaken from her slumbers and France would become part of the Fourth *Reich*. He hit on the ingenious scheme of using the French Foreign Legion to change his family name—that was the stratagem you so cleverly uncovered, *madame*.

"The day after the report came out, my grandfather, Philippe the Eighth, fled Paris and enlisted in the Legion under the name of Alphonse Malmaison, leaving behind Odile, his wife, and his infant son, my father; ODESSA looked after them financially. Château de Malmaison was the residence of Napoleon's consort, the Empress Josephine, so the family name he adopted has imperial overtones. Appropriately enough, the French word *mal* means evil, and *maison* is a house, and the house of le Sabre was indeed one of the most evil in France. As you surmised, *madame*, my grandfather used the law of *Français par le sang versé*—"

I supplied the translation, "French by spilled blood."

"Exactly, *monsieur*. That was how Alphonse Malmaison acquired French citizenship and became an army officer. Once he'd retired from the army, he became my grandmother's 'lover' and lived with her and my father. And when my father turned twenty, he married Nicole. I was born two years later, in 1969.

"At that time, my grandfather identified himself to my father and told him about his multigenerational plan for the le Sabre family. My father immediately agreed to leave, join the Legion, and change his name. He took one additional precaution: he instructed my mother to move to Lyon. If she'd stayed in Paris, someone who knew her there might associate her with Philippe the Seventh, her husband's grandfather. After all, Lyon is our second largest city, with many newcomers, and in France it's not done to ask new acquaintances about their past.

"My father paused, took a large swallow of cognac, smiled at me, and said, 'All the le Sabres are intelligent, so you must've worked out by now that I'm your father.' Without giving me a chance to respond, let alone embrace him as my parent, he continued. 'The time has come for you to protect the family name until France becomes part of the Fourth *Reich*. You need to enlist in the French Foreign Legion right away, taking on the name Claude Malmaison. Your new family name will identify you to the people who'll look after you in the Legion and ensure that you become a French army officer. Don't worry about your mother and me—the ODESSA people will continue to help us. You need to register your son tomorrow as Philippe le Sabre the Eleventh. And don't worry about him or Marie-André either, because

ODESSA will look after them the way they did when you were growing up with Nicole here in Lyon.

"*Monsieur-dame*, I want you both to know that I joined the Foreign Legion and changed my name not to protect the reputation of the le Sabre family but rather to terminate the le Sabre succession. I've never married and I never will. I am the tenth and the last Philippe le Sabre. I registered my son's name as André-Marie de Villiers. The accursed le Sabre name will die when I die.

"I left home two days after André-Marie was born and enlisted in the Legion. Needless to say, I've had no contact with my parents since then. I don't know if they're alive or dead, nor do I care. My mother and my father, my grandparents, and my great-grandparents were all followers of a hateful ideology, one that brought the world to war from 1939 to 1945 and destroyed tens of millions of individuals. Sadly, some people still share those beliefs; I cannot comprehend how that can be."

Changing to French, he shouted to the nurse still standing in the far corner, "Hey, Jules, tell the doctor I'm fine and I want to go home."

CHAPTER SEVENTEEN

"Poor man," I said, as we walked into our flat. "Imagine how he felt after his father's visit that evening, having to leave behind his partner, his son, his family, everything."

"You believed him, then?"

"What on earth are you talking about, Marina? Of course I believed him. What's not to believe?"

"Well, everything."

"Don't be silly. Give me just one example."

"Okay, here goes," Marina said. "Claude stated that his father had instructed him to take the name Claude Malmaison when joining the Legion. That specific family name was essential, his father told him, so that neo-Nazis in the Legion would help Claude to become a French officer."

"What's not to believe about that?"

"Don't you remember that Claude made it abundantly clear to us that he wanted nothing to do with neo-Nazis in general, let alone the neo-Nazis in the Legion? But when he joined the Legion, he took

159

on the family name Malmaison. If he really was such a staunch anti-Fascist, he should've chosen any other name, even Marjorie de Blanc, the pseudonym under which you wrote your first twelve bodice rippers. But your friend Claude picked Malmaison so that neo-Nazi sympathizers among the officers in the Legion would know his true identity and would help him to become a French Army officer. Claude was genuinely wounded in Zaire, but we know nothing about the circumstances regarding his father's and grandfather's injuries. I wonder if neo-Nazi officers in the Legion helped Philippe the Eighth and Philippe the Ninth to become 'Frenchmen by spilled blood' by providing false documentation."

Marina now shifted gears. "Let's discuss Philippe the Eighth, Claude's grandfather. According to Claude, right after Philippe the Eighth's son was born in 1947, the report of the legal enquiry came out and Philippe the Eighth learned some terrible things about his father. Except that in Philippe the Eighth's eyes they weren't terrible things, because Philippe the Eighth believed in the same vile ideology as his father, Philippe the Seventh. And what did Philippe the Eighth do when he learned about Philippe the Seventh? He instantaneously came up with a plan. Without even having to think, he said to himself, 'I must join the Foreign Legion, change my name, get wounded, regain French citizenship, become an officer, and promote the ideals of my father.' He bade farewell to Odile—or did he? That part of the story isn't clear—leaving her in the safe hands of ODESSA, and he joined the Legion. What a nice man Philippe the Eighth was, abandoning his wife right after giving birth to his infant son, and abandoning his son as well, for that matter.

"Next came Philippe the Ninth. He married Nicole. His wife gave birth to a son in 1969, and what do you know? Philippe the Eighth came to him the very next day and announced, 'No, I'm not your mother's lover. I'm actually your father. And you need to do exactly what I did. Rush off right now and join the Legion. Abandon your wife and your life here, as well as your infant son. You don't have to worry about leaving Nicole all alone in the maternity hospital, because ODESSA will look after her and the boy for the rest of their lives. And when you enlist in the Legion, you need to use the name Bertrand Malmaison so that the neo-Nazis will know that you are one of them.'

"And now we come to dear Claude. He's living in Lyon with his mother, Nicole, and this army officer who treats him like a son. For fifteen years, the man says nothing about being Claude's father. And then suddenly, in 1990, after Claude has been up all night and most of the next day in the delivery room with the mother of his child, and then presumably with Marie-André and the baby in the recovery ward, the man knocks on the door of the apartment, bearing cognac and surprising news. Even though Claude has been without sleep for about thirty-six hours, he listens raptly to his father spewing out his wish for world domination by Aryans and the extermination of the 'lesser races.' Then Claude dashes off to register his son's birth, and without bothering to say goodbye to the mother of his son, he skips off and joins the Legion two days after André-Marie was born, not having a worry or care in the world. After all, Daddy promised that ODESSA would look after the whole family.

"And I think you've overlooked one other remark Claude made. He claimed that the first time he learned about his family's predilection for Hitlerian beliefs was that infamous night when his father spilled the beans. So he fled from his parents, never to see them again. He explicitly mentioned to us that his mother shared those values. How did he know that?

"And another interesting question: Do you really think that Philippe the Ninth became a neo-Nazi literally overnight in 1969 when his father unveiled himself the day after Philippe the Tenth was born?

"Quentin, I realize that you're a writer of bodice rippers, so reality doesn't play a particularly large role in your life, but even you must agree that Claude's tale is pretty thin."

By the end of Marina's diatribe, I was as shocked as Claude had claimed to be that fateful evening in

1990. All I could manage was a sort of stutter. Then I asked, "So what did occur?"

"As Claude told us when he began his tale, I have to start at the beginning. And the beginning was Philippe the Seventh. He was more than merely a sympathizer; he was a Nazi through and through, deliberately following a course of action that led to the torture and death of thousands of his fellow countrymen and women. Claude's story is that Philippe the Eighth fled Paris the day after the legal inquiry released its report, which happened immediately following the birth of his son in 1947. Quentin, do you realize why all three men fled directly after their sons were born?"

"I've no idea at all. Please enlighten me."

"Here's a clue: they wouldn't have joined the Legion if their offspring had been daughters."

"Are you saying they stayed until they could register their sons with the family name le Sabre and then they fled?"

"Precisely, Quentin! You're remarkably clever, you know. But you have to be less gullible. And while on the subject of credulity, do you believe that the first time Philippe the Eighth learned the truth about his father was when they issued that report in 1947? Doubtlessly articles had appeared in the newspapers reporting the sworn testimony that had been given to the panel investigating the traitor. Why, Philippe the Eighth himself might have been a witness. In my opinion, he spent weeks, if not months, trying to come up with a way to change his name while still allowing the le Sabre line to continue. The trick was to wait until he was the father of a son, register the boy as a le Sabre, and then flee to the Legion. The date of publication of the report was either a coincidence or, more likely, quite untrue.

"Let's continue with Philippe the Eighth. Having come up with a clever plan—and no-one has suggested that any of the le Sabres were short on brains—he waited until his son was born in 1947. At that point, he carried out his plan. He registered the birth, thereby ensuring the continuity of the line of le Sabres, then joined the Legion, changing his name to Alphonse Malmaison. He'd obviously discussed his detailed multigenerational plan in advance with Odile, his wife. She had to have been a sympathizer too, or she'd have gone to the police and instigated a nationwide search for her husband. I've no doubt that when the French look for a missing person the Legion is high on their list of places where they think he may be hiding. Anyhow, not only was Odile in on the act, but Philippe the Eighth's preparations must've included setting up ties with ODESSA. Consequently, once he'd left for the Legion, Odile phoned their contact and funds started to arrive.

"That left Philippe the Ninth with Odile, his mother. She undoubtedly fed him neo-Nazi claptrap together with his mother's milk, and he grew up as committed to the ideals of Adolf Hitler as his father and grandfather before him. Once Philippe the Eighth had finished his five-year stint in the Legion, he became an officer in the French army and rejoined his wife under the guise of Alphonse Malmaison, her 'lover.' Their son married Nicole. But he wouldn't have proposed to her unless he knew that she was a full-blown neo-Nazi and would agree to follow his father's long-term plan. Once Nicole had produced a son in 1969, the cycle repeated. Philippe the Ninth joined the Legion under the name Bertrand Malmaison, and Nicole moved to Lyon to bring up the child we now know as Claude.

"I've no doubt that, despite his protestations to the contrary, Claude was also brought up in a fascism-loving household, and that he adopted that ideology."

"Wait a minute, Marina, now you're going too far. How do you know that?"

"For many reasons. He impregnated Marie-André de Villiers but, on his father's orders, he didn't marry her. Also on his father's orders, he gave their child her family name, not his."

"How can you say those things?" I asked. "On the contrary, Claude informed us that it was *his* idea to terminate the line of le Sabres."

"Aryanism is transmitted 'through the blood.' Bertrand must've found out something 'undesirable' about Marie-André's ancestry. Perhaps he discovered that one of her grandparents was Jewish. Whatever the reason, it was out of the question for Claude to marry Marie-André, and he certainly couldn't tell her anything about the plan for the future of the le Sabre family. As soon as Philippe the Tenth had registered the birth of his son the way his father had ordered, he left his girlfriend and joined the Legion, taking the *nom de guerre* Claude Malmaison. You see the pattern, don't you?"

"What pattern are you talking about?"

"Look at the new first names of Philippe the Eighth, the Ninth, and the Tenth: Alphonse, Bertrand, and Claude are in alphabetical order. I'm sure that's part of the plan."

"That's an astute observation, Marina. Tell me more."

"After Claude joined the Legion, Bertrand had Marie-André and her son killed."

"Now you're definitely going too far. Much too far," I said.

"Am I? Think back. Did Claude say one nice thing about his girlfriend or their child? Did he say, 'Poor Marie-André'? And he mentioned his son's name exactly once, when he spoke about registering his name—did you notice that?—and he never remarked how sad it was that he'd died so young. The idea was to destroy the unacceptable girlfriend and her child so that Claude could marry a certified Aryan and produce a strictly kosher le Sabre son, if I may put it that way."

"I can see so many holes in your theory that I hardly know where to begin. For example, if Claude were to remarry, the child's last name would be Malmaison, not le Sabre. But for the sake of argument, let's assume that you're right. In that case, where's the second wife and her son?"

"Do you remember the Zaire incident? Where was Claude wounded?"

"In the groin. But—"

"Yes, in the groin," Marina said. "And that's why he hasn't produced another son. And that's also the real reason why the le Sabre line will die out after ten Philippes."

"Hold on one minute, darling. I believe we have a problem with your explanation."

"That's impossible, sweetheart!"

"No, I think we have to resolve a genuine difficulty here," I said. "You're claiming that Claude knew who his father was from the time he was old enough to be taught not to call Bertrand 'father,' at least in public, because that would lead to the undoing of the whole complex plan."

"Correct."

"And his parents must've warned him in advance that Claude would have to leave Lyon and join the Legion once he'd produced a male heir and registered the birth of his son."

"Again correct," Marina said.

"And that means that no traumatic meeting with his father took place that evening. On the contrary, Claude got back from the maternity hospital and collapsed straight into bed, exhausted beyond all measure."

"Quite right."

"But if no traumatic meeting took place, how could this non-existent traumatic meeting have been the cause of his post-traumatic stress disorder? If no meeting took place, no trauma could've resulted from it."

Silence.

I couldn't help myself. I had to smile. Only the tiniest of teensy-weensy little smiles. I was simply unable to control my lips.

More silence.

After a long while, a small voice said, "Perhaps, darling, the traumatic incident occurred in Zaire."

"Formerly the Belgian Congo, then Zaire, and now the Democratic Republic of the Congo, or just the Congo for short?"

"Yes. There."

"And the incident that caused the PTSD was in reality the injury to his groin that made it impossible for the le Sabre line to continue?" I asked.

"Yes. That."

"I see. Well, Marina, I'm not yet ready to agree with everything you've said, but I do have to thank you for pointing out that hardly a word Claude spoke was true."

"Noted."

"In fact, I'm no longer certain he had nothing to do with the letter."

"Agreed."

I paused for effect. "And we're back to square one."

"Yes. Sadly. Very sadly."

"By the way, what made you suspicious of Claude's story? Everything seemed so natural to me."

"It was far too natural," Marina said, her self-confidence suddenly restored. "By all accounts, Claude was a tough Legionnaire, a hero of Zaire, a man's man and a soldier's soldier. Nevertheless, the police found him cringing under a bush outside Monet's garden, apparently curled up in a fetal position. His PTSD was so bad that they had to put him into a psychiatric ward and pump him full of an antidepressant, which can have all sorts of undesirable side effects. When we arrived to see him, he seemed to me to be in an extremely bad state. However, in the course of your telling him about the letter, he quickly recovered and reverted to the old Claude we knew. I've no idea whether episodes of post-traumatic stress disorder usually disappear as suddenly as they arise, but that's what happened here.

"Despite the fact that he'd just recovered from a serious case of PTSD and was still under the influence of the large doses of the antidepressant they gave him, his description of the family history was fluent and cogent. He never had to think of a year. He didn't confuse the various Philippe le Sabres. He never hesitated at any time. Did you ever hear him correct himself or apologize for forgetting to include one or other detail?

"Do you know, I'm going to go further. Twice in the last twenty-four hours, you've given an account of the threatening letter. You're a professional storyteller, a highly successful author, an international sensation. And yet Claude's narrative of his life was considerably better ordered and more fluent than your account of what's been happening to you and me. For example, as far I could determine, he never made a slip, whereas you did."

"A slip? *Moi?* You cannot be serious."

"To be precise, you told Claude that we visited the headquarters of the Legion in Sidi Bel Abbès."

"That's impossible! Why should I tell him that we went to Algeria when we didn't? Everyone knows that they moved the headquarters to, er, where we went, that suburb of Marseilles, you know, um, the place, with the woman with the computer and the commando badge and the paratrooper's wings. And that sergeant with gray hair who made the coffee. Very nice coffee. Very nice indeed. They moved a while ago, um, I can't recall exactly when they moved, but they moved, I know they did, and they—"

170

"Allow me to put you out of your misery, Quentin. The Legion has been based in Aubagne since 1962. Darling, the fact of the matter is that normal people make mistakes. And we occasionally forget facts, especially names, dates, and places. We tell stories in as logical a fashion as we can manage, but sometimes we come out with a piece of the plot too early or too late in the narrative. That's because we're human.

"But Claude did none of those things. His account was fluent and polished. He must've rehearsed that story over and over and over again until he could recite it perfectly, even under the influence of drugs. And that's what made me suspicious."

"But why would he do such a thing?" I asked. "Why would anyone put together a plausible—but almost completely false—family history and then learn it off by heart like that?"

"When Philippe the Eighth came up with his detailed plot, he must've been aware of the undeniable fact that, as Robert Burns so poetically wrote, 'The best laid schemes o' mice an' men gang aft agley.' When you draw up a complex stratagem for you and your descendants to follow for the next fifty or a hundred years, you have to take into account that things might go wrong. My guess is that an important component of the wide-ranging, long-term plan was that each successive Philippe le Sabre had to put together a credible cover story that he could use if an emergency arose, such as—"

"An attack of PTSD," I suggested.

"Precisely."

"Or what about an attack of PTSD within the framework of a police investigation of a threatening letter ostensibly signed by Philippe le Sabre the Tenth, also known as Claude Malmaison?"

"That's another good point. But we don't know for sure whether Claude even knew about the letter, let alone wrote it. The only thing we can rely on is that we can't rely on anything he says."

"Agreed," I said. "Now, are we ever going to go back to our favorite café where we can sit in the sun, watch the world go by, and be served delicious coffee by Claude Malmaison?"

"I think we should. He may let slip something about the letter, assuming he wrote it."

Before I could reply, my phone rang.

CHAPTER EIGHTEEN

I have an extremely simple mobile phone. It can handle one thing, and one thing only: telephone calls. For reasons that will shortly become clear, it's not a smartphone. In reality, it happens to be a particularly unsmart phone.

My phone has two circles. One is red, the other is green. Actually, I've noticed several other circles as well, but I never use them, and I don't even know what they're for. Marina once explained to me that when my phone rings I need to touch the green circle so that I can speak to whoever has deigned to phone me. The red circle, it seems, is what you have to touch when the call is over. It's quite simple and straightforward: green means go, red means stop, exactly like traffic lights. However, whenever the phone rings I go into a state of total panic. After all, my mobile phone isn't anything like the telephone I knew as a child, namely, a well-behaved black object made of polyoxybenzylmethylenglycolanhydride—or, to use its commercial name, bakelite—that had a

173

handset and a rotary dial and was connected to the wall by a wire. What I have now is a piece of electronic equipment, and I've never been particularly good with computers or digital watches or video games or things like that. Which is why I don't have a smartphone.

When my unsmart phone rings, the first part of the decision-making process is easy: the phone is making a noise, and in order to stop the din, I'll need to tap a button. I usually—but not always—get that initial step right.

The tricky bit is deciding which of the two buttons to tap. Remember, at this point in the saga I'm in a state of consternation bordering on hysteria. The phone is ringing, I want to make it stop, and I have to make an instant decision: red button or green button. What usually happens is that I look at the phone, and the exciting-looking red button is so much more inviting than that staid old green button. So I tap the red button and the noise stops. Which is a good thing. Furthermore, I've discovered that the more often I tap the red button the fewer phone calls I get, which is another good thing. These days I receive about one call a month, and for some reason it's always a wrong number. Probably my phone is malfunctioning in some way.

Anyhow, as I was telling you at the end of the last chapter, my phone was ringing. It was lying on the coffee table in front of me making this loud noise. I picked it up and stared at it the way a bacteriologist looks at a particularly malevolent microbe at the other end of the microscope. My wife, who claims to understand mobile phones and things like that, yelled, "Quentin, the green circle!"

Notwithstanding my state of panic, I was able to follow her instruction. Next came another tricky bit. But first, some essential background information.

In order to confuse us, historians claim that a variety of different people independently invented the telephone, including a chap called Johann Philipp Reis who in 1861 demonstrated his version of the telephone at a meeting of the Physical Society of Frankfurt. He used his telephone to transmit the German phrase, *"Das Pferd frisst keinen Gurkensalat,"* which means "The horse does not eat cucumber salad." My personal theory is that Reis's telephone had a serious design flaw, resulting in his listeners hearing that absurd phrase, whereas the truth of the matter is that Reis said something completely different, namely, "Mr. Watson, come here. I want to see you"—but in German. It is undeniable that Alexander Graham Bell patented the telephone, so he must've discovered it first. As the inventor, he had the right to decide what word people should say when they answer the phone, and he decreed that the telephone greeting should be "Ahoy!" Sadly, Marina strongly discourages my use of that word, so immediately after I tapped the green circle I said, "Hello!"

A voice I didn't recognize asked, "Is that Quentin?"

I grudgingly conceded that that was the case.

The voice continued. "It's Osbert, speaking from London."

I put my hand over the microphone—or more correctly, over the part of the phone that I thought was the microphone but which actually turned out to be something quite different—and hissed to Marina, "He says it's Osbert Oglesby. What's his real name again?"

She hissed back, "That *is* his real name, you idiot! Put the phone on speaker!"

"Is that the red button or the green button?" I asked.

In reply, Marina yanked the phone out of my hand. "Hello, Osbert. This is Marina. I'm sure I've warned you never to phone Quentin—he's mobile-phone challenged. Badly. If you wish to retain your sanity, I suggest that you phone me in future, the same way you've done in the past. I'm putting you on speaker so Quentin can hear you. What's up?"

"Wonderful news, Marina. The lawyers have finalized the contract, and the board of Megalodeon is happy with it. I'm about to email it to you, but I don't anticipate that you'll have the slightest difficulty with any of the terms. The studio is going to fly you to Japan in a week's time for the signing. First class, of course. And they'll put you up in a luxurious suite in the top hotel in Kyoto."

I grabbed my phone back from Marina. The fact that it was on speaker was entirely irrelevant. It was *my* phone, and Osbert—or whatever his real name was—had phoned *me* in the first place. That meant that I had every right to take it back.

"Did you say Japan?" I asked.

"Yes. Kyoto, to be precise. Air France flies nonstop from Paris to Osaka, and Kyoto is about thirty miles from there."

"Osbert," I said reluctantly, because I still didn't believe that anyone could be called Osbert Oglesby— it sounded like the sort of name you'd find in a case study in a textbook on object-oriented software engineering—"why Japan?"

"Because that's where they're going to film *She Loved the French Captain*."

"In Japan?"

"Yes. Not far from Kyoto. Why do you ask?"

"Have you read *She Loved the French Captain*?"

"I certainly have, Quentin. I'm your agent, remember. I couldn't possibly have negotiated on your behalf and obtained such a sweet deal for you if I weren't *au fait* with every last detail of your masterpiece."

"Correct me if I'm wrong, Osbert," I said, as calmly as I could manage, which wasn't calm at all, "but doesn't the action of my book take place during

Napoleon's retreat from Moscow? If I recall correctly, it begins with Napoleon at the gates of Moscow and ends with Napoleon in exile on the island of St. Helena. And I believe that Napoleon was born in Corsica. That makes him French. Not Japanese.

"In between, Captain Philippe le Sabre of the French Imperial Guard retreats across Europe from Moscow to Paris with Ludmilla, an utterly gorgeous Russian farmhand, whom he marries. In Paris. I don't recall anything about Japan in my book, Osbert. Do you?"

"You're quite right, Quentin, in every respect. But the people at Megalodeon Studios have nevertheless decided to make the film in Japan."

"Why don't they make it in Russia, Osbert? Are we perhaps talking about a different book, one that I haven't written yet and that I'm not going to write? Ever. The one I wrote is called *She Loved the French Captain*. And the key scenes take place in Russia. In the snows of winter. Not Japan. In the cherry blossom season."

"I hear what you're saying, Quentin. Yes, we're talking about the same book. But I can assure you that the studio has an excellent reason for deciding to create Russia in Japan."

At that point if I'd been talking on the old black bakelite phone at home I'd have slammed the handset down on the cradle, and that would've been *sayonara*. But I was holding my unsmart mobile phone. So I pushed on the green circle as angrily as I could and slammed the phone down on the coffee table.

Marina picked up the phone, cool as a cucumber salad that Ries's horse wouldn't eat, and checked to make sure that we were still connected to our agent. "Osbert, this is Marina. How much?"

"Pounds, euros, or dollars?"

"It doesn't matter; they're all worth about the same at the moment. And don't talk to me about our future share of the gross earnings or the net profit. I don't believe in counting my chickens before the eggs are hatched. What I want to know from you is this: When we fly home from Japan, what'll be the number printed on the check that I'll safely store in my handbag?"

The clear implication of that last remark was that if I put the check in my wallet I'd lose it somewhere between Kyoto and our bank in Paris. I felt egregiously insulted, notwithstanding the undeniable fact that Marina was completely right.

"Two and half million," Osbert said. "Less my percentage, as you know."

"Send me the contract as an email attachment. Now I'm handing the phone back to Quentin, who's calmed down fractionally after hearing the figure you mentioned, so that you can explain to him why they're making the film in Japan."

With the greatest reluctance, I took my phone back from Marina.

179

"Quentin," said the voice from London, "let me explain to you what this is all about. Every government in the world wants studios to make movies and TV programs in their country. Think what the *Lord of the Rings* Trilogy has done for tourism in New Zealand or the positive impact of *Game of Thrones* on Northern Ireland and Dubrovnik. Governments all over the world are only too keen to finance movies, in whole or in part, subject to certain conditions such as providing employment opportunities or advertising the features of the area to an international audience by filming in exterior locations. Yasuhara Prefecture, about twenty-five miles from Kyoto, has immense potential as a venue for movie making, but most studios don't seem to be aware of this fact.

"Owing to a quirk of nature, the landscape of the prefecture varies dramatically from place to place over a relatively small area. The region includes a desert that's ideal for filming westerns and a vast lake that can easily masquerade as a seashore. The prefecture has mountains, forests, rivers, caves, plains, mines, farms. It's quite incredible how many different types of scenery are found there. So no matter what sort of outdoor filming you want to do, Yasuhara Prefecture is an especially good location."

I decided to ask a pointed question. "What about snow-covered steppes?"

"I'm glad you asked me that," Osbert said. "Japanese ski resorts quite often have to resort to snow cannons and snow-grooming equipment. It'll be easy to recreate the wintry plains of western Russia, even in mid-summer. And I know what you're going to ask me next."

"What's that?"

"You're wondering how they can possibly do the destruction of Moscow by fire, aren't you?"

"Yes, how did you know?"

I heard a chuckle from the other end of the line. "Quentin, let's suppose that Megalodeon decided to make the movie in Russia, which is what you want. How would they film the burning of Moscow? Don't you think that the residents might get just a little upset if the movie makers burned down their city?"

"I hadn't thought of that."

Marina rolled her eyes. For some unknown reason, she does that a lot.

Osbert chuckled again. "They can make models and burn them. They can use computer-generated images. They sometimes construct buildings in the studio and then set them alight. Filmmakers have many different ways of fooling the audience into thinking they're seeing Moscow burning. Believe me, Quentin, the fact that most of the outdoor scenes are going to be shot in Yasuhara Prefecture will in no way detract from the movie. Most films aren't made in the location they depict, and the members of the audience don't know and don't care. A movie is an illusion, pure and simple.

"The question you should be asking me," he continued, "is this: Numerous places all over the world can recreate Moscow and the steppes of Russia for Megalodeon, so why have they chosen Yasuhara?"

"Okay, I'll bite. Why have they chosen Yasuhara?"

"Because the prefecture wants to become known all over the world as an outstanding site for movie-making, and they're prepared to pay Megalodeon a large sum of money to make their blockbuster there. I'm sure that the contract includes clauses ensuring that the studio has to hire a significant number of Yasuharans to participate in making the movie. That sort of condition is a win-win for the prefecture: it reduces local unemployment, and the area becomes known as a go-to place for making movies. And Megalodeon doesn't need to raise a truly gigantic sum of money to film *She Loved the French Captain*. Instead, they'll be able to do the job with only a vast amount.

"Now, I'm about to send you and Marina the program for the two-day signing extravaganza. All the events are designed to highlight what Yasuhara can offer filmmakers. Quentin, I'm afraid you're going to have to stay in the background; the public at large has no idea that you were the genius who wrote the book on which the movie is based. However, your charming wife will play a leading role. After all, she's ostensibly the author of the favorite book of an immense number of potential moviegoers all over the world."

Marina responded with her customary charm and exquisite tact. "Actually, Osbert, keeping Quentin out of the public eye is another win-win. He can be a little grumpy at times, isn't that so, darling?"

"I refuse to lower myself by responding to that scurrilous lie. I'm always amiable and delightful. Unlike actors who refuse to perform with children or animals for fear of being upstaged, I am a friend to every man, woman, child, and dog. Even cats. And guinea pigs. And hamsters. And meerkats. And—"

"Yes, we know, sweetheart. But Osbert will keep you company while I do what Megalodeon wants me to do."

"Thank you, Marina," Osbert said. "When you two receive the detailed program, you'll see that Marina has one engagement after another for two days. Quentin, on the first day, you and I will take a drive around the prefecture to see the different locations where they're going to film your masterpiece, after which we'll sample the local whiskey, which I can assure you is truly excellent. On the second day, Marina will sign the contract in front of the cameras, and then you'll sign on the relevant dotted line once the photographers have left."

Placing my signature at the bottom of the contract while seated on the platform of a cavernous Japanese auditorium, totally empty except for Quentin and me and a huddle of rapacious lawyers from New York, London, Hollywood, and the Cayman Islands, was

183

something forward to which I was not looking and out of which I wanted to get, as my pedantic friend Lancelot Aylesworth would've put it.

CHAPTER NINETEEN

The next morning, I went to see Gilles Despoir. "We're supposed to fly to Japan in about a week to sign a film contract. Do you know of any reason why we shouldn't leave Paris at that time?"

"How long will you be away?"

"The film studio has set up a dog-and-pony show for Marina. It's set to last two days. During that time, I've been firmly ordered to stay backstage and out of the limelight."

Gilles grinned broadly, but he didn't say anything, so I continued.

"I suppose that, having flown all that way, Marina will want to see something more of Japan than only Kyoto. I haven't discussed it with her yet, in the probably vain hope that the idea hasn't crossed her mind yet."

"It will," Gilles said. "Particularly when she and Priscilla next see one another or talk on the phone, which is probably happening right now."

"Yes, I think you're right. How long would Chunky Monkey deem appropriate for galivanting around Japan?"

"Two weeks, more or less."

"You have your answer, then. Would our spending a fortnight away from Paris cause a complication?"

Gilles looked glum. "With the current state of the investigation, it makes no real difference where you are. I suppose I should actively encourage you to leave France, just in case a homicidal maniac is trying to kill your wife, but we don't believe that one exists.

"I'm speaking unofficially, and I'll firmly deny having disclosed what I'm about to tell you, but here's our position. We've no doubt whatsoever that Claude Malmaison is Philippe the Tenth. The evidence is overwhelming, and he himself has admitted it. That said, we're equally sure he didn't write the letter, for the three reasons you gave in this very office last week: he's spent more than half his life trying to disguise the fact that he's a le Sabre; the writer claimed that the author of *She Loved the French Captain* 'despoiled and desecrated the family name,' and we know that's not the case; and finally, Claude is a highly trained killer who'd simply go ahead and kill Marina without warning her by writing a threatening letter."

I didn't want to tell Despoir that I'd successfully convinced the police but I hadn't yet managed to persuade myself, so I kept my mouth shut.

"I don't want to bore you with details," Gilles added, "but I think you should know that various investigators have put forward other good reasons. All in all, we're firmly convinced Claude is not the letter writer."

Then Gilles said, "I could tell you more about the case, if you're interested."

"I most definitely am. What did you find?"

"We haven't found anything; that's the whole problem. We know that Claude Malmaison didn't write the letter. That means that the person who wrote it wasn't Philippe the Tenth, and therefore the book doesn't besmirch his family honor. In short, most of what appears in that letter is nonsensical and irrelevant. That means that we need to ask the question: Why did the perpetrator write it? And we've no idea whatsoever.

"Without any clues, we can do nothing more. The police psychologists tell me that in all probability the writer poses no danger to your wife. But who knows? So if you want to travel to Japan, go right ahead. Actually, I'd encourage you to journey abroad. After all, Marina might worry less in new surroundings. Also, in the highly unlikely event that someone in France is actually trying to kill Marina, he won't be able to do anything while she's in Japan, and that gives us another two weeks to find him."

Gilles paused. He stared for a long while at the model of a sailing ship in a bottle mounted on the wall of his office. Eventually, he made eye contact with me. "The letter has another dimension to it. We've been talking about *who* might have written it and *why* they wrote it. But here's an equally important question: *How* did the writer obtain the information about the le Sabres?"

"Not from the internet. That we do know."

"I agree," Gilles said. "There has to have been some other source. The key issue is that the person who wrote that letter knows the entire family history. Either he or she discovered it somehow, which seems highly unlikely—where would they find the information?—or he or she is a member of the family. And the only two living le Sabres are Claude and his seventy-something-year-old mother, Nicole, neither of whom would ever divulge the family secret."

The expression on Gilles's face was gloomy. He stood and held out his hand. "Have a wonderful trip to Japan. It's possible that I'll have some information for you when you get back, but I'm not overly hopeful."

I turned to go, but as I reached the door, an idea struck me. I went back to my chair. "Gilles, something else has just popped into my mind. Tell me, have you interrogated Claude in depth?"

"No. He's in a psychiatric unit, suffering from severe PTSD, and he's heavily drugged with an antidepressant. The doctors reluctantly allowed us to ask Claude only a handful of basic questions and under their close supervision. The only important one was, Are you Philippe le Sabre the Tenth? Once he'd readily admitted his true identity, everything else could wait until he's fully compos mentis. Why do you ask?"

"When Marina and I went to visit him in Druny Military Hospital, he gave a detailed account of his family history, starting with the 1947 commission of inquiry that exonerated your grandfather—and vilified Claude's great-grandfather. At all times he was totally lucid."

"Totally lucid, you say? Notwithstanding his mental state and what the doctors had pumped into him?"

"His story involved the seventh, eighth, ninth, and tenth Philippe le Sabres. He never confused them, and not for one second did he hesitate or pause to think. He had every date on his fingertips. He related the story in strict chronological order with no omissions that he had to fill in later."

"Amazing!"

"Yes, indeed. Even more remarkable is that Marina analyzed what Claude had said to us. And when we got home, she showed that his entire story was a pack of lies from beginning to end."

"This may be important. Tell me the full story—omit nothing."

When at long last I reached the end of the saga, Gilles said, "Your wife is a remarkable person. I gathered from the way that you recounted Claude's tale that you didn't have the slightest suspicion that what he was telling you was actually a false cover story from start to finish."

"Correct. His account was most convincing, at least as far as I was concerned."

"Before we go any further, Quentin, I want to check where Claude was when his girlfriend and son were run over by that car. I've no doubt that he has an unbreakable alibi, but just to be sure, let me look it up quickly. Ah, yes, in 1995 he was in Bosnia–Herzegovina with the UN Peacekeeping Force. And at the time of the accident—if indeed it was an accident—he was part of the rapid-reaction force that was trying to break the siege of Sarajevo. It says here that we have photographs of him digging in on Mount Igman. Photoshop wasn't yet available in those days, so I have to accept that the pictures, which appeared in the French press, are genuine.

"Now let's get back to the case. If I've understood you correctly, nothing in Claude's story or, more importantly, in Marina's interpretation of Claude's story, ties him to the letter your wife received."

"Not directly, no. But indirectly . . ."

"Indirectly?" Gilles asked.

"It's the same as with the murder of his girlfriend and son."

Gilles raised his eyebrows when I used the M-word. However, the fact that he'd just checked where

190

Claude was on that day revealed that the French police major had exceedingly strong suspicions regarding the circumstances of the two deaths and the role Claude may have played in the incident.

"We now know of a group of people in France," I said, "who can best be described as neo-Nazis. They hero-worship a shadowy figure, Philippe le Sabre the Seventh."

"Quentin, I'm sorry to have to contradict you, but he wasn't a 'shadowy figure' of any kind. The traitor was the subject of a public legal investigation that went on for weeks. Numerous newspaper articles described each day's proceedings while the panel was hearing testimony from the various witnesses. And the final report was widely publicized."

"Yes, all that is true, but those events happened in 1947. Today, more than seventy years later, the name Philippe le Sabre doesn't even appear on the internet, much to their satisfaction. And I think that's why they sent the letter. They're angry that Marina has once again brought the name Philippe le Sabre to the attention of people all over the world."

"Hold on a minute," Gilles said. "Her book isn't about Philippe le Sabre the Seventh. We're keeping the contents of the letter—and, above all, the bit about the ten generations of le Sabres—strictly private. Why, you yourself informed me a few minutes ago that Claude Malmaison had no knowledge of the letter Marina received."

"That's why I used the word *indirectly*. I don't believe that while he was fighting in Bosnia–Herzegovina Claude was actively engaged in planning the murder of his girlfriend, Marie-André, and their son, André-Marie. On the contrary, in my opinion, everything was handled by the neo-Nazis. In fact, in order to protect Claude, they probably shared nothing at all with him about their intentions until after it had happened.

"In the same way, I believe that French fascists sent the letter to Marina. And again, they kept Claude out of the loop, precisely because he'd be the obvious suspect. Instead, he learned about the letter from us when we visited him in hospital."

Gilles did not look at all convinced by what I'd claimed. "I think your argument has a few weaknesses. First, you referred to Philippe le Sabre the Seventh as a 'shadowy figure.' If the vast majority of people have no idea who he was, how could a book praising the traitor's great-great-great-great-grandfather possibly change anything?

"And that leads to another issue. For all but a handful of people, Philippe le Sabre is a fictional figure. Many years ago, when I was at university, I went hiking in the Lake District. One day, I met a young woman named Jane Eyre. Was I supposed to say to her something along the lines of, 'Your name is the same as the title character in a work of fiction written by Charlotte Brontë. Are you related to the eponymous heroine?' On the contrary, like all sensible people, I realized that her parents had a warped sense of humor and that no connection of any kind between the two Jane Eyres existed. Let me spell it out to you explicitly: one was fictional, the other real. In the same way, not even a crazy neo-Nazi would dream that the hero of the historical romance novel *She Loved the French Captain*, a work of fiction, had anything at all to do with the seventh Philippe le Sabre.

"My third objection is that you claim that members of the cabal that murdered Marie-André and André-Marie are threatening to kill Marina. As we all agree, the letter isn't threatening anything; the writers only say they're going to do it. And if they're capable of killing two people in cold blood, one of them an innocent child of five, then they're perfectly capable of murdering Marina—so why send the letter?

"And I need to add something else, a further weakness in your argument that should reassure you. I don't believe that Marina's life is at stake. If neo-Nazis were even to try to kill her, the letter would become public, and the existence of the cabal would become public. And the last thing that a secret society wants is to be exposed to the light."

I sighed. Deeply.

"I'm sorry to say that I can't agree with your conclusions, Quentin. But we do need to have a written record of what Claude told you and Marina, as well as Marina's analysis of his story. Would you be prepared to give us a statement?"

Gilles's request took me aback. A few minutes before, he'd stated that as far he was concerned nothing in Claude's story tied him to The Letter. In addition, my wife's brilliant analysis was apparently equally unhelpful in that respect. I'd tried to point out to Gilles that an indirect link existed, but he'd firmly rebuffed me. Nevertheless, now he was asking me for an affidavit. Why? And if he wanted to know what Marina had said to me, why didn't he just ask her?

Before I could say anything, Gilles added, "I can see you're puzzled, and I'm pretty sure I know why. I'll find an assistant to take your statement. When you're finished, come back here and I'll explain everything."

Having lived in Paris for more than twenty years, my French is fluent and colloquial. That said, I was about to provide a written sworn statement of fact, part of which might be used to convict the person who'd written the letter that terrified the love of my life. I wasn't prepared to take the risk that I might use the wrong French word and thereby let the perpetrator off the hook, and I therefore insisted on giving my statement in English. Fortuitously, one of Gilles's assistants proved to be as fluent in English as Gilles is, and ninety minutes later I found myself back in Gilles's office.

"Quentin, when a car hits a pedestrian, we have to analyze the evidence in order to determine the cause of the accident. For example, the pedestrian may have crossed the road without looking, the driver may have been speeding or under the influence of alcohol, and so on. I used the word *accident*, because it rarely happens that a car is used as an instrument of murder or attempted murder. But when it does occur, it's usually blatantly obvious that the driver has used his vehicle for homicidal purposes.

"However, the death of Marie-André de Villiers and her son, André-Marie, falls into a different category. When it occurred nearly twenty years ago, all the evidence pointed to a hit-and-run accident at the pedestrian crossing outside the boy's preschool. While you were giving your statement, I went through the file with a fine-tooth comb, and I found no indication that any of the investigators even considered the possibility that this was an intentional killing.

"Then you raised the possibility—no, I'm wrong, that was Marina. Marina suggested that the boy wasn't registered as Philippe le Sabre the Eleventh because Bertrand had discovered that Marie-André wasn't of pure Aryan ancestry. And then, if I understood you correctly, Marina claimed Bertrand had mother and son killed.

"In the light of her suggestion, I felt that I should examine the evidence once again, with a view to reopening the case if I found anything suspicious. I asked you to give an affidavit so that we'd have on record what Claude said to you regarding the accident—precisely nothing. I didn't tell you why in case that might've subconsciously biased your statement. And someone will come to your home to get an affidavit from Marina."

"I see. And did you find anything suspicious in the file?"

"When a hit-and-run accident occurs, we almost always find the perpetrator's car. It can be much harder—and sometimes impossible—to find the driver, but we're usually successful in locating the vehicle within a few days. It isn't at all easy to completely dispose of a car. But in this case, nothing was ever found."

"Does the file comment on this?"

"No."

"What are you going to do now?"

"At this point, nothing. But once we've found who wrote that letter . . ."

CHAPTER TWENTY

When I got home, I realized I had forgotten my front door key. I rang the bell.

"The good news," I said to Marina as she opened the door, "is that Gilles has no objection to our traveling to Japan."

"And the bad news?"

"He wants a detailed statement from you. He's sending someone around to the flat."

Marina laughed. "Quentin, come into the living room so that I can introduce you to Lieutenant du Marque. She and I are working together on my affidavit. Gilles phoned me to set this up while you were giving your statement."

I shook hands with the lieutenant. Then I went to our bedroom and lay on the bed doing a cryptic crossword puzzle until I heard the police officer leaving.

I joined Marina in the living room. "It's time for another stiff armagnac."

"What's the problem now?"

"I can't make out what Gilles is up to. I went to see him, as we agreed, to make sure that he had no objection to our forthcoming trip. As I told you when I walked in, he's fine with it. And why? Because the police haven't the faintest idea who wrote the letter, so it doesn't seem to matter whether you're here or there."

"He stated that?" Marina asked.

"Not in so many words, of course, but that was the gist of it."

Marina rolled her eyes. "Go on."

"I asked him if they'd interrogated Claude in depth. He replied that the doctors had allowed them to ask only a few questions, including the important one: Was he Philippe le Sabre the Tenth? He readily admitted that he was. Everything else, Gilles said, could wait until the PTSD had been treated and the effects of the drug had worn off. So I gave him all the details of our visit to the hospital, how Claude had seemed clearheaded in every way, and about the pack of lies that Claude told us."

"Good."

"Then I informed Gilles that French neo-Nazis had written the letter to you and murdered Claude's girlfriend and their son. He utterly pooh-poohed my ideas, but next thing he's wanting detailed affidavits from us, for 'the file.' When I asked him what he's going to do about the car 'accident,' he declared that he isn't prepared to lift a finger until the letter writer has been unmasked. If that's the case, why didn't he wait until he's discovered who wrote the letter before getting affidavits from us? I think that Gilles was wrong. I believe that French fascists are responsible for the letter and for the murder, and I don't understand why he's not doing anything about it other than wasting our time with sworn statements regarding our visit to Claude. No, the time has come for us to take action."

"Precisely what are you suggesting?" Marina asked.

I suspected that she was only humoring me, but I pressed on. "We need to travel to Lyon to investigate the double murder."

"Which took place more than twenty years ago. And I should remind you that the police carried out an investigation at the time but came up with nothing."

"You're missing the key point," I said.

"And what's that?"

"The police were investigating an accident. This was murder."

"It probably was. But how do you propose to prove it?" my wife asked.

"We need to go to Lyon and make our own enquiries, armed with our secret weapon."

"Which is what?"

"Autographed copies of the French language edition of *She Loved the French Captain.* Those books will open every door."

"And what is your plan?"

"We take a taxi from here to Gare de Lyon. A high-speed train, or TGV, leaves every 25 minutes. After all, Lyon is the second city of France, so we're not the only people who want to travel there. For two hours, the train scythes its way through the glorious countryside on its way to Southeastern France, near the Swiss border, and—"

"I wasn't asking for a travelogue," a stern voice interrupted. "Once we've arrived in Lyon, what then?"

"We go to the nearest police station and, secret weapon in hand, tell *Monsieur l'agent*—"

"Or *Madame l'agent*, as the case may be," Marina interrupted again, displaying more knowledge of the French language in that one sentence than in the entire time we'd spent in France since our marriage.

I was too flabbergasted to do more than gaze at my wife in open-mouthed admiration.

"Go on, Quentin. What do you intend you say to him? Or her?"

"Well, er, I'll introduce you to him. Or her. And then I'll say that you're writing a book about an accident that took place in Lyon in 1995 and ask for their cooperation. And assistance. We are both fully aware that, all over the world—but especially in

France, the land of *amour*—everyone runs to fulfil the slightest wish of *Madame* Aver-smeet, the supreme writer of historical romance fiction."

* * *

That afternoon, Marina and I went to a travel agent who specializes in trips to Japan. He suggested a two-week itinerary that would enable us to see many of the major tourist sites as well as a couple of the more unusual places he'd visited and thought we'd enjoy. This included a night in a *ryokan*, a traditional inn. Marina thought this was wonderful idea. But pray tell me, dear reader, can you imagine me wearing a *yukata*—that's a casual summer kimono—and sleeping on a *futon* on the *tatami* mat flooring? I'm afraid you'll have to continue reading if you want to know what transpired in Japan regarding this touristic catastrophe-in-the-making.

Then an unpleasant idea struck me. "How safe is Japan?" I asked him.

"Extremely safe," he assured me. "Japan has one of the lowest crime rates in the world."

"Do many tourists get mugged?" I enquired.

"As I just told you, not much crime at all is committed in Japan. White collar crime seems to be a bit of an issue, but murder and other crimes of violence are extremely rare."

"What about grabbing tourist's handbags and stealing any checks that they may have stored there?"

The travel agent gave me a strange look. Marina quickly caught on. "Don't worry about that sort of thing, Quentin," she said. "Nowadays people don't pay with checks; they transfer money directly into bank accounts."

"Including large sums?" I asked her.

"Especially for large sums of money," she insisted.

I relaxed. "That's a load off my mind."

The travel agent, who understandably hadn't understood a single word of this, looked relieved. "Shall I finalize this itinerary?"

"By all means," Marina said.

Thinking about the forthcoming night we would spend in the *ryokan*, I shuddered.

CHAPTER TWENTY-ONE

The officer standing behind the counter at the Lyon police station had the build—and all the charm—of an angry Dobermann Pinscher, a breed developed around 1890 by a German tax collector named Karl Friedrich Louis Dobermann. Needless to say, dear reader, Dobermann Pinschers rarely feature in bodice rippers, and so I thought I'd take the opportunity to sneak the dog into this book. "Yes?" she barked.

"*Madame l'agent,*" I said, "this is *Madame* Marina Aver-smeet."

"Yes?" she snarled.

"The author of *She Loved the French Captain,*" I added.

"Yes?" By now she was all but foaming at the mouth, and her growl was so violent that I was seriously concerned that she was going to jump over the counter and bite me. Luckily, in the nick of time, an officer rushed from the inner office. He pushed his colleague aside and nearly knocked her over as he fawned over my wife.

"*Madame* Aver-smeet," he gushed, "we are so honored to have you visit our police station. Never before have we had so distinguished a visitor. And that includes the Dalai Lama, Angelina Jolie, the previous Pope, and the President of France, all of whom have been in this very room."

He spoke to his canine associate. "Madeleine, you have a degree in French literature. Surely you know of Marina Aver-smeet, the greatest author of our age? My wife and all her friends agree that *She Loved the French Captain* is the most marvelous book ever written."

Sadly, for Marina, this enthusiastic encomium was delivered in French, and I wasn't going to destroy the *gemütlichkeit* that now permeated the police station by interrupting his ardent paean in order to translate it into English. The mood lightened even further when his colleague, the literary critic, decided that she could no longer tolerate the company of Aver-smeet admirers and retreated, in a visible huff, to the safety of the inner office.

The police officer beamed. His perfect teeth gleamed in the fluorescent light. "Now, *Monsieur* Aver-smeet, how can I help you and your charming wife?"

"My wife is writing a book about a hit-and-run accident that took place in 1995 here in Lyon. A woman and her son were killed. We've come here to see the actual place where it happened."

"But why, *monsieur*? I know nothing of this accident, but any death is a tragedy, let alone a mother and her child. Such a book would be heartbreaking, not uplifting like *She Loved the French Captain*."

I was sure that the Lyonnaise would ask this question, repeatedly, so I'd prepared an answer.

"The book is about the love affair between the mother and her paramour. Only the very end is sad, but the tragedy of their deaths uplifts the quality of the pure love that went before it."

Dear reader, I can clearly hear you saying, *What utter rubbish!* Well, that's because you read that last paragraph in English. In French, however, it makes perfect sense. Go on, translate it, and you'll see for yourself.

Naturally, the police officer fully appreciated every nuance of what I'd said. "Indubitably!" he gushed. "The book will be even better than *She Loved the French Captain*, if that were possible."

I smiled because I'd just had an epiphany. I'd suddenly realized that the reason why French husbands were so enthusiastic about the book wasn't because their wives had rhapsodized endlessly about my bodice ripper. After all, in my experience, most husbands hardly listen to a word their spouses say. No, the explanation of their ardor was that the men of France were reading the book and savoring each word. Without a doubt, every red-blooded Frenchman would rather face death on the guillotine than admit that he'd even opened the book, let alone read it from cover to cover, but facts are facts.

I wondered wryly what would happen if the news ever got out that the person who wrote *She Loved the French Captain* was actually a man. My reverie was interrupted by the police officer.

"*Monsieur*, what was the name of the woman who was killed?"

"Marie-André de Villiers," I replied, much to my amazement. Imagine that: I'd actually managed to recall a name.

The police officer—who still hadn't introduced himself to us—tapped away at a computer. Within a few seconds, he looked up with a beatific expression on his face that seemed to say this was the very first time he'd ever successfully located a file. "I've found it. She and her son, André-Marie de Villiers, were killed at a pedestrian crossing at 122, Rue Calmette et Guérin in Lyon. It happened, exactly as you informed me, in 1995—on Tuesday, July 21st, to be precise. I'll print the whole thing for you."

He retreated to the inner office and emerged surprisingly soon with a stack of paper. I was impressed that the French equip even their suburban police stations with high-speed printers.

"*Monsieur* Aver-smeet, here's all the information we have on the accident. I wish *madame* every success in her new book. Finally, I must apologize for the behavior of my colleague who thinks that nothing worthwhile has been written since Sully Prudhomme won the first Nobel Prize for Literature in 1901. She has only herself to blame for never experiencing the sheer unbridled joy, ecstasy perhaps, of reading *She Loved the French Captain*."

We thanked him, left the police station, and looked for a café where we could sit and peruse the dozens of pages he'd given us. We turned left and walked for about five minutes. Across the road we spied a pavement café with an unusual feature. Above the awning was a panoply of window boxes, each resplendent with hundreds of petunias in red, pink, rose, puce, and purple.

"Darling," I said, "if their coffee is as outstanding as their flowers, we're in for a treat."

All the pavement tables were taken, but as we reached the café, a couple got up and left. We quickly took their places. I half expected to see Claude bustling up to the table. Instead, after a short time a middle-aged woman approached. She took our order without a word. A few minutes later she was back, still as silent as a Trappist nun. The coffee was in every way as outstanding as the flowers. And as for the praline tart, all I can say is that words fail me, which doesn't happen too often, as you well know, dear reader.

Our sheer joy of eating and drinking in a café in Lyon, the gastronomic capital of France—and therefore of the world—was rudely interrupted as I started to translate the file the police officer had printed for us.

"It says here that the father of André-Marie is *inconnu*. That means 'unknown.'"

Marina was as startled as I was. "What? But Gilles told us that Claude's name—or more precisely, Philippe le Sabre the Tenth—appears on André-Marie's birth certificate as the father."

I thought for a while. "No, that's not quite right. Gilles informed us that the hospital records reflect Claude as the father. He didn't mention the birth certificate."

"But Claude did. He told us that his father instructed him to register the boy as Philippe le Sabre the Eleventh, but he rebelled against his father's wishes. He stated that he registered his son as André-Marie de Villiers in order to ensure that 'the accursed name will die when I die.' If that were true, Claude would appear as the father on the birth certificate—I assume that only the father or the mother can register a child. And that means that Marie-André must've registered the birth. Quentin, is the son's birth certificate in that pile of papers?"

I paged through the wodge, and near the bottom I was delighted to find a copy of the document. "You're quite right. Here it says, '*sur la déclaration de la mère.*' That means 'on the declaration of the mother.' So as you correctly deduced, Marie-André was responsible for the birth certificate. In fact, the certificate is dated nearly two weeks after the date of birth. Marie-André waited until she'd fully recovered from the rigors of childbirth before going to the relevant government office to register the birth of her son."

"But that doesn't explain why the father is 'unknown.' Any ideas?"

"Nothing comes to mind," I said. "Marie-André was fully aware who the father of her child was. So what's going on?"

"I've just thought of something. Two different kinds of records are involved here. Hospital records are private—unless you obtain a search warrant or the like—and they're recorded while the patient is in the hospital. On the other hand, a birth certificate is a public document that's created at some time after the birth, when the father or the mother goes to a government office to make a declaration.

"The police were able to access the hospital records, and they reflect the fact that Claude was the father of the child. Those private records were started when Marie-André was admitted to the hospital and ended when she was discharged. Then, nearly two weeks after her son was born, Marie-André went to register the birth. I'm sure that, at that time, she stated that Philippe le Sabre the Tenth was the father. But the French fascists certainly didn't want the sacred name of le Sabre to be associated with the child in any way. So the public record was subsequently doctored."

"Can that be done?" I asked.

"Certainly! Every computerized record system has to incorporate a mechanism for correcting an incorrect entry. After all, human beings make mistakes, and it has to be possible to rectify a spelling error or fix a typo. But the problem is always the same: Who is allowed to make changes? If the system is badly designed, all sorts of people can alter official records."

"I think you've explained everything to my satisfaction, although I doubt if Gilles will be as easy to persuade."

Marina grinned. "Agreed. Let's take a taxi to the scene of the murder. Maybe we'll find something there to convince him."

* * *

Rue Calmette et Guérin, named after the two French immunologists who attenuated the bovine bacillus used to make the BCG vaccine against tuberculosis, was a long, straight, wide road. Marina stood in the middle of the pedestrian crossing.

"I can see a car half a mile from here, and the driver can see me just as clearly. Now I'm turning around, and the visibility is equally good in the other direction. You know, Quentin, this must be one of the safest pedestrian crossings in the whole world. The only way the driver of the car could possibly have hit the mother and son was if he deliberately tried to kill them. And I don't understand why the police didn't pick up on that point."

"Was it possibly weather related?" I asked. "Thick mist?"

"In July? Get real. Does the file mention the conditions?"

"Let me see. Yes, it says here that the weather was clear."

"No surprise there. Can you think of any reason, other than a deliberate killing, for the deaths?"

"Frankly—no," I replied.

"What did the coroner say?"

"They don't have coroners in France. That role is played by a *médecin légiste,* what we would call a forensic scientist. I think that the American term is something like 'medical examiner.' Anyhow, the *médecin légiste* didn't seem to come up with any sort of meaningful finding. All he reported was that they were killed as a consequence of the impact with the car."

"French neo-Nazis at work in Lyon?" Marina asked.

"I've no idea. Maybe."

"So what's our next step?"

"We need to read the police file carefully. Let's go back to our hotel."

CHAPTER TWENTY-TWO

The moment we returned to our hotel room, I studied the case file the policeman had printed for me. I suddenly realized that in presenting us with a copy he'd violated all manner of confidentiality laws. I just hoped that Madeleine, his canine colleague, hadn't observed what he'd done.

I've already told you someone had doctored André-Marie's birth certificate, and that made me wonder about the other documents. Accordingly, I started by looking at the copies of the official papers at the back of the file.

I found Marie-André's birth certificate and scrutinized it carefully. Nothing seemed to be out of the ordinary. Then I examined her death certificate. Again, everything looked reasonable.

Next, I quickly glanced through the entire file. As I'd expected, I encountered no mention of the father of her child nor any reference to his family. Then I noticed that the address of the deceased was given as

Apartment 7, Number 34 Rue Évariste Galois, La Mouche quarter, Lyon.

Again La Mouche! First the treachery of Philippe le Sabre the Seventh had resulted in the execution of Gilles Despoir Senior, alias La Mouche, and now we'd discovered that the partner and child of Philippe le Sabre the Tenth had been living in the La Mouche quarter when they were murdered. Was this merely another coincidence—or something more?

Then I slowly and carefully went through the entire file, line-by-line. As Gilles had hinted, it appeared that someone in the Lyon police force had decided from the outset that this was to be treated as a run-of-the-mill traffic accident. For example, I could find no record of any serious attempts to locate the car, let alone the driver. As far as I could tell, the detectives had started to go through the motions but quickly threw in the towel. Then I noticed a total absence of witness statements in the file. Did that mean that no one saw the incident? Or was all evidence of that kind suppressed?

Now I understood why Gilles had told me he wasn't prepared to reopen the investigation until he'd identified the letter writer; he would've had to start again from scratch, some twenty years later. Marina and I had come to Lyon on a fool's errand, and I was the fool.

I explained the situation to my wife.

214

"What about her apartment?" Marina asked. "Is it possible that someone in the building remembers her?"

"After nearly twenty years? I doubt it."

"It's the only lead we have. After we've come all this way, surely we need to give it a try?"

Half an hour later we found ourselves in Rue Évariste Galois, a street lined with an interminable succession of elderly apartment blocks, each barely distinguishable from its neighbor. The four-story concrete buildings with identical windows stood cheek by jowl. The blank façades were unsullied by ornamentation or decoration of any sort. I felt as if I were walking through a cemetery, with giant tombstones on either side.

When we reached Number 34, I noticed a plaque fastened to the right of the entrance. It read, *In memory of Jean de Villiers, a leader of the Maquis. He died in 1944 for France and Liberty.*

"So," Marina said, "Marie-André's grandfather led a rural guerrilla band of partisans during the Nazi occupation of World War II. What a tragedy: Montague boy meets Capulet girl, boy falls in love with girl, boy impregnates girl, boy learns about girl's grandfather, boy's associates kill girl. And their child."

"Why didn't Claude just drop Marie-André as soon as he discovered she was the granddaughter of a Maquisard leader?" I asked. "Why did he stay with her until the child was born and then flee to the Foreign

215

Legion? And why didn't Marie-André ask the police to find the father of her baby?"

Marina pondered for a considerable time before answering. "My guess is that, from the start, Claude was simply making use of Marie-André. He didn't love her, and he certainly never had any intention of marrying her. Then she fell pregnant. An abortion would've simplified matters, but clearly that didn't happen.

"The family must've decided that the best way to make the problem go away was for Claude to tell Marie-André that she would receive ample financial support for herself and her child as long as they needed it, provided she agreed to sever all ties with the le Sabres. Most importantly, she would have to declare on the birth certificate that the father of her child was 'unknown.'"

"So the birth certificate wasn't doctored after all?" I asked.

"Probably not. Anyhow, Philippe the Tenth stayed with her until the child was born, then he left for the Foreign Legion to become Claude Malmaison."

"Why?" I asked.

"The family wanted to ensure that no one could find a way of linking him to his son, André-Marie."

"But he was present at the birth."

"That's true," Marina said, "but hospital records are private—or so they assumed."

"Are you saying that they ordered him to join the Legion at a cost of breaking the chain of ten successive men named Philippe le Sabre?"

"As far as they were concerned, Claude could always father another boy, this time with a more suitable woman, one who believed fervently in the perverted values of the le Sabre clan. The child's last name would later be changed from Malmaison to le Sabre."

"And why did they kill Marie-André and André-Marie?" I asked.

"My guess is that the fact that Jean de Villiers was Marie-André's grandfather came to the attention of the French neo-Nazis. They couldn't possibly allow Marie-André to reveal the fact that Philippe the Tenth had fathered a child with the granddaughter of a leading Maquisard. So they organized the murder, and to protect Claude, arranged for it to take place while he was fighting in Bosnia–Herzegovina."

"That all fits nicely together. Well done! Shall we go in?"

The interior of the building was as grim as the exterior. It seemed to me that the apartment blocks in Rue Évariste Galois had been solidly constructed inside and out, but without spending a single unnecessary penny. The foyer of Number 34 was immaculately clean and in an excellent state of repair, but I thought of it as bare, bleak, and barren.

Apartment 7 was up two flights of stairs. We knocked. After a significant wait, an elderly male voice asked, "Who's there?"

I thought quickly. "A friend of Marie-André de Villiers."

The door flung open. A man in his mid-eighties stood before us. His clothes were old and somewhat disheveled, his hair unbrushed. He obviously hadn't shaved for some days, but his blue eyes were crystal clear and piercing.

"What did you say?" he shouted.

I repeated what I'd said.

"Come in!" he ordered. "Sit down."

As far as I could tell, the room hadn't been cleaned for months. Dust coated the wooden surfaces. Newspapers were scattered everywhere, some discolored by the sun, and I noticed a plate caked with dried-out food scraps lying on the floor in one corner. Marina and I cleared the debris from our chairs as unobtrusively as we could.

The man seemed oblivious to our presence. Then he suddenly spoke. His accent was unmistakable; I was certain that he was a graduate of one of the *grandes écoles*, the small, elite, highly selective higher-education establishments that for decades have educated France's leaders in both the public and the private sector.

"I haven't heard Marie-André's name spoken in this room for many years," the man said. "Who are you?"

We introduced ourselves.

The man switched to faultless English with only an innuendo of a French accent. "From your names, I gather you're British."

We nodded.

"And why have you come to see me?" he asked.

I spoke without thinking. "We're investigating her murder, in the hope of finding who sent my wife a threatening letter."

Dear reader, please consider what I'd just said. Addressing a perfect stranger, I'd alleged that Marie-André had been deliberately killed. Also I'd suggested that what had happened two decades before was somehow connected to a letter that Marina had recently received.

To my amazement, the man's face lit up and he nodded knowingly. "My niece and her son were incontrovertibly murdered. The police tried to hush it up and pretend that it was an accident. But it was a revenge killing."

"By French neo-Nazis?" I asked.

"Yes, certainly. But I know nothing about a letter."

Remembering the plaque on the outside wall, I asked, "Are you a son of Jean de Villiers, the Maquis leader?"

"Yes, I am. My parents moved into this apartment soon after they were married in 1932. My father was twenty-four years old at the time. I was born here, as was my younger brother Lucien, Marie-André's father. Then the Germans came. When they introduced Compulsory Work Service in 1943 to provide forced labor for Germany, my father fled to the mountains, the French Alps; it's not that far from here to Switzerland. There he encountered hundreds of other men and a number of women as well. Men aged between seventeen and sixty were subject to labor conscription. It's true that women were rarely conscripted, but if they were caught engaging in subversive activities, they were sent to labor camps in Germany.

"While they hid in the mountain forests, my father organized them into a highly effective resistance group. They acquired weapons, moved Jews and downed airmen along escape routes into Switzerland, and engaged in acts of assassination and sabotage against the Germans. Their greatest strength was their ability to engage in effective guerilla warfare. His group was responsible for the deaths of hundreds of German soldiers.

"Until then, my father apparently hadn't shown any leadership abilities at all, but in the Alps he was able to meld his Maquis band into an effective fighting force. As you probably know, they were a heterogenous bunch of people, including socialists, communists, and anarchists, people who under normal circumstances wouldn't cooperate with one another in any way. However, my father had the gift of focusing on commonalities. The result was that his Maquis group was so competent that it became a primary German target.

"I won't bore you with the details—you can read about it in my book—but in January 1945 the Gestapo set a trap, captured Jean, tortured him, and shot him; they sent my mother, my brother, and me to a concentration camp. By some miracle, we all survived. We returned to this apartment after the Liberation."

The man, who still hadn't introduced himself to us, stopped talking as suddenly as he'd started. I glanced at Marina. She made a small chopping gesture with her right hand to indicate that I should just keep still.

The three of us sat quietly for some minutes. Then he resumed speaking as if nothing had happened.

"Lucien left home when he married; Marie-André was his only child. I, on the other hand, have remained a bachelor all my life, and I came back and lived in this apartment after our mother died.

"Then my niece moved in with me; her relationship with her parents was somewhat unfriendly. In more detail, they wouldn't have anything to do with her from the moment she started going out with the man who now calls himself Claude Malmaison. That was fully understandable: her father's father had died for the values of France, but Marie-André was associating with a family that in public was all sweetness and light, but in private espoused the vilest of neo-Nazi views. But she chose to follow her heart, not her head. After André-Marie was born, she continued to live here.

"As I told you before, the murder was an act of revenge. Yes, they'd discovered that Marie-André was the granddaughter of a Maquisard, but that wasn't the key issue. You know now that my father commanded a highly successful guerilla group. However, after the Liberation, the military discipline that he'd instilled broke down. Suspected collaborators in the greater Lyon area were subjected to vigilantism and summary justice at the hands of members of the Maquis band that Jean had founded and led. The murder of Marie-André and André-Marie was a reprisal, a retaliation for the deaths of so many of their fascist fellow travelers after the occupation. It's true that they waited for fifty years after the war ended to take revenge, but neo-Nazis have long memories.

"By the way," he continued, "did you see the plaque to Jean on the wall outside?"

We both nodded.

"The government put it up a couple of years after the war. It proved to be a source of great comfort to our mother."

He paused again for a minute or two, looking vacantly at one of the yellowing newspapers lying on the floor. Then he looked up. "The rest you know, I think."

Without waiting for a response, the elderly man got up from his chair and walked slowly to the front door. As Marina and I left, we thanked him profusely. But I don't think he heard us. His mind was wandering with his father in the French Alps; dodging German patrols; seeking out suitable drop zones for parachutes to deliver explosives, radios, and small arms; and carrying out acts of sabotage.

* * *

We walked out of that depressing building together. "What precisely have we achieved?" Marina asked. "We came here to prove that French fascists were behind the deaths of a mother and her child, and also that members of the cabal sent me the threatening letter. Even if everything we've just heard is true—and I do realize that that's not necessarily the case—we still haven't found any actual evidence of any kind to back either assertion.

"Furthermore, even if we could show beyond all reasonable doubt that neo-Nazis killed Marie-André and her son, that doesn't automatically mean that the same group was responsible for the letter and, therefore, for the threats to my life. If you were in

Gilles's shoes, would you reopen the case more than twenty years later?"

"Probably not."

"Precisely."

"What you're saying is that we've wasted our time coming here."

"I'm afraid so."

"Let's go home. We need to pack for the dog-and-pony show in Japan."

CHAPTER TWENTY-THREE

Five items were artfully arranged on the gleaming wooden table in our suite at the Mikado Hotel in Kyoto: an exquisite porcelain vase containing two chrysanthemums; a glass bowl of exotic fruit, with two plates, knives, and napkins to its side; a large white envelope; a tall brass cylinder crammed to capacity with red roses; and a bottle of Scotch whisky.

The card propped up against the glass bowl was typed. It seemed that the fruit was a gift from the general manager of the hotel, Mr. Mori, to welcome us to his establishment. He'd signed twice. First in Latin letters, then in Kanji script. That was a nice touch, I thought.

The card that lay on the table next to the vase of chrysanthemums was also typed. It informed us that everyone in Megalodeon Studios was absolutely delighted that we were in Kyoto and if we needed the slightest thing we had only to ask. Unfortunately, the card failed to specify whom to ask or what number to call. Also, it was unsigned. Not a promising start.

Next, we opened the large white envelope. It contained our detailed program for the next two days. It seemed to be identical to what Osbert Oglesby had emailed us that night after he phoned us from London.

I'm sure that you've guessed who sent us the red roses. If not, dear reader, you didn't read Chapter Five with sufficient care and attention. On the other hand, you've actually got as far as Chapter Twenty-Three. You're more than halfway through this book, which is quite an achievement, under the circumstances.

The roses, as I'm sure you realized, were from Adrien Legendre, who was still on my lengthy list of two suspects: Adrien and Claude. The possibility that anyone else might possibly be responsible for the letter was out of the question, in view of Chekhov's Gun; no one else was mentioned in Chapter One. The gushy note that accompanied the flowers was handwritten, and I freely admit that Legendre had a beautiful script. The note was signed "Adrien" and, underneath, "Room 2404."

Finally, I examined the whisky. It was my favorite whisky of all time, eighteen-year-old Lochervan, "the crowning glory of the whisky maker's art." My mouth watered just looking at the label. Then I looked at the note, which read "Room 1906," written in a familiar-looking hand that I just couldn't place. Then it came to me.

"Lancelot's here!" I yelled.

"Where?"

"Room 1906. Where's the hotel phone?"

"We're having dinner with Osbert tonight."

"Correction: You're having dinner with Osbert. I'm about to phone Lancelot. In Room 1906. And then he and I will go to dinner together. I assume that once I find the phone I just dial 1906?"

"Darling, days ago we agreed to have dinner with Osbert. He'll be terribly disappointed if you're not there."

"Is that so? I think he'll be absolutely delighted. He's expecting me to spend the whole meal complaining that for the sake of authenticity the film has to be made in Russia. Which I fully intend to do."

"Sweetheart, I'll tell you what. Why don't you phone our mutual friend and ask him to join our *ménage à trois* tonight?"

"Marina, you're speaking French at last—how absolutely bloody marvelous! As a reward, I'll do as you say, on two conditions."

"Which are what?"

"Firstly, that you show me where the hotel phone is. And secondly, that you explain to me which buttons to push to connect to Room 1906."

"I'll do both with pleasure. And why don't we invite Adrien to join us? I'm sure he and Lancelot will get on well."

"Yes, it certainly seems like we're going to have a wonderful dinner party. Lancelot has an extremely low opinion of people who earn their money via commissions, so the probability of his hitting it off successfully with Osbert is zero. Or less than zero. Also, Adrien is an actor, Osbert is an agent, guaranteeing another sure-fire recipe for a social disaster. They'll probably try to strangle one another between the starter and the main course—if not within five minutes of meeting one another. Finally, people in Lancelot's social circle aren't exactly Francophiles, which means that he'll spend most of the evening insulting Adrien. All in all, this is going to be the most disastrous meal since the unwelcome appearance of the ghost of Banquo broke up the intimate little dinner party held in Lord and Lady Macbeth's utterly charming castle in Inverness."

* * *

Contrary to my gloomy expectations, the dinner was a rip-roaring success. If you've read *The Book Buyer*—and if you haven't, you probably should, because you'll laugh your head off—you'll know all about Lancelot. A reviewer of *The Book Buyer* accurately described Lancelot as "an eccentric, wildly rich newspaper owner." Lancelot lives in Varenne, a town in the so-called "Stockbroker Belt," the area on the periphery of London where many wealthy traders live in large houses and commute to the London financial district. There he single-handedly produces a local weekly newspaper called the *Varenne Bugle*. Why? I've no idea. But that newspaper is everything to him, despite costing him an ever-increasing amount of money every year. He's a gourmet—and an overweight gourmand to boot—and he loves fine wines. Lancelot lives in a huge mansion, and—you may be surprised to learn—he's read almost all the leather-bound books in his vast library. Despite his height and his girth, both on the large size, he insists on driving a top-of-the-line sports car. His clothes are scruffy and neglected, but were handmade by top tailors and bootmakers. A considerable time ago. Lancelot is about sixty-five years old, but some of his garments seem to be older than he is. However, with all that, the *Varenne Bugle* remains his passion and his obsession.

Marina and I were the first in our party to arrive at the restaurant. Kyoto, with a population of under two million people, has seven restaurants that have earned three Michelin stars. In contrast, the twelve million people who live in the metropolitan area of Paris, the home of *haute cuisine*, have to make do with only ten three-star establishments between them. The availability of fine food in Kyoto was one thing;

getting a reservation at the last minute was quite another. Typically, if you want to eat at that sort of place, a booking made several months in advance is essential. Preferably longer. A lot longer.

Fortunately, the Japanese translation of *She Loved the French Captain* had been published a month or so before. All I had to do was to ask Marina to pick up the phone and call the concierge—my wife knows how to do things like that—and tell him that Marina Haversmith wanted a table for five at Yemyo, which we'd heard was outstanding even by Michelin three-star standards. She also asked him to send up a copy of the Japanese translation of the book for her to inscribe and present to Nobukazu Takahata, the chef at Yemyo, to give to his wife.

An hour later we were escorted to the best table in the restaurant, overlooking the Oi River, with the densely wooded Arashiyama Mountains forming a dramatic backdrop. Hardly had we sat down when Adrien Legendre joined us. He was carrying a single long-stemmed red rose, which he presented to Marina before kissing her on both cheeks in the French style. Seconds later a server arrived at our table. She was carrying a delicate porcelain vase, tall and thin—the vase, that is, not the server. I assumed that she'd seen Adrien carrying the flower as he entered the restaurant and had rushed to acquire a suitable receptacle.

Shortly after Adrien had taken his seat, Lancelot arrived. He amazed me by addressing the film star in fluent, colloquial French. After all, Lancelot had been educated at one of those elite British boarding schools where they learn nothing but Latin and Greek.

Quickly realizing that Marina couldn't understand what he was saying, he immediately switched to English. That was another surprise. In my opinion, Lancelot has high-functioning autism—which may explain why he speaks so pedantically, refusing to break even the least important grammatical rule of eighteenth- and nineteenth-century English, no matter how obscure—so he's rarely aware of other people's feelings. This time, however, he caught on at once.

I asked him where he'd acquired his French skills.

"My parents felt that I should learn the language in case I decided to become a diplomat. Of course, diplomacy is one of many fields that are entirely beyond me—as you both know, I open my mouth only to change feet. But I thoroughly enjoyed spending my school holidays every summer in a small village on the coast of Brittany. I acquired a love of France, a love of the French language, a love of the French people, and as a consequence of a love for one particular French person, a nasty dose of the clap. I was unaware of the fact that the object of my affection had been generously sharing her favors with about half the village.

"Oh, I'm so sorry, Quentin," he quickly added, "I should never have used the word 'clap' in front of an author of bodice rippers, let alone his wife. What circumlocution would you have employed to avoid offending the delicate sensibilities of your readers?"

"My dear Lancelot, you know that sex doesn't play even the tiniest role in the imaginary worlds we writers of historical romance fiction create. The closest we come to that sort of thing is when the handsome hero 'takes' the utterly gorgeous heroine. And without sex, no sexually transmitted diseases are possible."

"Quentin, life is a game of give and take. I took Françoise, and I've just informed you what she gave me."

That was yet another surprise. A few weeks with Lancelot had convinced me that the man was, and always had been, as celibate as a hermit monk. It's true that he'd once referred to a police pathologist as a "distant cousin of my late wife," but his vast house in Surrey was totally devoid of memorabilia or photographs of the woman in question, or of any other woman for that matter, so I assumed that he'd been joking about a deceased spouse—Lancelot has a highly developed offbeat sense of humor. And now I was learning that as a schoolboy he'd "sowed his wild oats," an expression that you'll never find in a bodice ripper.

At that moment, Osbert Oglesby joined the party. Interestingly enough, even though my wife had spoken to him many times on the phone and the two of them had exchanged innumerable emails, neither Marina nor I had ever met the man in person. We acquired him as our agent when film studios started bombarding us with offers for the movie rights to *She Loved the French Captain*. Marina had consulted the lawyer who'd wound up her paternal grandfather's estate, and he'd strongly recommended that we engage Osbert to protect our interests.

Our agent turned out to be a small man with a face that was dominated by large round glasses with blue plastic frames. He brushed his black hair right across his head from one side to the other, a technique that some men who are losing their hair use to cover the large bald patch on the top of their skulls. In Osbert's case, however, it was obvious that his entire scalp was covered by a lush hirsute tropical forest, so I've no idea why he combed it the way he did. It was hard for me to estimate his age, because his spectacles made him look young and his hairstyle made him look old; the best I could do was to come up with a range of between thirty-five and fifty. Then I looked at his clothes. Once more I was struck by a contrast, in this case between his conservatively cut charcoal pinstripe Saville Row suit and his shirt and tie, the latter items both in an identical yellow-orange fabric decorated with large crimson tropical flowers. So I gave up on the guessing game and sat back and waited for open warfare to break out between Osbert and our other two guests, followed by duels to the death with *katana* swords at dawn in a Japanese glade ringed by cherry trees.

Adrien was the first to fire point blank over open sights. "Osbert, I don't think I ever thanked you properly for sorting out the contract. You handled those lawyers absolutely masterfully. I assume that the final wording is yours, not theirs?"

Osbert smiled modestly.

"Do you have any legal training?" Adrien continued.

The demure smile stayed firmly in place while Osbert replied, an impressive feat. "Dealing with lawyers has provided me with all the legal knowledge I need. Most members of the profession are outstanding people who put the interests of their clients front and center, and the contracts they draw up are models of their kind. I used some of what I've learned from them when I worked on that contract. That said, as with all occupations, some lawyers are less than outstanding, and I've acquired a treasure trove of useful information from the documents they've produced for my clients. Above all, I've learned what clauses should never be in my clients' contracts under any circumstances whatsoever, and what wording superficially looks fine but needs to be changed because it could prove to be calamitously detrimental to the authors whom I represent."

"You mean like an iceberg," Lancelot suggested. "One-tenth visible, nine-tenths lurking below sea level, waiting to tear an unwary ship apart."

"Oh, no," Osbert said, "much worse than that. At least you can see a small part of an iceberg ahead and take diversionary measures. Continuing your naval analogy, those clauses are like a U-boat wolf pack massing below the surface, waiting to torpedo a World War Two convoy crossing the Atlantic. Above water you can see nothing that would warn you about what terrors lurk in wait underneath."

And that remark got me thinking yet again about that infernal letter. On the surface, the tenth Philippe le Sabre was threatening to kill Marina because she'd insulted the le Sabre clan. But if Claude hadn't written it, who had? And why had the perpetrator written it? The answer to that second question, like a Nazi submarine pack, remained hidden beneath the surface.

CHAPTER TWENTY-FOUR

We were finishing the last drops of our second cups of coffee. Lancelot had temporarily excused himself, presumably to powder his nose. As he passed behind me on his return to the table, he leaned forward and mumbled, "I need to talk to you back at the hotel."

I suddenly realized Lancelot hadn't told us why he was in Kyoto. I'd assumed he'd come to celebrate the signing of the contract, but his furtive request seemed to imply he was there for some other reason.

My curiosity got the better of me, as it always does. "Gentlemen and Marina, tomorrow is going to be a long day. Perhaps we should think of calling it a night. I'll just settle with the restaurant."

Lancelot was firm. "No need. I have just taken care of everything, including a car that is waiting outside to take us all back to the hotel."

The joviality of the evening persisted during the drive back in the large black limo that Lancelot had summoned. However, I know Lancelot well, and I could sense a note of concern in his voice. Something was wrong.

As the five of us walked into the lobby, Lancelot spoke to Marina, "I should like to borrow your husband for a while. We shall be in my room."

When the lift reached the nineteenth floor, he and I got out, bidding a cheerful goodnight to Marina, Osbert, and Adrien. Lancelot opened the door of his suite, indicated that I should enter, then made straight for a bottle of you-know-what and poured each of us a hefty glass of the eighteen-year-old. He handed one glass to me, and we sat down.

Being Lancelot, he got down to brass tacks instantly; the phrase "small talk" isn't in his otherwise voluminous vocabulary, just as contractions like "I'll" or "you'd" are totally absent from his speech. And you'll never hear him split an infinitive. Or end a sentence with a preposition. Or break any other of the mostly forgotten rules of Georgian or Victorian English grammar.

"Only one thing in my life," he said, "is more important to me than the *Varenne Bugle*, and that is my friendship with you and Marina. Well . . . maybe they are equally important," he added with a wink. "But why did you not tell me about the letter? I would have been on the very next flight to Paris."

"I didn't want to bother you. And the French police seemed to have the matter under control."

"You did not want to bother me? Is our friendship that fragile? And please do not talk to me about the French police. Why, those clowns could not—"

"Just a minute," I interrupted him. "How did you find out about the letter?"

"I am a newspaperman, as you are well aware. And we newspapermen ferret out the news."

"Come on, Lancelot, no public information was out there for anyone, let alone a news hound like yourself, to discover. If any sort of leak had occurred, Marina Haversmith's smiling face would've graced the front page of every newspaper in the world, not just the *Varenne Bugle*. My wife is the darling of all women on the planet, if not the galaxy. Riots would've broken out in Rome. The women of São Paulo would've donned sack cloth and ashes. The president and the vice president of—"

"Enough! I get the drift of what you are trying to say. Fine, I shall come clean. My grandniece telephoned me."

"Your grandniece? I didn't know you had any relatives. As far as I can recall, during the many weeks that I stayed with you in Varenne, no one related to you either by blood or by marriage crossed our path."

"We are not what you might call a particularly close family. It so happens that I had not heard from Priscilla for years."

"Just a minute, Lancelot. You have a grandniece named Priscilla?"

"Yes, I do. It is not a particularly attractive name, but it is a lot better than Lancelot, I can tell you."

"And this niece of yours, what's her last name?"

"Murgatroyd. She is my grandniece, the grand-daughter of my older sister Iseult. Priscilla and I do not share the same last name. Is anything wrong with that?"

"Has she recently married?"

"If she has, she did not invite me to the wedding."

"Was she phoning from Paris, by any chance?"

"Yes, she was. How else could she have heard about that letter?"

"From her husband?"

"That is possible. Many women hear things from their husbands. The converse, however, is much rarer. After all, men seldom listen to a word their wives are saying."

"Lancelot, it may interest you to know that Major Gilles Despoir of the Regional Directorate of the Paris Judicial Police at 36 Quai des Orfèvres in Paris, the person who's in charge of the investigation, is married to an Englishwoman. And her first name just happens to be Priscilla. And that Priscilla just happens to be Marina's nearest and dearest friend. Do you think that Gilles's wife and your informant might be connected in some way?"

Lancelot's glass fell on the carpet, spilling every last precious smidgen of eighteen-year-old Lochervan it had previously contained. His mouth dropped open. His bushy eyebrows shot up. For the first time since I'd met him, Lancelot Aylesworth was rendered totally speechless.

"Let's start at the beginning," I suggested. "Your grandniece, Priscilla Murgatroyd, a relative with whom you've had no contact whatsoever—for how long? Five years? More?—suddenly phones you from Paris."

Lancelot nodded. He doesn't usually nod in acknowledgement—he almost always answers—but he was still bereft of the power of speech.

"'Hello, granduncle Lancelot,' she said, 'I'm phoning you from Paris. Do you know why?'

"'I have no idea, grandniece Priscilla,' you answered. 'Why are you telephoning me from Paris after five or more years of cruel neglect of your beloved elderly relative?' Lancelot, now please tell me what happened next."

He tried to swallow, failed, reached for his glass, and saw that it was on the floor, empty, with its contents spewed onto the carpet. He got up from his chair, picked up his glass with difficulty, refilled it, and sat down again.

After two mouthfuls of the golden elixir, his voice returned. "She told me that she had heard a story that would interest me as a newspaperman. She asked me if I remembered Marina Haversmith. I replied that I had spent several weeks investigating Marina as a murder suspect, so it would be hard for me to forget

240

her. And then Priscilla informed me about the threatening letter."

"When was this phone call?"

"Oh, a few days ago. The moment Priscilla hung up the phone I packed a suitcase. I was about to telephone for a taxi to take me to St. Pancras station so that I could hop onto the next Eurostar Express to Paris, when my eye caught a story in *The Times* still lying, unread, on my desk. It seemed that Marina was about to sign a movie contract in Kyoto. So I hopped onto the next plane to Osaka instead."

"Why didn't you phone me?"

"You do not have a phone. Do you not remember the trouble we had in Belfast when that hoyden of a drug chemist refused to accept that anyone could possibly not own a mobile phone? And da Cunha, the man they arrested in Lisbon, was equally skeptical."

"I have big news for you, Lancelot. Marina bought me a phone, and she insists that I carry it around with me at all times. As I'm sure you realize, I've no idea how it works and no one ever phones me, but the fact of the matter is that I do have my own mobile phone."

"What is your number?" Lancelot asked eagerly, taking out his smartphone.

"I've no idea. If you want to know that sort of thing, you need to ask Marina."

Lancelot sighed deeply and returned his phone to his pocket. "What are we going to do about that letter that someone sent to her?"

241

"Same answer as before: I've no idea. That's the other reason I didn't want to bother you with this. We've no clues at all other than the fact that either a waiter named Claude Malmaison—who's actually the tenth Philippe le Sabre—wrote it, or else he didn't. And if he didn't, the writer is someone who somehow learned about the ten generations of le Sabres. And that's all I know. What did Priscilla tell you?"

"My grandniece's description of the circumstances surrounding the letter was brief to the point of taciturnity. Moreover, she seemed to be in a tremendous hurry to get off the telephone, which was somewhat surprising after five years of mutual noncommunication. So I flew here to give you my moral support and also to inform you in no uncertain terms that if another letter arrives you are to let me know at once."

"Of course I will. But I think it would be better if you didn't tell Marina the real reason why you're here in Kyoto. If she learns that her best friend betrayed a confidence, it may lead to insurmountable complications."

CHAPTER TWENTY-FIVE

Before I met Marina, for twenty years I sat in a rented room on the fourth floor of an apartment building in Paris writing historical romance fiction. I don't mean that I sat there continuously for twenty years; occasionally I got up from my chair and even more occasionally I went outside for a walk or to buy food. And sometimes even wine. But by and large, however, I spent most of my waking hours sitting and writing.

I know what you're thinking, but that solo existence boasted a few advantages. One was that I didn't need to talk to perky women; I hate, loathe, and detest perkiness. And another was that I had no need to have any interaction with women who talk in high-pitched squeaky voices. My negative attitude towards high-pitched squeaky voices is even stronger than my feelings regarding perkiness.

Why do I tell you about this, you ask? Well, the next morning at nine o'clock, Osbert, Lancelot, and I were comfortably seated in the lobby of the Mikado

Hotel. Through the wide plate-glass windows of the hotel, we saw a large, black, chauffeur-driven car draw up. A young woman emerged, sashayed into the hotel, and approached us. Yes, the original plan was for only Osbert and me to tour Yasuhara Prefecture, but Marina had arranged with the studio for Lancelot to join the two of us for the day's excursion.

"Are you Mr. Oglesby?" she asked me.

I pointed.

"Are you Mr. Aylesworth?"

I pointed again.

"Then you must be Mr. Pakenham. I'm Carmela, originally from Carmel-by-the-Sea, California, but now a proud resident of Japan. I'll be your guide as you visit Yasuhara Prefecture, the Japanese Hollywood."

I was delighted that our guide was so intelligent. After I'd identified two members of our triumvirate as Osbert Oglesby and Lancelot Aylesworth, she'd immediately—and totally correctly—deduced that the third one had to be Quentin Pakenham. What was less pleasant, at least as far as I was concerned, was that Carmela was ultra-perky, with an extremely high-pitched squeaky voice.

The rest of the day was sheer torture. Carmela proceeded to explain, in excruciating detail, the movie-making potential of what seemed to me to be every square inch of the Prefecture.

244

It didn't start well. Before I could even fasten my seat belt, she'd already made it abundantly clear that, irrespective of whether I wanted to make a western, a romantic comedy, a thriller, a buddy cop movie, a tearjerker, or a space opera film, I was in the right place. Yasuhara Prefecture was indubitably the absolutely ideal location for any movie of any genre, but especially for historical romance fiction movies. She urged me, repeatedly, to impress on my wife how important it was for all her future world bestselling books to be filmed there.

After what seemed like a lifetime, the initial on-slaught belatedly ceased and a blessed silence reigned. Before she could resume her sales pitch, I informed Carmela that an author's personal predilection for a specific location is entirely irrelevant, even for the world's leading writer of historical romance fiction, because such matters are exclusively in the hands of the movie studio. I hoped that by explaining every-thing to her in words of one—or at most two—sylla-bles, the Yasuharan Ron Popeil would leave me alone and turn the blowtorch of her proselytizing on behalf of the Prefecture onto Osbert. Or Lancelot. Or both of them.

No such luck. I assumed, for want of a better ex-planation, that her employer, the Yasuhara Prefecture Film, Music, and Digital Entertainment Office, had instructed her to do a selling job on poor Quentin, regardless of how he responded, and to leave lucky Lancelot and opportune Osbert unscathed.

I still get nightmares from that voice. Carmela squeaked and perked from nine in the morning until just after five in the afternoon when the limo stopped at a Kyoto whiskey bar. I turned to her and said, "Thank you for a wonderful day, Carmela. But drinking whiskey is a task for men."

Yes, dear reader, that was an extremely offensive sexist remark on my part, and I apologize unreservedly to you, especially if you happen to be a member of the fairer sex. But by that point I had only two choices open to me: blatant sexism, or murder by strangulation using my bare hands. And I chose what I considered to be the lesser of the two evils. Of course, your mileage may vary.

* * *

As you will soon see, the following day was worse. Much worse. It started the same way: Carmela arrived at nine o'clock at the Mikado Hotel in the same black limo. This time she took Osbert, Lancelot, and me to the conference center, the venue for the all-day signing extravaganza; Marina had also arranged with Megalodeon Studios for Lancelot to be her guest at the ceremony.

The morning was devoted to presentations that highlighted the moviemaking potential of Yasuhara

Prefecture. Everything was in Japanese, but foreigners like us were issued with headphones so that we could listen to a simultaneous interpreter. I was pleased that they offered a wide choice of different tongues because the speeches were so repetitious that I soon began to listen to them in languages that I don't understand, like Dzongkha and Tswana.

After a lavish lunch in the banqueting hall, we returned to the auditorium for more boring talks and to watch clips of movies that had been made in Yasuhara. I didn't recognize any of the movies, let alone any of the actors. After six or seven videos, I suddenly realized that these weren't scenes from movies at all, but rather clips that had been put together to resemble scenes from real feature films. The minions of Yasuhara Prefecture had made sure that they incorporated at least one scene from every movie genre, including, I'm delighted to report, a historical romance movie. But not just any bodice ripper. Definitely not.

The three of us were seated near the back of the huge auditorium, bored to tears—at least I was. And then it happened: a video set in Olde England around the time of the Civil War. That's the English Civil War, which took place around 1650, not the American Civil War, which was fought more than two hundred years later.

We saw a woman wearing an old-fashioned long white nightdress and carrying a three-branched candelabrum walk downstairs to the main room of an inn, where a man dressed as a Cavalier stood waiting in front of the fireplace. His long flowing hair was arranged in ringlets. He wore a wide-brimmed black felt hat trimmed with a large white ostrich plume. His elaborate collar and cuffs were of fine lace, and his jacket was elaborately embroidered in a blaze of bright colors. Beneath his nose lurked a luxuriant mustachio, the ends twisted up. His sword was in its scabbard; he'd casually thrust a flintlock pistol into his sword belt.

"Osbert," I whispered softly at the top of my voice, loudly enough for the people back in Paris to hear me, "they're doing the key scene from *Love in the Days of King Charles*."

"Do I know that book?"

"It's the one I wrote before *She Loved the French Captain*. It sold quite well."

"Do you think someone might buy the movie rights?" the ever-practical Osbert asked.

But by this time, shocked faces were looking at us. Apparently, it isn't done in Japan to talk during a presentation, even an obvious—and obnoxious—sales pitch.

At about half past three, they eventually ran out of video clips and presentations, and I must confess that I wasn't overly upset when that happened. Now the stage was rearranged for the signing ceremony. The curtains parted, and I saw Marina standing behind an intricately carved wooden lectern. She was wearing an elaborate kimono. Her hair was arranged in a *shimada*, a classic Japanese hairstyle somewhat similar to a chignon. In addition, her coiffure was decorated with traditional *kanzashi* ornaments. Even though we were still seated on our original seats near the back of the auditorium, we could see Marina clearly, magnified on the huge screens on either side of the stage. The applause was thunderous, presumably led by the women in the audience who'd read the book. Which is another way of saying all the women in the audience.

But the best was yet to come. My wife proceeded to give a speech in Japanese—and this from a woman who can't even manage to successfully order a cup of coffee in French. I soon worked out what they'd done—it was extremely clever. The previous day, while Osbert, Lancelot, and I were out touring Yasuhara Prefecture, Marina had put on the identical kimono with her hair arranged exactly as it was for the signing ceremony. Then, the organizers put Marina in front of that same wooden lectern facing a video camera and asked her to read a speech in transliterated Japanese. Do you know how newsreaders manage to read the news while staring directly into the camera? Modern technology is unbelievably fantastic. The words that the newscaster is supposed to say appear on a teleprompter screen, and a reflector placed slightly below the camera lens enables him or her to read the teleprompter while apparently staring unwaveringly into the camera. That meant that Marina could read her script in transliterated Japanese while seemingly looking straight at the audience.

Next, they arranged for a Japanese actress whose voice is somewhat similar to Marina's to read the same speech, synchronizing her words to Marina's lips. Then, during the actual ceremony, Marina stood in front of the audience, silently reading from the transliterated Japanese text on the teleprompter in front of her while the two huge screens showed her reading the speech and the sound system played the actress's voice. It was a most ingenious trick, and I have the utmost admiration for the technicians who carried it out so impeccably. Only if someone observed that Marina's lips occasionally were fractionally out of sync with the sound would he or she realize that the virtual Marina on the screen had been recorded earlier.

After the hysterical applause at the end of her speech finally abated, Marina walked over to a table on the left side of the stage and sat down on an ornately carved wooden chair in front of an equally ornately carved wooden table. She was joined by a man bearing a thick leather folder. He looked like a caricature of a high-powered American lawyer as portrayed in TV shows: tall, somewhat portly, wearing a three-piece suit, power tie, and cascading waves of gray hair. He placed the folder on the table, opened it, handed a gold pen to Marina, and indicated where she should sign. Marina made her mark, the audience clapped frenetically, Marina waved, and the curtains closed. That was the last formal item for the day, so the attendees filed out of the auditorium, talking excitedly amongst themselves, for some unknown reason. The three of us remained in our seats until Carmela came to escort us onto the stage.

Lancelot stood in the wings while Osbert and I joined Marina. We signed on our respective dotted lines. In more detail, Osbert picked up the pen and signed calmly and resolutely; I panicked until the lawyer showed me where to place my signature. Then the lawyer signed on behalf of Contrapuntal Howitzer Limited.

We were joined by a shortish woman of about sixty. I was struck by her beautifully cut short brown hair with subtle blonde highlights, the string of enameled wooden beads around her neck, and the warm smile on her face. Her clothes were simple and unassuming, the sort of garments that enable the wearer to fade into the background if she so wishes. She introduced herself to us as Francesca and warmly congratulated Marina and me. She apologized for having only just arrived in Kyoto, but it seemed her plane had had a minor mechanical fault of some kind that took much longer than anticipated to fix. Then she sat down on the chair, picked up the gold pen, and signed on the remaining dotted line. Osbert told me afterwards that Francesca was the long-time head of Megalodeon Studies; a more pleasant and unpretentious studio mogul would be hard to find.

And that was that. I looked around for a troop of waiters, dressed in white ties and tails, bearing trays of vintage champagne and huge mounds of caviar on ice on white gloved hands—the trays would be on the white gloved hands, not the ice—but nothing like that happened. Instead, various men in expensive-looking suits who'd been standing silently in the wings started drifting away in twos and threes.

My kimono-clad, *kanzashi*-coifed wife joined me. "Darling, the money should be in our account in Paris within seconds. We're rich!"

"Wonderful!" I said and kissed her. "Without you, the lawyers would still be arguing about the contract. You're marvelous!"

My unbridled and unfettered joy became slightly bridled and partially fettered when I saw Carmela walking perkily towards us. She squeakily informed us that it was time to return to the Mikado Hotel to relax, unwind, and prepare for the gala dinner. Hah! I thought. That's where they're going to serve us the vintage champagne and huge mounds of caviar. On ice.

We retrieved Lancelot, and Carmela led the four of us to the limousine. The driver took longer than I'd anticipated to transport us back to the hotel, because the rush hour traffic in Kyoto is horrendous, but after what seemed like hours, we finally arrived. As we walked into the lobby, Mr. Mori, the general manager, came up to us, beaming.

"How nice to see you again, Mr. and Mrs. Pakenham—or should I say Ms. Haversmith? My wife loved your book from beginning to end. Would you mind autographing it?"

Lancelot and Osbert excused themselves and went up to their rooms while Mr. Mori led Marina and me into his office, where a copy of the Japanese translation was waiting.

"Thank you so much. My wife will be absolutely thrilled. By the way, a courier letter arrived a few minutes ago. I'll just get it for you."

I took the envelope absentmindedly, and we rode up in the lift. It was obvious that the unending strain of the previous two days had totally exhausted Marina. I unlocked the door of our suite, and she stumbled through the living area into the bedroom where she flopped onto the bed, still in her elaborate embroidered kimono, which must've cost thousands and thousands. Of pounds, euros, or dollars. And the *kanzashi* ornaments were still in her hair.

"Quentin, I am never ever going to be able to get off this bed, let alone manage to survive a lengthy formal dinner. I'm going to sleep now—wake me tomorrow morning. No, make that the day after tomorrow. I've never been so tired in all my life."

Then I became conscious of the envelope in my hand. It was addressed to Marina, but she clearly didn't have the energy to open it, so it was up to me. La Poste is the French postal service, and like the postal service in many countries, it offers a courier service. The way to tear open a La Poste courier envelope with the greatest of ease involves pulling a clearly marked tab, but I've never quite mastered the technique. Accordingly, I walked over to the table in the living area to get a knife from a fruit plate to slit the envelope open. As I picked up the implement, I noticed the name of the sender: Philippe le Sabre.

I slashed the envelope open. Inside was an identical copy of The Letter.

CHAPTER TWENTY-SIX

By now, dear reader, you know me well enough to be able to predict with certainly what happened next. Yes, you're quite right, I panicked.

After running around for a few seconds like a chicken with its tail feathers on fire, I rushed to the table in the living area. Why? Because I remembered the card from Megalodeon Studios that stated that if we ever needed anything we only had to call them. I grabbed the card. Then I remembered that the card bore no name, let alone a telephone number.

Next, I examined the card that was propped up against the fruit bowl. It was from Mr. Mori, the general manager of the hotel. But calling in the Japanese police, which Mr. Mori was sure to do, was the very last thing I wanted. Japan had nothing whatsoever to do with The Letter; the only reason that the copy had arrived in Kyoto was because the intended recipient, Marina, just happened to be in Japan. Even in my state of terror, dismay, and confusion, I was nevertheless able to comprehend that getting Japanese law enforcement involved would be a surefire step on the road to disaster. Japan was out of the picture, but I couldn't speak a word of Japanese to make that point clearly and unambiguously to the Kyoto Kops.

Finally, I picked up the card that came with the whisky. It read 1906. Through the dense brain mist that invariably accompanies my frequent panics, I somehow managed to remember that Lancelot was in Room 1906. I knew where the room phone was because I'd used it to phone Lancelot two days earlier.

I grabbed the phone. I dialed 1906, but that didn't seem to help. Then I remembered the old saying: if all else fails, read the instructions. And on the base unit of the telephone, I saw lots of words, including the following: "To call another room, dial 8 followed by the room number expressed as a four-digit number." And for people like me, they gave explanatory details. "For example, to call Room 917, dial 80917." In my panic, I was about to dial 80917, when I happily remembered what I'd done before. I dialed 81906.

As you are no doubt aware, the word "dialed" is nonsense; nowadays we have push-button phones. But I've never seen an instruction that reads "Push 81906"—it always says "Dial." I've no idea what's going to happened when the last person to have used a telephone with a dial finally dies.

I must apologize to you, dear reader, because I've gotten slightly sidetracked. Here's where you and I were: I'd just pushed the buttons marked 8, 1, 9, 0, and 6, in that precise order. I waited for a long while, then I heard Lancelot pick up the phone. I cannot recall the last time I was so relieved to hear the word "Hello."

"Hello, Lancelot," I responded. I was about to add, "It's me, Quentin," but I remembered just in time that Lancelot is incapable of disobeying any rule of English grammar, no matter how archaic the rule or how stilted the result—it's all part of his autism, if that's what he has—and I didn't want to antagonize him, so instead I said, "It is I, Quentin. Could you please come to our room right away?"

"What's the number?"

"I've no idea. How do I find out?"

"Why not ask Marina?" Lancelot suggested. "I'm sure she knows."

"I can't. She's fast asleep, totally exhausted, and I don't think I'll be able to rouse her for hours and hours."

"Right. Let's try Plan B. Can you open the door to the corridor and read the number on the outside without locking yourself out of your room?"

"I can try. Hold on."

I put down the phone without cutting Lancelot off—a major feat in itself—unlocked the door, jammed it open with my left foot, read the number on the outside, memorized it, removed my foot, and closed the door. With me on the inside.

"I'm back again. It's Room 2306."

"Well done, Quentin! I'll be with you shortly."

True to his word, a few minutes later I heard a light tap on the door. I deduced that considerate Lancelot didn't want to wake Marina, unaware that nothing softer than the sounding of the Last Trump could possibly rouse Sleeping Beauty before morning. Dear reader, I'm fully aware that a mixed metaphor is lurking dangerously in the previous sentence—you're not supposed to commingle 1 Corinthians 15:52 with the fairy tales of Charles Perrault—but I was still in a state of acute panic, so you'll have to sort that one out by yourself.

"Thank you for coming, Lancelot," I said, and handed him the envelope and its contents.

"Is the wording the same as the previous one?"

"It seems to be identical."

"And the signature?" he asked.

"The police experts say that the last one was computer-generated. I assume that this one is too."

"I see that the sender stated that his name is Philippe le Sabre. How macabre!"

"What did he give as his address on the envelope?" I asked.

"Rue Ludmilla, in the Eighteenth Arrondissement. No house number."

"Given that the heroine of *She Loved the French Captain* is a farmhand named Ludmilla, I'm pretty sure that no such street is to be found in the Eighteenth District or, for that matter, anywhere else in Paris."

"Quentin, it's addressed to Marina Haversmith, Mikado Hotel, Kyoto. Now, that is truly fascinating."

"How so?"

"For many reasons. I doubt if anyone named Marina Haversmith is registered at this hotel. The sender made the reasonable assumption that the hotel staff would know that your wife was the intended recipient."

"Yes, that's true," I said, "but you must remember that Yasuhara Prefecture publicized the signing extravaganza worldwide, so I don't think the use of that name is particularly significant, especially since so many of the staff of the hotel are women. Anything else?"

"Yes, and this is most important. How many people knew you were staying at the Mikado Hotel?"

"I'm sorry to be so argumentative, Lancelot, but in my opinion, that's even less relevant. The Mikado is the top hotel here in Kyoto, so it would be the obvious place where the studio would lay on a suite for Marina. And I've just had another idea. There are other hotels here that are nearly as fancy as this one, but for all we know, he sent courier letters to those establishments as well."

Lancelot sighed. "I think you're right. The only fact that we can deduce from the label on the envelope, which happens to be printed, is that the sender was aware you were going to be in Kyoto. And millions and millions of people must've known that."

"You're quite right. The letter and its envelope are probably totally useless as evidence. That said, we have to take them back to Paris right away so that the forensic experts can get their hands on them."

A look of horror appeared on Lancelot's expressive face. "My sainted aunt! Never mind *their* hands—we got *our* hands on them. We forgot all about fingerprints. And what about DNA? We should never have touched the envelope, let alone the document it contained. A fine pair of detectives we turned out to be!"

CHAPTER TWENTY-SEVEN

S oon after Lancelot left our room, the hotel phone rang. It was Carmela to tell us she was in the lobby to escort us to the gala dinner. I explained to her that Marina was exhausted and fast asleep and please to make our apologies to one and all. Much to my surprise, Carmela was most sympathetic. It seemed that, in addition to being an expert at the hard sell, she had a soft heart. She gave me the number of her mobile phone and insisted I call her at any time of the day or night if Marina needed a doctor. I thanked her warmly and rapidly revised my unreasonable prejudice against perky women with high-pitched squeaky voices.

The next morning, after sleeping more than twelve hours, Marina started to stir. I phoned down to room service for breakfast. Once she'd had her first cup of coffee, I told her what had happened.

"You managed to phone Lancelot all by yourself? How perfectly marvelous, Quentin! I'm so proud of you. Maybe someday you'll even learn to use your mobile phone. And wasn't it lucky that Lancelot came to Kyoto to be with us for the signing ceremony? I shudder to think what you'd have done last night without his help."

Marina was obviously still half asleep, otherwise she'd have focused on the slightly more important aspect of what I'd just related to her, namely, that she'd received another copy of the threatening letter. The perpetrator was still out there, still determined to achieve whatever it was the scoundrel wanted to achieve. And we still hadn't the foggiest idea what that might be.

I required Marina's full attention, so I decided to try mild shock treatment. "Darling, don't you think that Gilles Despoir will want to see the new letter?"

As I'd hoped, mention of the name of the police major brought Marina to a state of wakefulness. She shuddered the way a long-haired dog shakes itself when it gets out of the water. A look of horror appeared on her face.

"We need to get back to Paris right away. Phone down to the concierge and tell him to put us on the first plane back home."

"Certainly, darling, but how do I contact him?"

Marina rolled her eyes. Yet again. I sometime wonder if she uses them more for rolling than for seeing. She picked up the hotel phone from the bedside table and started tapping away. A brief conversation ensued.

Eventually she turned to me. "Let's start packing. The car taking us to the airport will be downstairs in an hour's time."

"What about Lancelot?" I asked.

"What about him?"

"Don't you think he'd want to come along with us?"

Marina's eyes widened. "Of course he would! How could I be so thoughtless? I'll sort it all out while you get to work on the suitcases."

Three minutes later Lancelot strode into our suite. Perhaps the word *strode* is just a little too strong; after all, when you're carrying a hundred and fifty pounds or more of excess weight, striding is somewhat difficult. On the other hand, Lancelot wanted to make it plain to Marina and me that he had something important to say.

"Why are you returning to Paris?" he asked.

I was taken aback. "We have to get this evidence to the French police."

"Yes, I understand that," Lancelot said. "Even though two bumbling amateurs—sorry, Quentin, but you and I have to face the facts—contaminated the paper. And the envelope is of no evidentiary value because a variety of people whose fingerprints and DNA are not on file in France handled it. I'm thinking of the Japan Post Service employees who processed the item, Mr. Mori and employees of the Mikado Hotel, and so on.

263

"You're absolutely right," he continued. "The envelope and the letter need to get to Paris. But why do you have to take them?"

"Are you saying," I asked, "that we should put the evidence in an envelope and pay the Japan Post Service to rush it to Paris just as quickly as they can manage?"

"Precisely. That is exactly what I am saying. And before we do that, you need to photograph the letter and both sides of the envelope and send the pictures as email attachments so that the police can get moving right away. In addition, you and Marina—and possibly I, too—will need to phone your police contacts in Paris and tell them what has happened and that they should stand by for a courier delivery of the new letter."

"Just a minute." Marina said. "What if the French police want to interview us face-to-face?"

"That's highly unlikely," Lancelot insisted. "What on earth could you tell them? You received another letter, Quentin and I messed it up, and we are sending it to Paris with our apologies. Remember, the sender is in France, not Japan. Hopefully, the police can work with La Poste and obtain information about whomever posted the envelope—a person who probably has nothing to do with the writer. No, Marina, everything is under control in Paris. At the same time, I know of two good reasons why you should stay in Japan for a while."

Then Lancelot sat down in an easy chair. "That is better. Much better." His face revealed his relief at being able to take it easy after all that vigorous striding.

"Well?" I said.

"Well, what? Oh, you mean my two reasons. You were in Paris for two weeks after receiving the first letter, but no other letters arrived. You travelled to Kyoto, and now we have another one. I am prepared to stick my neck out and aver that were you two to have stayed in Paris you would not have received the identical second letter. Do you know why?"

Marina and I dutifully shook our heads.

"Something is decidedly odd about that letter. It does not contain a threat. I have received threatening letters in my time, plenty of them, and published several in my newspaper. A genuine one goes along the lines of, 'Pay me a thousand pounds, or I shall tell your wife,' or, 'If that dog of yours barks at four o'clock in the morning just once more, you and your animal will be in very big trouble.'

"In other words, the recipient is instructed to do something—or not to do something—and if he or she disobeys, he or she will suffer in some way. But this letter to Marina carries no such demand. It simply says that she has besmirched the family name and he is going to kill her.

"And that bit also makes no sense. If he wants to kill Marina, why does he warn her? She could get protection every second of the day, or move to a secret location, or take all manner of evasive actions.

"In other words, this is not a threatening letter, and he has no intention of murdering Marina. What, then, is its purpose? In my opinion, the writer wants Marina to do something. I have no idea what that 'something' is, and I do not think anyone does: not you two, not the French police, no one other than the letter writer. We all know that if Marina were aware of what it was she would do it right away and bring this nightmare to a speedy end. The writer must give her more facts.

"But the second letter," Lancelot continued, "contains no more information than the first. Why not? My guess—and it is only a guess—is that the writer is on the horns of a dilemma. If he were to provide additional facts to Marina, then by so doing he might reveal himself.

"Marina, you need to get a third letter, one with more information. If you and Quentin were to stay in France, I very much doubt if you would ever get to the bottom of this matter. The malefactor undoubtedly knows the French police are looking for him. One slip, and they will pounce like a puma. A fingerprint or some DNA, and it will all be over. But if he were to send a letter abroad, the only risk would be someone seeing him dropping the letter into a postbox. And even then, he has probably arranged for

someone else to do the actual mailing, with an extremely clever cover story."

"And what's your second reason why we should
stay in Japan?" I asked.

"I am 100 percent certain that Marina is in
absolutely no danger. As I explained, if you genuinely
intend to kill someone, you do not announce it in
advance. But suppose I am wrong—unlikely, but
possible. If the killer is in France and you are in Japan,
that makes it just a little hard for the murderer, does
it not?"

I know I shouldn't have mentioned it, but I
ignored the little voice that told me to keep silent.
"Lancelot, what if the killer is in Japan? He may have
come here before we did, leaving behind the second
letter for his probably totally innocent stooge to mail.
At least we have police protection in France. What are
the chances that the Japanese police would take any
action at all, let alone go through the evidence with a
fine-tooth comb? You must remember that the name
le Sabre is associated world-wide with the hero of a
work of fiction; the fact that ten generations of
Philippe le Sabres have lived in France is a closely held
secret for now. Worse, the last three generations
changed their last names to Malmaison. Could you see
a senior police officer here in Japan taking that letter
seriously? As a result of the publication of the
Japanese translation of *She Loved the French Captain,*

everyone in this country would treat the letter as a joke."

"So what are you saying, Quentin?" Lancelot asked. "Stay here or go home?"

"Despite the infinitesimally small probability of a risk to my darling Marina, but a risk nonetheless, we need to play the odds. If we were to go back to Paris, I doubt if the matter would ever be cleared up. But if we stay here in Japan for a while, the culprit may make a mistake.

"And now you need to phone the French police right away," I added.

Marina pulled a face. "That wouldn't be particularly good idea."

"Why not? They need to know what's happened."

"Quentin, it's the middle of the night in Paris!"

"In that case, I tend to agree with you. As far as I'm concerned, the French police need to be standing by twenty-four hours a day waiting for a call from you. But under the circumstances, perhaps you should wait."

Lancelot spoke up. "Marina, I seem to recall that Quentin informed me that a specific officer is responsible for this case, one Police Major Gilles Despoir, a man married to Priscilla, my grandniece and your good friend. And—"

"Lancelot, I never knew that Priscilla was your grandniece—how perfectly wonderful! Why didn't you tell me?"

268

"The occasion never arose. Anyhow, I am sure that Gilles is fast asleep, tucked up in his bed in Paris. No emergency has arisen that requires us to wake him. While he is in dreamland, clutching his teddy bear tightly to his chest, his minions will be poring over the email I am about to send them. When he wakes, fresh as a daisy, his underlings will no doubt brief him to prepare him for your call later today."

"I'm pleased you agree that we need not trouble Gilles right away," Marina said, "if only because your call would rouse Priscilla."

"True. I doubt if she would like to hear from me in the middle of the night."

"Lancelot, I know Priscilla better than anybody in the whole world. Your waking her will unquestionably precipitate World War III. Or a phone call from her redoubtable mother, who I assume would be your niece?"

Lancelot shuddered in horror. "Anything but that. Anything."

"Fine," I said. "But while your formidable female folks sleep the sleep of the just, we need to decide what we're going to do next."

"Before we do that," Lancelot said, "I have to know: Are all of us in agreement that your trip to Japan triggered the second letter?"

Marina and I nodded emphatically.

"Good. Now, Marina, unmake the travel arrangements you've just made."

"Heavens! I forgot all about that. The car will be here in five minutes."

"Sadly, the driver will have to forgo the honor of driving the world-famous Marina Haversmith to the airport."

My wife picked up the phone, tapped a few buttons, spoke the magic words, and lo! the travel arrangements were unmade.

Lancelot nodded approvingly. "Now, we somehow have to tell the writer of The Letter that you, Marina, are staying in Japan for a while, waiting for another communication from him that hopefully will contain additional information that will enable you to determine what it is he wants from you."

"How do we do that?" I asked. "We don't know who he is, so how do we communicate with him?"

"Let us think this through," Lancelot said. "The writer discovered you were staying in a hotel in Kyoto. How did he manage that?"

"I can only assume," Marina said, "that he heard about my trip via the media. Television, perhaps. More likely via the internet. Or possibly even in a newspaper."

"I agree," Lancelot said. "But how did the information get to the media? And the answer is that the publicity machines of Megalodeon Studios or Yasuhara Prefecture—or both—informed the world that you were coming to Kyoto."

"And your point is?" I asked.

"We should make use of the formidable public relations strengths of one or both organizations. Preferably both. That way we can—"

The room telephone rang. Marina walked over and picked it up. "Tell him, um, tell him, er, tell him we're exhausted from the last two days. No, please put him on the line."

She put her hand over the microphone. "It's our guide—for our tour of Japan." Marina pulled a face.

"Mr. Matsumoto? . . . Yes, I know . . . I'm awfully sorry, but the last two days have been impossible . . . No, it's fine . . . Come back tomorrow, please . . . No, just cancel everything for today and put the charges on our bill . . . I apologize again, but we simply cannot make it today."

She put down the phone. "We have a two-week itinerary all set up, with a car and driver-guide. A Mr. Matsumoto. He seems terribly nice, and his English is perfect. Why don't you join us? I'm sure that we can find an extra room for you at our hotels. Let me get the paperwork; I printed out the itinerary before we left Paris. Oh, good. I see a telephone number here, a travel agency, I assume. The country code is +81, so it's a Japanese travel agency—exactly what we need. I'll just get them to organize everything."

"Please tell them to charge everything to my card," Lancelot said.

My wife nodded as she continued to study the itinerary.

"What if a hotel listed on our itinerary is full?" I asked Marina, with an ulterior motive.

"Then we're going to have to find another place to stay," she replied. "But I would imagine that, with the Japanese translation of your masterpiece flooding the country, every reservations clerk would lean over backwards to accommodate us."

Dear reader, I'm sure that you're way ahead of me and that you've worked out what I was hoping would happen. These inns—apparently, the Japanese plural is *ryokan*—are generally small and hard to get into. People come back to the same *ryokan* year after year, and the host gives those customers preferential treatment, for obvious reasons. I was hoping that the *ryokan* where we were going to stay was fully booked and that the host of the *ryokan* was too traditional a Japanese to have heard of Marina Haversmith and, even if he or she knew all about my wife, the host was too honorable a person to eject a customer with an existing reservation.

That was the selfish Quentin Pakenham speaking. The kinder, nicer Quentin couldn't imagine his friend Lancelot walking around the *ryokan* in a *yukata*. Apart from the question of dignity, something with which Lancelot is liberally endowed, we still had to find a *yukata* to fit his girth, another item with which Lancelot is liberally endowed. I was pretty certain they don't make *yukata* in his size. I hope you noticed that the plural of *yukata* is still *yukata*. I've just found out why: most Japanese nouns don't have a plural form.

Luck was with me—and Lancelot. The Japanese travel agent phoned back later that afternoon and Marina put her on speakerphone. "Mrs. Pakenham, I'm delighted to tell you that I've managed to find a room for Mr. Aylesworth at all your hotels. The car-hire company will provide a larger car, so the three of you will be most comfortable. Mr. Matsumoto was delighted to learn that he now can show our beautiful country to an extra guest. I've prepaid the third admission at all the sites. The bad news is that the *ryokan* is full. That was the reason it took me longer than I would've liked to get back to you. I've tried to find another *ryokan* for you, but there doesn't seem to be a traditional inn located within a reasonable radius that's even half as nice as the one where you have a reservation. One alternative would be for you and your husband to stay at the *ryokan* and I could find a nice hotel for Mr. Aylesworth"—I shook my head as violently as I could while glaring at Marina—"or the three of you could stay at a super luxury resort about forty miles away. I've put a hold on two suites for you."

Marina looked at me. I nodded as energetically as the pain in my neck from the earlier shaking would allow. Considering that I was experiencing extreme agony in the entire region south of my ears and north of my shoulders, the nod wasn't especially enthusiastic. But I did my best.

"Cancel the room at the *ryokan*, please, and we'll take the suites at the resort."

I somehow managed to smile through the unspeakable agony.

CHAPTER TWENTY-EIGHT

I forgot to tell you that, while the three of us were waiting for the travel agent to reorganize the details of our trip, we spent the day hard at work trying to come up with a plan to persuade the letter writer to supply Marina with more information.

"First things first," Marina said. "We have to publicize our trip. The perpetrator has to learn exactly where I'll be for the next two weeks. That part should be quite straightforward. As soon as I get the new itinerary, I can forward it to the public relations departments of both organizations, and they'll tell the world where we'll be staying."

"Darling, I'm not so sure that's such a good idea," I said. "I'm still concerned that the writer may want to kill you and that he may be in Japan. I certainly don't want everyone knowing the names of our hotels. The culprit knows—or seems to know—that we're staying in luxury accommodation. Even though the exact amount we received for the movie rights hasn't been made public, the gossip columnists are all in agreement that we received a seven-figure check. Alternatively, he may think that Megalodeon Studios is paying for our holiday in Japan. Either way, it would be reasonable to conclude that we're staying at only the finest hotels.

"He's clever enough to realize where we are this very minute. I don't mind letting people know which cities we're visiting, but I don't think we should supply any more information than that. Why should they know the day we arrive in say, Tokyo, and the day we leave? All we should make public is the names of the places we're visiting in the order we're visiting them and leave it at that."

Marina was unhappy with my cautious approach. "What if a particular city doesn't happen to have one spectacular hotel? Courier letters aren't cheap—we're talking a hundred euros a time, if not more—and he's not going to dispatch five or ten in the vague hope of finding us in one or another hotel in a Japanese city. Remember, we have to strongly encourage the writer to communicate with us. I think we're going to have to release the names of the places where we're staying. They're all top hotels, so they'll have good security. The only precaution we need to take is to tell each manager that Marina Haversmith will be staying in their hotel under the name of Mrs. Quentin Pakenham, and I'm sure he'll organize a team of Olympic champion samurai warriors to protect me."

And I, in turn, was unhappy with her nonchalant attitude, especially her flippant reference to the Japanese military nobility of feudal times. Nowadays, the only place you find samurai is in historical romance novels, and this was a most inappropriate time for her to take a dig at bodice rippers. Surprisingly, I didn't rise to the bait. Instead I asked, "Are you confident that will be sufficient to ensure your safety?"

"We're in agreement that it's highly unlikely he wants to kill me, or even harm me, and he's probably still in Paris anyway. The chances of anything happening to me are infinitesimally small, and I want this whole thing to be completely cleared up before we get back home. And that means we need to tell him where we're staying."

I turned to Lancelot for moral support. Much to my amazement, he looked at me rather strangely. I have to tell you that I'd never before seen that particular expression on his face, and I just couldn't make it out. It was a mixture of cunning and amusement, with an overall hopeless attempt at a look of pure innocence to try to disguise what he was actually thinking. No question about it, Lancelot was up to something. But what?

"Marina," he said, "why not give the complete itinerary to Gilles, with a request that he ask his Japanese counterpart to keep an eye on you? I fully agree that trying to tell the Japanese police the full story of the ten generations of Philippe le Sabres would be a bad mistake. But you are a major celebrity; the whole world loves Marina Haversmith. Asking the Japanese National Police Agency to protect you from overeager fans would not be unreasonable, would it?"

I weighed up the pros and cons of his suggestion for a moment: plenty of pros, no cons of any significance that I could see. "Yes, I think that's a good idea. In fact, it's a particularly outstanding idea. Marina, don't you agree?"

"Certainly. And it couldn't do any harm. I'm sure it's standard operating procedure for hotel security to liaise with the local police."

"In that case," Lancelot said, "when you speak to Gilles later today, why not ask him to arrange it?"

The weird expression was still on his face. I could see he was trying to maintain the innocent look—and failing dismally. I know him far too well.

"I have a further suggestion," Lancelot said. "Marina, I suppose we're going to stay at nine or ten different places?"

"Eight, if I recall correctly. Why?"

"Will you please do me a favor?"

"Certainly," Marina replied.

"I am going to ask you to do something, but I do not want you to ask me the reason for my request."

"I'm utterly mystified," Marina said. "But please go ahead. What do you want me to do?"

"We are now in Kyoto. I assume that we are going to end up in Tokyo, and we shall fly home from there. Is that correct?"

"Yes. We're flying out of Narita Airport."

"What is to be our penultimate overnight stop in Japan?"

Marina consulted her pile of papers. "The travel agent may change things around at the last minute. For example, she may find a splendid *ryokan* for the three of us."

I shuddered. I hoped that Marina hadn't noticed.

Lancelot nodded. "I appreciate that. But what does the current version of the itinerary say?"

"We're going to be staying in some place called Hakone, wherever that is. We go from there to Tokyo."

"Fine," Lancelot said. "When you give the list of places where we are staying to the studio and the people from the prefecture, would you please omit Hakone?"

Marina and I looked at one another, utterly mystified. I was about to speak, but Lancelot put his index finger to his fleshy lips.

We said nothing for about ten seconds. Then the ever-practical Marina asked, "But what if she changes the itinerary?"

"That would not be a problem. All I want you to do is leave out the penultimate destination, wherever it finally turns out to be."

"And what about the information that I'm to give to Gilles, for him to forward to the Japanese police?"

"Gilles must receive the full itinerary in all its glory—every stop, every hotel. And if you make the slightest change, no matter how minor, you need to pass it on to him as well. For your own safety, it is absolutely vital that you forward to him everything that the travel agent sends you, without exception. The only way that the Japanese police can protect you is if Gilles gives them the fullest information possible. What I am saying is that you are responsible for your security.

"When I asked you to omit Hakone," Lancelot continued, "I was referring to the list of destinations that you will give to the public relations people. Start at Kyoto, naturally, and end with Tokyo. But please 'overlook' Hakone; instead, inform them that we're coming to Tokyo one night earlier. And this is most important: Gilles must not know that you are deliberately going to 'forget' to tell the publicists about that one stopover. Will you do that for me?"

We looked at one another again, shrugged in unison, and then nodded.

"Thank you. Now let us all go downstairs to that sushi restaurant on the second floor."

Right after we ordered, Lancelot excused himself. As soon as he was out of earshot, I said to Marina, "What was all that about? Have you even heard of this Hakone place?"

"No. But I don't think that this is about Hakone."

"What do you mean?" I asked.

"Remember what happened. Lancelot asked us what the second-to-last overnight stop would be. He didn't care where it was. And when I explained to him that the travel agent might modify the itinerary and put us up somewhere else, that didn't seem to be an issue. His sole concern appeared to be to find out where we're spending the night before we get to Tokyo, and he didn't seem to care if it's Hakone or somewhere else."

"Odd, isn't it?"

"That's only the half of it," Marina replied. "What about his insistence that we don't ask him any questions? And that we don't tell Gilles about it? This is truly weird."

"I stayed with him for weeks at his house outside London. During that time, he never once acted this way. I don't think he shared every piece of information with me, but he never displayed any secretiveness, and he certainly didn't play games like this."

"Could it have anything to do with the fact that he's overseas?"

"While I was his guest in Varenne, we made short trips to various places: first to Liechtenstein via Switzerland and back. Not long after that, we flew to Belfast. A week later we travelled to the Republic of Ireland, and from there to Portugal. Nothing like this

281

ever happened. And now he's not only acting mysteriously, he specifically asked us not to question him about it."

"I can find only one way to put it, Quentin. The fact of the matter is that he doesn't trust us. Either of us."

At that moment, Lancelot came back to the table. We smiled at him, he smiled back. And that was that.

After lunch, the three of us returned to our room to continue the discussion and wait for the travel agent's phone call. And you already know all about that.

CHAPTER TWENTY-NINE

T he sun was descending on the far horizon in the Land of the Rising Sun when Marina phoned Gilles Despoir at nine in the morning, Paris time.

"Gilles, I'm speaking from our hotel room in Kyoto. Quentin is with me, and so is Lancelot Aylesworth. We're on speakerphone."

"So you're Priscilla's granduncle Lancelot," Gilles Despoir said. "She's told me all about you."

"I think that is extremely unlikely. If she had told you *all* about me, there would not be slightest doubt as to what will happen in two weeks' time when our plane from Tokyo lands at Charles de Gaulle Airport: Your colleagues would arrest me and put me on the first plane to London, with unambiguous instructions never to set foot in France again."

Gilles chuckled. "Let me rephrase that. My wife has mentioned just a few things about you, all exceedingly complimentary."

"That is so much better. Now let us get down to business."

"Before we do that, Lancelot—may I call you Lancelot?—I need to thank you for the report you sent us in the middle of the night. Combined with Marina's photographs, my colleagues were able to start working on this right away."

"Have they discovered anything?" our friend asked.

"Yes and no. We've learned that the La Poste envelope was dropped into the box outside a post office in the Eighteenth Arrondissement, not the same one that he used for the first letter, but another box less than half a mile away. No CCTV cameras are located anywhere near either post office, which may be why he chose them."

"Did he send letters via courier to any other hotel in Kyoto?"

"We haven't checked whether he used a different courier service, which seems unlikely, but we do know yours was the only one sent via La Poste. And that's also interesting. It implies he knew where you were staying," Gilles said.

"Or," I interposed, "he simply assumed the studio would insist on putting Marina Haversmith up at the best hotel in town."

Gilles wondered about my suggestion for a second or so. "You may be right. And if you are, then the only thing we've learned from this episode is that the person who sent the letter is very clever. But we knew that anyway."

I got down to brass tacks. "Can you tell me whether the prime suspect is still Claude Malmaison, and if so, is he still in the military hospital?"

"Good question," Gilles replied. "We've looked into that aspect of the case in depth. What I can tell you is that he's still in Druny Military Hospital. And the only visitors he's had are you and your wife. As you may have noticed when you saw him, his room doesn't have a telephone. Or a computer. Let alone a printer. One way he could've been responsible for that second letter is if he somehow managed to bribe a nurse or a doctor to go to his apartment, print out another copy of the letter, and dispatch it by courier to Japan. Alternatively, he may have planned for two or more copies from the beginning and given instructions to an accomplice to send them at specific times to wherever you might be. But all of that seems far beyond the bounds of plausibility.

"What I'm saying is that it would've been impossible for him to send the second letter himself or even to arrange for someone else to dispatch it to you. Now that I come to think of it, that must mean he had nothing to do with the first one either."

Lancelot took over. "We feel that the letter is not threatening as such. Instead, we think the writer wants Marina to do something, but we have not been able to determine what that is. Do you agree?"

"Certainly," Gilles said. "We've come to a similar conclusion. And we also have no idea what he wants."

"Good," Lancelot continued. "The problem, as I see it, is that the second letter was identical to the first. Consequently, Marina still has no idea what the person who wrote the two letters wishes her to do. If she continues with her trip to Japan, it is possible she may receive a letter with additional information. Obviously, it is of critical importance that the perpetrator finds out about Marina's trip, otherwise he cannot communicate with her in writing. In fact, lots and lots of people need to know about it, or else sending a letter would incriminate the writer. We have come up with a way to publicize the trip, making use of the public relations departments of the studio and the prefecture, the two groups that have been telling the world Marina came to Kyoto to sign the contract. But even that is not going to help unless Marina can also somehow persuade the writer to give her additional information. And that is the real difficulty."

No one said anything. No solution of any kind came to mind.

After a while, Lancelot spoke again. "If I may, I would like to raise a different point. Gilles, what would happen if the police were to publicize the letters?"

"The women of France would undoubted lynch the entire police force," Gilles said gloomily.

"Be serious," I said. "This is no joke for Marina and me."

"I'm being perfectly serious. I don't have to tell you two about the depth of feeling for *She Loved the French Captain* and Marina Haversmith worldwide, but especially in Paris, the City of Love.

"And another thing," he added. "Even if we managed to calm the female populace, the effect of putting a letter like that in the newspaper would be to bring out the copycats. We'd be inundated with thousands of similar letters. No, Lancelot, that's probably the last thing we'll do, after we've tried everything else. And even then, we won't do it.

"However, I like your other idea, but with one proviso. Before you let the publicists run wild, I need to have the fullest details of your trip. I agree it's possible that the writer is in Japan and that he intends to harm you, Marina. I appreciate that it's most unlikely, but I'm not prepared to risk it. I must insist you send me everything you have regarding your itinerary so I can arrange for protection from the Japanese National Police Agency. They'll maintain a discreet presence at your hotels, and they may even lurk in the background at the various tourist sites you visit. Will you do that?"

"Certainly. I have a detailed itinerary. I shall forward it to you right away. Keep in touch!"

CHAPTER THIRTY

"Our trip starts tomorrow," I said brightly. "The plan for today was for us to wander through the streets of Kyoto, relaxing after two hectic days of signing the contract and posing for publicity photographs. It's now late in the afternoon. We've done nothing all day but discuss the letter, eat a sushi lunch, and talk some more about the letter. Does anyone feel like dressing up and hitting the town?"

This suggestion was met with total silence.

"Drinks in the bar?"

The other two shook their heads.

"We've had two ultra-hectic days, plus the second letter and all that implies," Marina said firmly. "Let's go to—"

"What happened to Adrien Legendre?" I suddenly interrupted.

Marina and I looked at one another. Neither of us spoke.

288

I turned to Lancelot. "At our dinner two nights ago, did Legendre tell you why he's in Kyoto?"

"No. Why?"

Now, all I'd said to Lancelot when Adrien, bearing a single red rose, joined us at the dinner table was something along the lines of, "Lancelot, this is Adrien Legendre. In the movie, he's going to star as Philippe le Sabre." As I far as I could recall, the broad variety of topics we'd discussed that evening didn't include any aspects of Adrien's professional work. I hadn't mentioned Chekhov's Gun to Lancelot. And Marina, the arch sceptic, definitely would've stayed a million miles away from that topic. She has no compunction in private about treating me like the idiot I am, but she'd never make fun of me to one of our friends. With all this in mind, I surmised Lancelot knew nothing of the connection between Adrien and ourselves.

"Lancelot," I said, "we need to fill you on something."

Marina took over. "We signed the film deal with Megalodeon Studios because they have Adrien Legendre under contract, and we felt he'd be the perfect person to play the lead role of Captain Philippe le Sabre."

No doubt, you're fully aware the previous sentence isn't strictly accurate. All decisions relating to Legendre were made by Marina alone. Naturally, I didn't dream of correcting her.

"We encountered contractual difficulties," she continued, "and we decided to invite him to dinner to see if we could sort the problem out."

Again, this wasn't strictly accurate. To be quite frank, it was a barefaced lie. As you know, we—yes, this time it really was both of us—invited Adrien to dinner with the hope he'd accidentally let slip a remark that would prove he was the criminal. However, if Marina had informed Lancelot that we strongly suspected Legendre was responsible for the letter, she'd have to tell him our sole reason for our suspicion was Chekhov's Gun, and as I've just told you, she had no intention of going there. Nor did I.

Marina resumed. "During the course of a most pleasant evening, Adrien came up with a brilliant solution to the critical legal issue. Without that dinner, the Megalodeon lawyers wouldn't have approved the contract and the two of us wouldn't be in Kyoto now. Then when we arrived here, we found a vase crammed to capacity with red roses on the table in our suite. The note indicated they were from Adrien, who was staying in our hotel. That night, the five of us went to dinner: you, Quentin and I, Adrien, and Osbert. It was a delightful evening, I'm sure you'll agree. You'll certainly recall that the conversation was wide-ranging. But one topic was never raised, namely, why Adrien Legendre was in Kyoto. I can only think that we all assumed he was there for the extravaganza that culminated in the signing ceremony. After all, that was why the rest of us were in Kyoto. It was almost like going to the Olympic Games and bumping into a friend in the host city. You'd never ask him 'What are you doing here?'—because you'd assume he was there for the international sporting event."

I suddenly came up with another reason why the friend was at the Olympics. In reality, he was a spy who wanted to use the cover provided by hundreds of thousands of sports fans from all the world to surreptitiously hand over the plans of the top-secret highly experimental thermonuclear exploding grelbin device to an agent of a foreign power. But I firmly decided not to say a word. After all, I write historical romance fiction. I would never lower myself by getting involved with anything as crude and crass as a spy thriller. Let alone a detective story. Heaven forfend!

I realized my mind was wandering and I'd better concentrate on what Marina was saying.

". . . and we've just realized that none of us have seen Legendre since the dinner. He certainly wasn't on the stage in that hall when we all affixed our signatures to the bottom of the contract; presumably he has a separate agreement with Megalodeon Studios. Perhaps he was at the celebratory dinner last night. I can phone Megalodeon and find out if he was there, but I've no idea how to contact them."

"Last night, while you were sleeping, Carmela gave me her mobile phone number," I said. "She certainly would know about Legendre."

Carmela answered right away. Before Marina could ask about Adrien, she had to repeatedly reassure Carmela that she (Marina) had suffered from nothing worse than total exhaustion and that she was right as rain after a good night's sleep followed by a relaxing day.

"Was Adrien Legendre at last night's dinner?" Marina eventually managed to ask.

Carmela seemed puzzled. "No. Should he have been there?"

"Surely he flew here for the signing ceremony?"

"Not at all. He's a great actor, as we all know, so much so that Megalodeon Studios has signed him up for the lead role in three pictures with an option for two more. But Megalodeon intended you to be the sole star of the show here in Kyoto. From a viewpoint of publicity, it's hard to focus the public's attention on both a world-famous author and a heartthrob actor at the same time. Once they've made the movie, we'll run an international publicity campaign for Yasuhara Prefecture featuring all the leading actors— but the director hasn't decided yet who's going to play Ludmilla. Quite frankly, Marina, I wasn't even aware that Adrien Legendre was in Kyoto."

Marina quickly thanked her and hung up.

"How about that? She didn't even know that Adrien was here. Or is here. We don't know if he checked out. I'll ask Mr. Mori."

Two minutes later she had her answer. "Adrien arrived here one day before we did and left the hotel the morning after our dinner at Yemyo two nights ago."

By now, Lancelot was champing at the bit. "Why would Adrien come to Japan, announce his presence at the hotel via the vase of red roses he sent to your room, have a wonderful dinner, and then disappear if he had nothing to do with the signing? It does not make sense to me."

"It certainly doesn't," I said. "Without a doubt he came to Japan for some reason other than the signing. So, why did he contact us?"

Marina looked puzzled. "Why wouldn't he contact us?"

"Speaking for myself," I said, "if I'd come to Kyoto for a reason I'd prefer to keep secret, I'd go out of my way to avoid people whom I know. I'd be especially careful not to stay at the hotel where they were staying. I'd make some excuse to avoid having dinner with them. And I certainly wouldn't send them my trademark dozens and dozens of red roses."

"Maybe it was an insurance policy," Marina suggested.

"What do you mean?"

293

"Suppose," Marina replied, "that Adrien Legendre had to be in Kyoto at the same time as us and for a reason he wanted to keep secret. But what if we bumped into him by chance? He couldn't claim he didn't know we were here. Every single person in the whole wide world was apparently aware of the signing of the contract for the filming of everyone's favorite historical romance novel, so the star of the movie could hardly claim ignorance, could he? So, he deliberately stays at our hotel, sends the roses, and dines with us."

"But what if we'd asked him what he was doing in Kyoto?" I asked.

Marina rolled her eyes. "Don't you ever listen to what I say? When you bump into a friend in the host city while the Olympic Games are underway, you don't inquire what he's doing there. Adrien has been extremely clever. If anyone had asked him why he was in Kyoto, all he had to say was, 'The contract for the most important movie of my career is about to be signed.' That statement happens to be 100 percent truthful, and no one would challenge it."

"Except, perhaps, someone who knew that Adrien wasn't actually going to sign the contract," I said.

"That's most unlikely," Marina replied. "The overwhelming majority of people go to the Olympics to be present at the opening and closing ceremonies and to watch the various events. Comparatively speaking, only a small percentage are there to compete. Adrien flying to Japan simply to be present when other individuals were affixing their signatures to the document isn't particularly odd. After all, that's why Lancelot came to Kyoto. The difference, obviously, is that Adrien wasn't at the ceremony."

Lancelot, who'd hardly said two words since I'd raised the subject of Legendre, now supplied another two. "Phone Gilles."

CHAPTER THIRTY-ONE

"Gilles," Marina said, "you're again on speakerphone with Quentin, Lancelot, and me. We think we may have a lead. As everyone knows, Adrien Legendre is starring in our movie as Captain Philippe le Sabre. He was here in Kyoto."

"That comes as no surprise. Weren't you all supposed to be there to sign the contract?"

"No, that's not the case. Adrien has his own separate agreement with Megalodeon Studios, as do each of the actors. In fact, one of the organizers of the ceremony didn't even know Adrien was in Kyoto. But he wasn't at the signing. He checked into our hotel a day before we did; he had dinner with us the night we arrived; and he checked out the next morning, the day before the ceremony."

"What reason did he give for his trip to Japan?"

"That's the whole point," Marina said. "We never asked him, and he never volunteered."

"He might have been in Kyoto for a perfectly innocent reason that he chose not to share with you. Something personal, perhaps."

"True. But he might also have been there to organize the second letter."

"Which someone sent from Paris, not Kyoto," Gilles said. I felt that he spoke rather pointedly.

"You're right about that," Marina replied, choosing to ignore the underlying tone in the French police officer's voice.

"And another thing," Gilles said. "I don't have to tell you that Adrien Legendre has a huge fan base here in France. If I were to initiate even a highly confidential inquiry, it would soon become public knowledge and my superiors would call me in and ask me to explain my actions. I'm sorry, Marina, but based on what you've just told me, no way could I justify any sort of probe, even on an unofficial basis."

Marina's disappointment as she disconnected the call was palpable.

Lancelot volunteered another two words. "What now?"

Before either of us could answer, he went on. "Tell me again why you suspect Legendre of sending the letter."

I looked at Marina with an expression of desperation on my face, to be met with an identical look from her. I grasped at straws.

"It all started when every filmmaker in the world tried to buy the movie rights to *She Loved the French Captain*. We decided to go with Megalodeon because they'd signed up Adrien to play the role of Captain Philippe le Sabre.

"Then," I continued, "a disputation of lawyers from Megalodeon got involved. They insisted that it was legally unclear who owned the copyright for the book. That brought everything to a screeching halt. Next, all the parties involved jointly filed a lawsuit so that the courts could settle the matter one way or the other. While the juridical battle raged on, the first letter arrived.

"We soon worked out, just as you did, that this wasn't a threatening letter. We therefore concluded it was sent to frighten my wife—and it certainly succeeded in that respect. Next came the obvious question: Who wanted to frighten Marina?

"We discussed the issue for a long while and finally decided, on the basis of little more than unfounded guesswork, Adrien was responsible and his objective was to scare Marina into settling the lawsuit at all costs so that the movie could be made, even if it meant her giving up her rights to lots of money. So we invited him to dinner and—"

"Let me get this quite straight," Lancelot said. "You determined, based on hardly even a hunch, that Adrien had sent the letter to frighten Marina into settling a lawsuit. Having arrived at that extraordinary conclusion, you invited him to dinner. Are you both stark staring mad?"

"You see, Lancelot, we wanted to trap him into a—"

"I do not have the slightest doubt: you and Marina are certifiably insane. There is a good reason why we have police. Their job is to investigate crimes and find the perpetrator. Individuals like yourselves who think themselves smarter than trained detectives and try to solve crimes are nothing short of deranged lunatics who—"

"Tell me, Lancelot, after someone murdered Sir Henry Haversmith, who decided to play detective and find his killer?"

He didn't respond for a long while. Then Lancelot cleared his throat, but he didn't say anything. Eventually, he spoke. "That was different."

"Different how?" Marina and I said simultaneously.

"Sir Henry was a friend of mine."

"And that entitled you to investigate his death and find the murderer?" I asked.

"Certainly."

I persisted. "Because he was your friend?"

"Yes, indeed. Sir Henry was a close friend for decades. That gave me the right."

"Well, Lancelot, Marina is my wife. Doesn't that mean I have an even greater right to determine who sent her the letter?"

The silence that now reigned seemed unending. After a long while, Lancelot wisely decided to revert to the previous topic. "And what happened when you invited him to dinner?" he asked brightly.

Equally wisely, I ignored the fact that he'd changed the subject. "He quickly came up with a way of resolving the copyright issue in its totality, with no negative repercussions or adverse consequences. On the contrary, the lawyers representing all four parties quickly agreed on the wording of the contract. And they didn't charge us for their weeks of unnecessary work."

"And that proved he wrote the letter?" Lancelot asked.

"Yes. No." I replied.

"Which is it?" Lancelot asked. "Believe it or not, you cannot have it both ways."

"He couldn't possibly have found the solution to the copyright dispute then and there at the dinner table. He must've worked it out earlier, and that means he could easily have informed the lawyers about his brainwave before coming to our dinner party. The fact that he pretended to solve the issue during the meal proved he was up to something."

"But how do you know that the *something* up to which he was was the threatening letter?"

This time neither Marina nor I said anything for long while.

Now Lancelot moved in for the kill. "You stated that Adrien could not have possibly solved the legal

300

problem at the dinner table. How can you be sure of that?"

More unresponsiveness from the two of us.

"What might have happened was that Adrien thought hard about the copyright obstacle for a while but without success. When he met the two of you in person, something fell into place and he came up with the answer to the issue with the contract."

"That's possible," I ventured.

"It certainly is. Putting it all together, here is what we know: Adrien may have written that letter, but we have absolutely no evidence whatsoever in that regard. I freely concede that his behavior here in Kyoto was suspicious, but again we know of nothing whatsoever to tie him to the second letter either."

Marina and I had the grace to look ashamed.

"However," Lancelot continued, "it should not be too hard to find out why he came to Kyoto. Get your agent on the line, ask him to contact Adrien's agent, and ask Adrien to phone you."

"What do I ask Adrien when he calls back?"

"I would suggest you say to him that you did not see him at the signing and you were wondering if he was ill. He probably will say that he was fine. At that point, you need to throw caution to the wind and ask him what he was doing in Kyoto."

Marina looked enthusiastic as she dialed Osbert's number. Ten minutes later, Adrien phoned her.

301

CHAPTER THIRTY-TWO

"Adrien, are you okay?" Marina asked.

"And why shouldn't I be okay?" Lancelot and I heard over the speakerphone.

"But you weren't at the signing."

"Was I supposed to be there?" Adrien asked. "My agent didn't say anything about that. And I don't recall any of the Megalodeon people telling me I had to attend the ceremony."

Now came the first personal question. To continue with the Olympic Games leitmotif, let me just say that the manner in which Marina handled it closely resembled the way a champion hurdler sails effortlessly over the barriers.

"But wasn't that why you came to Kyoto?" she asked. Her delivery was smooth, very smooth.

"No. I just happened to be there at the same time as you."

Now for the especially tricky one. Even when talking to a close friend, it's hard to ask a personal question. But when the famous Adrien Legendre is at the other end of the line, it can be almost impossible.

Marina aced it. Instinctively she knew that the hackneyed opening, *I hope you don't mind my asking,* would result in an exquisitely polite paraphrase of the obvious response, *Actually, I do mind your asking.* Instead, she jumped right in, boots and all.

"Then why are you in Kyoto?"

I hope you noticed that, by using the present tense, Marina didn't give away that she'd discovered Adrien had left the Mikado Hotel two days before. And that seemed to do the trick. He immediately replied, "Marina, I'm back in Paris. I flew to Kyoto to find a house to rent."

Marina gasped. I hoped that Adrien hadn't heard her sudden intake of breath. But she recovered quickly.

"You mean you came to Kyoto to find somewhere to stay during the filming? Won't Megalodeon Studios put you up in a luxurious suite, presumably here at the Mikado Hotel?"

"Yes, that's standard operating procedure. But I hate hotels at the best of times. And when making a movie, I far prefer to rent a comfortable house where I can relax."

As you well know, dear reader, I'm not the most perceptive person. But in this case, I quickly realized the situation: Adrien didn't want his innumerable fans to know he preferred male companionship, and a famous movie star doesn't get much privacy in a hotel.

And then I really felt bad that I'd even suspected him of being the malefactor. I caught Marina's eye and made a sharp downward chopping motion with my open right hand to signal she should terminate the conversation right there and then and leave the poor man in peace.

Much to my amazement, I heard Marina saying, "Adrien, that's a brilliant idea! As you know, we're coming here for the filming, and I think we definitely need to follow your example. Who's your real estate agent?"

I was stunned. Marina now knew why Adrien had been in Kyoto, so why did she want to prolong the agony? In any event, this was the first I'd heard of our going back to Kyoto while they made the film. On the contrary, Marina had made it abundantly clear to me that I wasn't to make any suggestions regarding the filming of *She Loved the French Captain* to Adrien or anyone else, so why would we want to be in Kyoto for several months to witness the film company massacring my beautiful historical romance?

I was even more stunned when I heard Adrien stutter. "Well, um, well, I can't seem to find her card. Where is it? I know I put it somewhere. I must've left it behind when I flew back home yesterday. I'll have to call you back." And he rang off.

Marina looked at me in triumph. "I knew it! Adrien was lying."

"How could you tell?" I asked.

"His reply was over-polished. He sounded like an actor delivering a line he'd rehearsed one time too many."

Adrien had certainly fooled me, but not my clever wife. I quickly realized I'd better continue my invariable policy of telling the truth to Marina, because she seemed to be equipped with some sort of built-in lie detector.

Lancelot joined the conversation. "I can see no point at all in your telephoning Gilles again. The fact is that we do not know why Adrien came here, he is not going to tell us, and his prevarication is proof of absolutely nothing—other than he prepared a cover story for his trip."

Now it was my turn to sigh. "Lancelot," I asked, "what do we do now? Marina and I simply have to know the identity of the writer. We can't go on like this. We can't drop the investigation—any more than you were willing to forget about finding the murderer of your friend Sir Henry Haversmith. What do you suggest?"

"Mr. Matsumoto will be at the hotel tomorrow morning at nine o'clock to take the three of us on a tour of Japan. My advice to you is to forget about the whole thing for two weeks and have a wonderful holiday. By the time you get back to Paris, the mystery may have been solved."

And then I remembered Lancelot's weird request. He'd instructed us to omit Hakone from the copy of the itinerary that we were to give to the studio and the prefecture. As Lancelot himself, the ultimate grammar freak, would've put it: Up to what was our friend?

As I was trying to work that out, Marina's phone rang. It was Adrien Legendre. "I've found her card. It was in my wallet the whole time. I've just photographed it and emailed the picture to you. Please give Mrs. Fujiwara my warmest regards. I'm sure she'll find a place for you to stay during the filming that's as marvelous as the house she found for me. Amazingly, it was built in the thirteenth century, during the Kamakura period, as an urban merchant's house, or *machia*. The attention to detail and the craftsmanship are nothing short of astounding. I'll send you some of the photographs I took."

I mentally crossed Adrien Legendre off my long list of suspects, which by then had been whittled down from two names to just one: Adrien Legendre. And then I suddenly realized Legendre wasn't the only person who'd benefit financially from frightening my wife into signing an unfavorable contract.

"We've been at it all day," I said. "We're all emotionally drained and physically exhausted. We'll have to get up early tomorrow morning to start our tour with Mr. Matsumoto. But I must tell you something that you indubitably need to know."

Neither Marina nor Lancelot showed the least interest in what I wanted to say. Lancelot just looked straight ahead, avoiding making eye contact, while Marina rolled hers. No surprise there.

"Fine," I said. "Let's talk about it tomorrow morning after a good night's sleep."

But the next morning, I somehow never had a chance to discuss my epiphany. Lancelot phoned to say he was having breakfast in his suite and would meet us downstairs just before nine, and Marina seemed to be busy packing every time I tried to talk to her. From time to time, dear reader, I actually started to wonder if my two travelling companions were trying to evade me.

Somehow all three of us found ourselves and our luggage in the lobby of the Mikado Hotel just before the appointed time. There we had the pleasure of meeting Mr. Matsumoto, whom I can best describe as a scholar and a gentleman. The scholarly component was revealed by his encyclopedic knowledge of his country, its history, and its people. His gentlemanliness manifested itself in the amiable way that he explained everything and, just as importantly, through his realization that it wasn't necessary to show us every square inch of Japan beginning each day at cock-crow and ending way after midnight. On the contrary, the earliest we ever left our hotel was the civilized hour of nine o'clock, he never rushed us, and the day's touring always ended by half-past five. As a result, we saw only the very best that Japan has to offer the tourist, and we learned in depth about every site he showed us.

We decided the first day not to discuss the identity of the letter writer in front of Mr. Matsumoto. He'd feign deafness, without question. That said, he'd undoubtedly be offended that we were more interested in our own affairs than what he was showing us. Out of politeness I kept silent all day, during which we visited only the choicest of the nearly two thousand temples of Kyoto.

The sun was ready to set when, at dinner at our hotel in Nara, I had my initial opportunity to broach my discovery. I waited until we'd ordered our meal. Bracing myself for eye-rolling, or worse, I leaned forward in my chair and spoke my piece.

"We suspected Adrien Legendre because we surmised that he needed money and wouldn't be able to gain financially from his starring role in *She Loved the French Captain* unless Megalodeon made the movie. And nothing could happen until we'd signed the contract. But Legendre isn't the only person who'd benefit if someone frightened my darling Marina into signing."

Neither of my table companions seemed particular excited by what I'd just stated. Lancelot looked around to see if the bottle of wine he'd ordered was on its way. Marina opened her handbag, took out her iPhone, and laid it on the table.

"Don't you want to know who it is?" I asked. Underlying my voice was more than just a hint of petulance.

I expected them to look at me intently, waiting for me to reveal the name. But all they did was turn their heads towards me.

"Can't you guess?" I taunted them.

Bad mistake. They just didn't care.

I couldn't keep silent. "What about Osbert Oglesby?"

"Why Osbert?" Lancelot asked. His voice was flat.

"Because he's our agent. Because he received what I consider to be a usurious percentage of what the studio paid us for the film rights, but not a penny until we signed the contract."

"Dearest one," Marina said, her tone of voice revealing loads of sarcasm embedded in those two words, "it would be the best possible news if Osbert were responsible for the letter, which I'm sure he wasn't. If you're correct, which you aren't, then the nightmare would be over. But unfortunately it isn't."

"But how can you be so sure that Osbert is innocent?" I asked.

"Quentin, until the first letter arrived you had no idea that a real person named Philippe le Sabre ever existed, let alone seven or ten generations of them."

I nodded.

"I know that you searched the internet scrupulously when you wrote your masterpiece. But no Philippe le Sabre appeared, not even the arch traitor of the German occupation of France."

I nodded a second time.

"But if you couldn't uncover anything about the le Sabres, how did Osbert learn enough about the family history, including the name changes, to be able to write the letter?"

I wondered about that for a while.

"Maybe it wasn't Osbert, then?" I ventured.

"Yes, darling, you're right. Maybe it wasn't."

CHAPTER THIRTY-THREE

D ear reader, if you're hoping that I'm about to give you a detailed account of our visit to Japan, I'm afraid you're going to be bitterly disappointed. After all, I write historical romance fiction, not travelogues. You may want to know that my next book is going to be entitled True Love in the Court of the Mikado, and the tale will be set in the Muromachi period, which Mr. Matsumoto informed us lasted from 1333 to 1568. But the story won't take place in Japan. Rather, it will be set in a region that'll be vaguely reminiscent of Japan, a beautiful location that has no actual existence except in the mind of the reader. That's how it is with all bodice rippers.

Even though I'm not going to describe our wonderful trip, I need to tell you about two incidents that occurred. The first took place during our visit to Hiroshima. At the Peace Memorial, Mr. Matsumoto outlined to us why the United States decided to use nuclear weapons against Japan in August 1945. He explained that his country was on the brink of defeat, with American bombers roaming the skies unhindered and the economy in ruins. Nevertheless, the Japanese people refused to surrender because they'd been indoctrinated to believe that it was an honor for them to die for Japan and for the Emperor. Peace attempts were out of the question, because overzealous Army officers immediately assassinated anyone in the Japanese political leadership who even mentioned the word "surrender." A conventional invasion of Japan would've resulted in the deaths of about half a million Allied troops, and between five and ten million innocent Japanese civilians would've been killed. The decision was therefore made to drop the two atomic bombs, Mr. Matsumoto continued, to save lives on both sides and bring the war to a rapid close.

But before he could say anything more, a tall, thin, white-haired Japanese man suddenly interrupted Mr. Matsumoto and started screaming at him in Japanese. Attendants quickly removed the protester, but our delightful, erudite guide was clearly embarrassed by what had happened. He stood silently for a while, trying to regain his composure. Then he said, "Some Japanese people, to this day, refuse to accept what I've just shared with you. They insist that Japan was winning the war and could easily have repulsed any conventional invasion by the Allies. They also say that the United States dropped the two nuclear weapons on Japan to intimidate the Soviet Union at the beginning of the Cold War. Sadly, the end of World War II did not mean the end of fascism in Japan."

That evening at dinner, I rather rudely interrupted a conversation between Lancelot and Marina by asking, "Do you remember what Mr. Matsumoto told us?"

By this time we'd heard many tens of thousands of words from our superlative guide, so my question was greeted by two blank stares. So I quickly added, "About fascists in Japan, I mean."

Marina misunderstood. "I hope that the police are going to charge that man who abused our guide that way. It was totally uncalled for. If he disagreed—"

"No, that's not what I meant. It's about the letter."

"What on earth are you talking about?" Lancelot asked. "We've been extremely careful. Mr. Matsumoto knows nothing about the letter. What have you said to him?"

"No, Lancelot, this has nothing to do with Mr. Matsumoto."

Now it was Marina's turn again. "But you just asked us if we remembered what Mr. Matsumoto told us. If he said something to us, how can it have nothing to do with him?"

"Let's start again from the beginning," I said. "Mr. Matsumoto informed us that fascists are still active in Japan. The second letter was posted in Paris. We therefore arrived at the conclusion that no one in Japan was involved. But maybe we were wrong."

Marina and Lancelot both looked at me as if I were as mad as a March hare.

"The letter was sent from Paris," Marina said, "not Japan. As you just stated."

"True," I replied. "But how did the sender know where we were staying? We decided that he'd assumed the studio would arrange for you to stay at the top hotel in Kyoto. But what if we were wrong?"

Lancelot didn't seem to be convinced. "Quentin, am I hearing you correctly? Are you suggesting that someone in Japan told the perpetrator where you and Marina were staying in Kyoto? And that the informant is a Japanese fascist?"

"Yes, that's exactly what I'm saying."

"It certainly is possible that Marina is being followed here in Japan," Lancelot said, "but why on earth are you suggesting Japanese fascists are involved?"

"Because," I replied, "French fascists killed Claude's girlfriend and child. And the le Sabres, including Claude, are fervent neo-Nazis."

That statement did not sit well with Marina. "What Quentin just stated is factually correct. But no evidence of any kind exists to suggest that any French fascists, let alone Claude, are behind the two letters I've received."

Now it was Lancelot's turn to be unhappy. "Just a minute. That's the first I've heard that French fascists were behind the death of Marie-André and André-Marie. What evidence of that have you found?"

"We spoke to Marie-André's uncle," Marina replied, "and he told us."

"Did he produce any actual proof?"

Neither Marina nor I responded.

"So all you have regarding the deaths—not murders, at least not at this stage—is hearsay. And unless you can come up with a plausible mechanism by which Claude could have sent the second letter, no ties exist between any fascists—French, Japanese, or of any other nationality—and the letters. Am I correct?"

Marina and I had nothing to say.

* * *

The second incident I have to tell you about happened when we arrived at our hotel at Hakone. In case you were wondering, Hakone is a resort town noted for its hot springs, its open-air sculpture park, and its views of Mount Fuji in clear weather. It rained for the entire time we were there, and none of us were particularly interested in plunging into hot springs, so our visit to Hakone was somewhat less than successful. More accurately, it was an unmitigated disaster because waiting for Marina at the reception desk of the Paradise Hotel in Hakone was a letter.

The organizational skills of Mr. Matsumoto and the Japanese travel agency were superb. For example, when we arrived at a hotel, we would hand our passports to Mr. Matsumoto. The hotel staff then escorted us to a comfortable lounge where they served us drinks while Mr. Matsumoto did all the paperwork for us. If a check-in clerk required a signature, our guide would bring the form over. Once everything was signed and sealed, the manager would personally escort Marina Haversmith, her husband, and their friend to our respective suites, where our luggage was waiting for us, and return our travel documents to us there.

However, for some reason, the staff of the Paradise Hotel were unable to cope with this delightful scheme, and I found myself standing next to Lancelot at the reception desk, compelled to register as guests in the conventional way. The receptionist bowed politely. Then she handed me an ominous-looking La Poste courier envelope. I looked behind me. Marina was standing next to a pillar about ten yards away, staring into space.

I quickly handed back the envelope, saying in an undertone, "I'll come back and pick this up later."

All the Japanese people I encountered on the trip were unbelievably polite and helpful, the one obvious exception being the angry man at the Hiroshima Peace Memorial I've just told you about. It therefore came as no surprise that the receptionist took back the envelope and bowed again without saying a word. More importantly, she didn't ask any questions that Marina might have overheard, thereby alerting her to the situation. I glanced at Lancelot; his face was totally wooden.

We found our room and waited for the porter to bring up our luggage. As soon as our suitcases were on the luggage racks, I turned to Marina and said, "This isn't good enough. We've paid for ultra-luxurious treatment, but we're not getting it here in Hakone. I'm going downstairs to have a word with Mr. Matsumoto."

I don't know whether Marina picked up the lie; she probably did.

Lancelot was waiting for me near the reception desk. "Does that envelope contain what I think it does?"

"The only way we could tell," I answered, "would be to open it, and I'd rather not make that mistake again. I think the best thing to do would be to ask the manager to fold it in half, unopened, put it in a Japanese Post courier envelope, and send it posthaste to Gilles."

"And if it turns out to be perfectly innocent, Gilles will scan it and email it back to us as an attachment. Presumably, we'll be at our Tokyo hotel by then."

"I was wondering what would happen if it wasn't from the letter writer," I said. "But I'm sure that it's from him."

"I agree."

I looked at Lancelot. Again, I saw that strange facial expression, the one he had when he asked Marina not to tell the studio or the prefecture people we were going to spend a night in Hakone. You may remember that back in Chapter Twenty-Eight I described his demeanor as "a mixture of cunning and amusement, with an overall hopeless attempt at a look of pure innocence to try to cover up what he really was thinking." I've tried and I've tried to avoid repeating myself, but I simply cannot improve on what I wrote there.

The hotel manager was extremely helpful, dispatching a bellgirl to the nearest branch of the Japan Post Service with our courier letter now inside an envelope addressed to Gilles Despoir. I thanked him, and we left his office.

I said to Lancelot, "Let's go to the bar for a whisky. Sadly, they probably won't have eighteen-year old Lochervan, 'the crowning glory of the whisky maker's art,' but Yamazaki Single Malt Sherry Cask was the World Whisky of the Year for 2015."

After a few sips of Yamazaki, which proved to be absolutely delicious, we were ready to talk. At least I was.

"Lancelot," I asked, "why did you ask Marina to keep this destination secret from everyone except the police here in Japan and in France?"

Much to my surprise and disappointment, Lancelot wouldn't reveal anything at all. He frowned. "Have you forgotten? I specifically asked you not to ask me that question."

"Can you tell me anything at all about what's going on?"

"I am afraid not. But I am sure that Gilles Despoir will explain everything when you get back to Paris in only a few more days' time."

"At least can you tell me who wrote the letters?" I asked. My voice revealed an unmistakable note of desperation.

"That depends on the contents of that envelope. And no one knows that—other than the sender."

"Who happened, by a strange coincidence, to have mailed the letter in the Eighteenth Arrondissement. For the third time. And he gave his street address as Rue Travailleuse Agricole."

"I noticed that, too. What does that tell you?" Lancelot asked.

"His previous address was Rue Ludmilla. You may recall that Ludmilla, the utterly gorgeous heroine of *She Loved the French Captain*, is a farmhand."

"Which is *travailleuse agricole* in French."

"Precisely," I replied. "And I can guarantee you that no street with that name can be found anywhere in Paris. Or elsewhere in France, either."

"So, Quentin, do you think that envelope contains a third letter from the person purporting to be Philippe le Sabre?"

"I don't think it, I know it, and with 100 percent certainty. And so do you."

That strange expression reappeared on Lancelot's face. He took another sip of Yamazaki but didn't say anything more.

The conversation was over. We finished our drinks and went back upstairs.

"What did Mr. Matsumoto say?" Marina asked.

"I couldn't find him. But I bumped into Lancelot; we went to the bar for a whisky."

"Did they have Lochervan?"

"Sadly, no. But the Yamazaki was wonderful. Utterly superb."

"As good as Lochervan?"

"That would be impossible. But it definitely was marvelous.

CHAPTER THIRTY-FOUR

I don't remember too much about our stay in Tokyo. Instead of concentrating on Mr. Masumoto's descriptions of the marvels of modern Japan, I couldn't keep my mind off two inescapable facts. Firstly, the perpetrator was still at large and continued to send letters to Marina. Secondly, no one seemed to have the slightest idea regarding the identity of the writer. From time to time, I've read about police investigations where they interview literally thousands of suspects to try to determine who the culprit is, but in this case, it was pointless to interview anyone at all. No one had yet found a helpful clue. Neither the paper on which the first two letters were printed nor the computer hardware and software that produced them were of any use in narrowing down the field of suspects, and I had no doubt that forensic investigation of the third letter would prove to be equally fruitless. That meant that the suspect could've been anyone in the whole wide world, except for one vital detail: the writer had intimate knowledge of the le Sabre family secrets.

That pointed to Claude Malmaison. But he couldn't possibly have sent the second or third letters from the secure psychiatric ward in the Druny Military Hospital, so he was unequivocally innocent. And as for his mother, all her life Nicole had done everything she could to hide the family history, and her son had been equally assiduously hiding the past. The very idea that a le Sabre might do anything that would jeopardize their detailed multigenerational plan seemed ludicrous. And yet, who else possessed the knowledge needed to be able to write the letters? My head was splitting, and I found it hard to stay polite and friendly in my responses to my travel companions when they included me in their conversations.

It seemed like a lifetime, but three days later, at about seven o'clock in the morning, we found ourselves back at Charles de Gaulle Airport in Paris. As we were collecting our luggage, Marina's phone rang. Before she could answer it, an angry policeman carrying a submachine gun marched over and demanded to know why she hadn't switched off her telephone. He pointed to the sign on a pillar that instructed all passengers to turn their phones off. Actually, for security reasons, it's the rule in every immigration and customs area all over the world. Marina was unable to use her lack of knowledge of French as a defense, because the sign was large and in multiple languages, including English, and even incorporated an unambiguous graphic. Worse, for some reason the authorities had assigned a monolingual policeman to airport duties, so any meaningful communication between him and Marina was impossible.

As always in such situations, I stepped in as translator. But this policeman wasn't having any of it. He threatened that he would arrest me on the spot if I didn't shut up at once. Then he demanded to see Marina's passport. Unfortunately, British passports display only the married name of the bearer, so the official had no idea he was dealing with the immortal Marina Aver-smeet.

At this point, Lancelot had a brainwave. He opened his hand luggage, took out a copy of the French translation of *She Loved the French Captain*— and I've no idea why he was carrying it around with him, let alone how he'd acquired it—and pointed first to the author's name and then to Marina. And that settled the matter. Marina felt so bad about what had happened that it didn't occur to her to commandeer Lancelot's copy, sign it, and give it to the policeman for his wife, girlfriend, partner, mistress, paramour, or significant other.

We collected our suitcases and headed out of the terminal building to hail a taxi. We'd obviously invited Lancelot to stay with us in our two-bedroom apartment, and he'd equally obviously thanked us for our kindness but firmly insisted on staying at Hôtel le Manchester, pointing out that he'd always stayed there when in Paris. We shared a taxi for the trip to the city. As the driver accelerated wildly rushing to get to the highway, Marina retrieved her lost call and discovered that Gilles had rang.

She immediately phoned him back. "We're in a taxi on the way home. We'll come and see you just as soon as we've dumped our luggage at our flat."

"Please don't hurry on my account. The third letter was identical to the other two, and we haven't found any useful forensic evidence. Also, I'm sorry to have to tell you that we've made no progress at all during the past two or three weeks since you've been away."

"What on earth are you talking about?" Marina demanded to know. "What third letter?"

Gilles was taken aback. "The one that you received in Hakone and sent back, unopened, for us to check for fingerprints and DNA."

"What letter? I've no idea what you're talking about."

"Marina, you received a third courier envelope in Hakone, and you sent it to me without opening it."

"I did no such thing. Quentin, what's all this about a third letter?"

"Darling," I said, "I didn't want to worry you unnecessarily, so I just sent it to Gilles."

From the time the first letter arrived, Marina had understandably been under a severe strain, and the longer the police were unable to determine who was sending her death threats, the harder it was for her to cope. The incident with the policeman in the arrivals hall, though minor by comparison to what she'd been forced to endure, had added to the cumulative stress, and learning about the third letter was the last straw.

Dear reader, I'm sure you won't be the least bit surprised when I tell you that Marina started to lose it completely. I quickly grabbed the phone, told Gilles that I'd call him back, and for once managed to terminate a call successfully. I'm not going to be specific about what happened next. All I'll share with you is that things got most unpleasant in the taxi, and I was extremely relieved when the driver drew up outside our apartment building.

Marina was in such a bad state that I summoned a doctor, who prescribed a strong sedative. In retrospect, I should've insisted on a course of the appropriate medication from the time Marina received the first letter, but—like everyone else—I have twenty–twenty hindsight. Luckily, the drug started working by mid-afternoon, and Marina decided that the three of us had to go and see Gilles. I tried to persuade her to postpone the meeting until the next day, after a good night's sleep, but Marina would have none of it. She wouldn't give me a reason;

she just kept repeating that she had to meet with Gilles.

I phoned Lancelot.

"Are you alone?" he asked.

"Yes."

"Are you sure Marina can't hear what I'm saying?"

"Yes, I'm quite sure."

"Let me just say that I think it would be far better if we met tomorrow, or even later. What I have to tell Gilles may upset her."

I wanted to ask him what he'd learned, but I had to raise a far more pressing issue. "Lancelot, for the last ten minutes I've been urging Marina to wait until tomorrow, but to no avail. She's about to summon a taxi to take her to Gilles's office. I'm coming along with her because I've been unable to dissuade her no matter what I tried. It's up to you whether you'd like us to pick you up on the way."

Not surprisingly, Lancelot insisted that he accompany us.

Gilles was visibly shocked when he saw what the stress had done to Marina. "Are you all right? Why don't we postpone this meeting? Truly, I have nothing new to tell you."

Marina tried to smile but failed. "Gilles, you're most kind, but I think I would go mad if I had to wait any longer. Tell me about the third letter."

"Marina, as I said to you when we spoke this morning, I have nothing new to tell you. The third letter was identical to the first two. We still haven't found any forensic evidence, and we don't know who dropped the letter into the box. In short, nothing has changed."

"Not exactly," Lancelot stated. His voice was a mixture of sadness and triumph.

We all stared at him. For the first time since her collapse, Marina looked hopeful.

"Gilles, I laid a trap for the perpetrator. I saw it this way. I was convinced that the person who wrote the letter was trying to compel Marina to go public. Yes, I am fully aware that is the last thing the police want; you have explained to me about copycat letters. Nevertheless, I believed that the miscreant was steadily increasing the pressure on Marina in the firm expectation that she would go to the press in a desperate attempt to stem the flow of threatening letters."

"But why?" I asked. "Why does he want publicity?"

"That I do not know. Yet. But I was certain Marina would receive at least one other letter in Japan, and my guess was that it would arrive somewhere near the end of the trip. So I asked Marina to send out two different versions of the itinerary. The police— meaning you and your Japanese counterparts—would receive fullest details. But the version for public consumption had one omission: our penultimate stop, Hakone.

"And when I saw the third letter waiting for us at Hakone, I knew who the writer was."

Gilles, Marina, and I sat spellbound without saying a word. In detective stories, when the sleuth announces *I know who the culprit is!* everyone leaps up and shouts *Who?* But in real life, it's quite different. Learning that everything is about to be revealed takes your breath away and you're unable to move, let alone talk.

"Only the police knew about Hakone," Lancelot continued, "and the Japanese National Police Agency obviously had nothing to do with it. After all, the first letter arrived before anyone outside Megalodeon Studios knew that they were going to make the movie in Japan. It had to be the French National Police."

Again, in a detective story, at this point Gilles would jump to his feet and scream, *How dare you accuse me of sending the letters?* But Gilles wasn't a character in a novel. So he just stared at Lancelot with a dazed expression. Again in retrospect, I think he knew what Lancelot was going to say next.

"However," Lancelot continued, "no member of the French police knew enough about the le Sabre family to be able to write the letter. And that includes Gilles, who would be the most obvious suspect. Yes, his grandfather and namesake was killed as a consequence of the actions of Philippe le Sabre the Seventh. But until the first letter arrived, Gilles knew nothing about the next three generations, let alone the previous six. As far as you were concerned, Gilles, precisely one Philippe le Sabre existed: the arch traitor of World War Two, the man who murdered your grandfather."

Gilles simply sat there, his face white. He was breathing heavily. And I could see sweat starting to build up on his forehead.

Lancelot looked down at the carpet as he added, "Only one person had access to information about our stay in Hakone *and* knowledge of the le Sabre family—my niece, Priscilla."

I stared at Gilles. I expected him to look surprised and indignant, but he just sat calmly in his chair. I wondered if he'd known for some time, or perhaps he'd merely suspected, that his wife had written the letters.

Finally, Gilles spoke quietly. "I think we need to go to my apartment. I believe Priscilla is at home."

CHAPTER THIRTY-FIVE

Priscilla's voice was emotionless, her features expressionless. "I sent that letter to you because of *Wikipedia*."

"What's *Wikipedia* got to do with anything?" Marina asked. Her voice was equally impassive because she was still under the influence of the powerful sedative the doctor had prescribed.

"Have you read the *Wikipedia* article on French collaborators during the Second World War?"

"No," Marina replied. "Did you send the letter because of the contents of that article?"

"No such article exists."

I couldn't believe my ears. "That's unbelievable! There has to be one. How can *Wikipedia* overlook what happened?"

"No, Quentin, that's not the way *Wikipedia* works," Marina said.

She turned to Priscilla. "Why didn't you write the article?"

"Impossible. Anyone could change what I wrote, deliberately incorporating false information. The result would be far more damaging than having no article at all.

"In any event," Priscilla continued, "*Wikipedia* does include short subsections on French collaborators within more general articles like 'Collaboration with the Axis Powers during World War II.' That entry describes what happened in thirty European countries, including France. In one subsection, they named a few of the worst French collaborators, like Petain, Laval, Bousquet, Touvier, and Papon, but essentially made no mention of the thousands of others who were convicted in open court. And they totally omitted the worst of the worst: Philippe le Sabre the Seventh. Furthermore, as you yourself know because you checked, the name of the ultimate collaborator appears nowhere in the internet, which is why you came up emptyhanded when you did a Google search."

Despite the effect of the tranquillizer, Marina was sufficiently alert to be able to maintain the fiction that she wrote the book. "I looked up every name before I included it in *She Loved the French Captain*. If I found a person on the Web with the name that I wanted to give to a character, I immediately made up a different name. I've no wish to be sued."

Priscilla nodded. "I understand. And that's why you had no qualms about calling your hero 'Philippe le Sabre.'"

"Yes, that's it. But you still haven't explained why you wrote the letter to me."

"Haven't you ever wondered why the name 'Philippe le Sabre the Seventh' isn't on the internet?"

"No, I haven't. It's not the sort of thing that I think about. But now that you come to mention it: Why isn't it there?"

"Because," Priscilla said, "ever since the end of the Second World War, the members of the far-right in France have tried to do everything they could to try to 'rehabilitate' the collaborators in the eyes of the French people. For example, Jean-Marie le Pen once stated, 'Was General de Gaulle more brave than Marshal Pétain in the occupied zone? This isn't sure. It was much easier to resist in London than to resist in France.' That quotation appears in the *Wikipedia* article on le Pen.

"Above all, those fascists have done everything they could to keep Philippe le Sabre out of the internet. Why? Because he was the worst of the worst. Some people say that perhaps, just perhaps, maybe you could condone a strictly limited number of the acts of a few of the less culpable collaborators on the grounds that they genuinely believed they were acting in the interests of the French people. Myself, I think that's a load of utter rubbish, but I've heard otherwise sensible people arguing along those lines. But nothing whatsoever can justify what le Sabre did. Once the French people discover those facts, the far-right's efforts to rehabilitate the collaborators will come to naught."

"Are you saying," I asked, "that the neo-fascists in France have conspired to keep le Sabre off the internet and out of *Wikipedia* in particular?"

"That's exactly what I'm saying," Priscilla replied. "If I'd written the article, dozens of people would complain that the entry was offensive. Facts would be altered; my article would be vandalized. In short, it would be just me against the French neo-Nazis. And as has happened far too many times in the past, the bullies would win through sheer weight of numbers.

"And that's why I sent the letters to your wife. I was hoping that she'd go to the newspapers and the facts about Philippe the Seventh would then come out in an irrefutable form. But for some reason, that didn't happen."

"And is that why you contacted me, after five years of no communication of any kind?" Lancelot asked.

"Yes. You're a newspaper proprietor. I was hoping you'd investigate the story and publish it. Why didn't you?"

Lancelot chose not to respond to Priscilla. I think he realized it would be a waste of breath.

Marina broke the long silence. "Priscilla, why didn't you express yourself more clearly?"

I noticed that she'd called her friend by her given name, not Chunky Monkey. It was obvious the friendship was over—permanently. And then I realized Priscilla had been responsible for terminating it when she decided to send the first letter. After all, someone who makes use of another person, even for a good cause, is no friend.

"I didn't want to give myself away, which would've happened if I'd supplied more details."

"So you just kept sending me the same letter again and again?" Marina asked. "Albert Einstein once stated that the definition of insanity is doing something over and over and expecting a different result."

Priscilla's granduncle, Lancelot Aylesworth, is my dearest friend. But, as I think I've told you, one aspect of his behavior certainly is bizarre: his refusal to break any rule of English grammar, no matter how antiquated, or to use any colloquialisms or contractions. I think he has high-functioning autism, or perhaps Asperger syndrome. Also, Priscilla's mother is apparently the embodiment of a control freak. In other words, Priscilla's family tree definitely includes some odd fish, if you'll forgive the mixed metaphor. But was Priscilla certifiably insane, as my wife was alleging? I couldn't make up my mind.

I decided to change the subject and turned to Gilles. "What happens now?"

The answer came instantly. "Nothing."

"Nothing? Gilles, what do you mean?"

"I know of no evidence against Priscilla. She was extremely careful, so no forensic evidence has been found; we've examined and re-examined everything over and over again. But you need to know more."

He glanced at his wife, who sat immovable, staring straight in front of her. It seemed to me that she had somehow transported her essence to another realm, and only her physical body remained in the room. Perhaps that was why Gilles was talking about her as if Priscilla had been transmuted into an inanimate statue.

"As far as I know," Gilles continued, "no proof has come to light that Priscilla knew anything about the le Sabre family, with the obvious exception of the traitor. I've no idea where she found her facts, but I'm convinced it wasn't in one single location. She's an experienced and highly skilled researcher, as you know. She probably spent months putting the pieces together from numerous different sources, possibly including those nine boxes that were lying in the outbuilding of my aunt's farm in Picardy. And she told you that she's visited the military archives at both Vincennes and Châtellerault.

"I know for a fact that her book on the conflict between Winston Churchill and Charles de Gaulle resulted in many doors being opened to her. For example, she was invited to meet certain important individuals who usually never talk to historians. Those contacts might have led to her being invited to access private archives. But the bottom line is this: in my opinion, I don't think we'll ever be able to discover how she came up with her information about the other nine le Sabres.

"As I said before, no evidence against her exists. None whatsoever. And without evidence, the *juge d'instruction*, the investigating magistrate, cannot possibly bring charges. Furthermore, Priscilla can make a strong argument that the letter isn't threatening. In fact, everyone else in this room has made that point repeatedly. If Priscilla were to claim the whole thing was a joke, that would be the end of it. But this case would never get far."

"And what's going to happen to Claude Malmaison?" I asked. "I assume he's still locked up in Drury Military Hospital. Is he going to have to spend the rest of his life there?"

"He'll go home today."

"How can you be so sure?" I enquired.

"A medical certificate from the psychiatrists, dated about two weeks ago, is lying on my desk. It states that he's fit to be released and that he's a danger neither to the public nor to himself. Attached is a letter awaiting my signature that declares that, based on the facts at my disposal, Claude is incontrovertibly not the author of the letter. As soon as I return to my office, I'll sign the letter and fax the two documents to the Minister of Police."

"And what are you going to say when Claude asks why he was kept in the psychiatric ward for two weeks for no good reason?"

Gilles looked shocked.

In the ensuing silence, Marina, Lancelot, and I got up and left without saying another word.

AFTERWORD

This book is a work of fiction. None of the characters are based on real persons, either living or dead. This includes the three characters we first introduced in *The Book Buyer*, namely, Quentin and Marina Pakenham and Lancelot Aylesworth, as well as Gilles and Priscilla Despoir, Claude Malmaison, and Adrien Legendre.

To the best of our knowledge, no person named Philippe le Sabre has ever existed. More specifically, Philippe le Sabre the Seventh is in every way a figment of our imagination. So are "La Mouche" (Gilles Despoir senior) and Jean de Villiers and the members of his family. However, the La Mouche quarter is an actual location in the Seventh *Arrondissement* (administrative district) of Lyon; the excursion vessels on the River Seine in Paris, the Bateaux Mouche, were originally constructed in the boat yards of La Mouche.

Boulevard Nicolas Bourbaki does not exist, because as any knowledgeable mathematician will tell you, Nicolas Bourbaki does not exist. Nor does Rue

339

André Weil. Or Rue Szolem Mandelbrojt. Notwithstanding André Weil's and Szolem Mandelbrojt's affiliation with Nicholas Bourbaki. Who does not exist. Also, you won't find Rue Calmette et Guérin in Lyon, perhaps because Doctors Calmette and Guérin conducted their pioneering research developing the BCG vaccine at the Pasteur Institute in Lille. And there's no Rue Évariste Galois in Lille either. Nor in Lyon. And you'll struggle in vain to locate Rue George Quatre in Paris.

The military and police personnel are all fictional. This includes Captain Léopold Montmorency-Fosseux, as well as "Doudou" and the innumerable members of his improbable family.

In Chapter Eighteen, Quentin says that the name Osbert Oglesby sounds like "the sort of name you'd find in a case study in a textbook on object-oriented software engineering." That's because Osbert Oglesby is the name of the subject of a fictional case study in *Object-Oriented and Classical Software Engineering, Sixth Edition* (McGraw-Hill, 2005), a textbook written by one of the co-authors of this story.

Equally nonexistent are Yasuhara Prefecture; its Film, Music, and Digital Entertainment Office; and Megalodeon Studios. None of the commercial establishments in this book are real, including bookshops, hotels, restaurants, cafés, and the like. In particular, Lane Hookham Press, Contrapuntal

Howitzer Limited, and the *Varenne Bugle* are all figments of our imagination.

Furthermore, Druny Military Hospital and its staff are fictitious, as is its namesake, Dr. Olivier Druny—but Marshal Joseph Gallieni and his eponymous Métro Station are real.

When we started to write *Chekhov's Gun* in 2017, we discovered that *Wikipedia* had no specific article on French collaborators during the Second World War. By the time you read this novel, however, such an article may have appeared.

When we wrote the book, there was no Mikado Hotel in Kyoto, no Paradise Hotel in Hakone, and no Hôtel le Manchester in Paris. Sadly, the Yemyo restaurant is equally fictitious.

Quentin Pakenham believes that his friend Lancelot Aylesworth has Asperger syndrome or high-functioning autism. In fact, the compilers of the current edition of the *Diagnostic and Statistical Manual of Mental Disorders* (DSM-5, published in 2013) folded the previously separate subcategories of the autism spectrum, including Asperger syndrome and high-functioning autism, into the broader category of autism spectrum disorder (ASD).

To answer a question posed by a reader of an early version of the manuscript, polyoxybenzyl-methylenglycolanhydride is indeed the scientific name of bakelite.

The phrase "top-secret highly experimental thermonuclear exploding grelbin device" in Chapter Thirty occurs repeatedly in the "Double Oh Orson" and "Pinfinger" episodes of the animated cartoon series *Garfield and Friends*. One of the co-authors of this book avidly watched every one of the 121 episodes of the series with his daughter, then even more avidly re-watched them all on DVD with his grandchildren. More than once. He hopes that his grandchildren will enjoy Chapter Thirty when they are older.

Finally, for information on purchasing eighteen-year-old Lochervan whisky, "the crowning glory of the whisky maker's art," please see the Afterword of *Double Two* by Steve Schach and Sharon Stein.

ACKNOWLEDGEMENTS

Novels have provoked a great many sermons, almost invariably of the fiery and condemnatory variety. The converse appears to be considerably less common; indeed, we have been unable to find a previous instance of a sermon inspiring a novel. As stated in the Preface, the idea for this book came to us after we heard Rabbi Dr Benjamin Elton of The Great Synagogue, Sydney elucidate a point in his weekly sermon by alluding to the literary principle of Chekhov's Gun. We wondered how Rabbi Elton might react when we told him that his erudite preaching had triggered a light-hearted romp like *Chekhov's Gun*. Happily, he agreed to write the Preface for the novel that his words had serendipitously inspired. We thank him warmly for his kind remarks.

Fine art photographer Raphael Shevelev created the double portrait that appears on page 347. After seeing the work, photographic historian Dr. Anne Hammond wrote, "This is extraordinary. I don't know of any other photographer who has been able to merge two portraits into a double portrait . . . I think of the composite photograph . . . as combining and averaging the unique markers of personality, whereas you have preserved them and lovingly linked them . . ." We thank Raphael for allowing us to reproduce his masterpiece in this book.

Our developmental editor, Michael Mann, read the manuscript as meticulously as always, and we warmly thank him for his many helpful comments and criticisms. Once again it has been a delight to work with our publisher, Jennifer Chesak, of Wandering in the Words Press. And for the tenth time, we thank her for designing a striking cover.

SHARON STEIN

Sharon Stein is a pediatric radiologist. Born in Cape Town, South Africa, Sharon was a professor of radiology at Vanderbilt Children's Hospital in Nashville, Tennessee and an examiner for the American Board of Radiology. She is a former president of the Southern Pediatric Radiology Society. In 2009, Sharon moved to Sydney, Australia with her husband, Steve Schach, to be with their grandchildren. She is an accomplished cook and baker who loves to share her recipes and techniques. This is her seventh thriller co-written with Steve Schach; Wandering in the Words Press published the first, *Coopers Island*, in October 2013.

STEVE SCHACH

Steve Schach, a native of Cape Town, South Africa, moved to Sydney, Australia, in 2009, after twenty-six years as a professor at Vanderbilt University in Nashville, Tennessee. Before he began writing thrillers, Steve wrote thirteen best-selling software engineering textbooks, which are used in universities all over the world. Down Under, Steve intended to become a full-time grandfather, and limit his intellectual activities to solving cryptic crossword puzzles and avidly watching Sesame Street with his grandchildren. However, the urge to write proved to be far too strong to overcome. Wandering in the Words Press has previously published nine of his thrillers, most recently *A Case of Wine* in October 2019, co-authored by Sharon Stein.

Sharon Stein & Steve Schach

www.ingramcontent.com/pod-product-compliance
Lightning Source LLC
Chambersburg PA
CBHW020242200626
46816CB00001BA/90